LIFE BELONGS TO THE LOUD

LOW FICTION

This fictional work is from the mind of the author and any
similarities contained to actual persons, places, events is
coincidental. Any & all real events are used fictitiously.

LIFE BELONGS TO THE LOUD

Paperback ISBN: 979-8-9908145-0-9
eBook ISBN: 979-8-9908145-1-6
Audiobook ISBN: 979-8-9908145-2-3

Design & Layout done by Forrest Lonefight

Check out the Original Soundtrack at:
www.forrestlonefight.com
This OST is meant to be an interpretation by the author and should not in
anyway dictate literally what the reader experiences. It is an entirely different
medium to enjoy.

In memory of Grandpa,
You seated in the backroom at a makeshift desk lit only by a dusty
fluorescent light as you wrote on reams of yellow legal notepad, that
is the image of what "Burning the midnight oils" is to me.

PT I

CHAPTER ONE

I keep coming back to the guitar. Even when it's left me starving, heartbroken, and hating life; the sound resonates, I always return.

I find the guitar as one of the most perplexing and rewarding things you can discover at an early age. A chord, or a riff can take you back to those archetypes, memories, and milestones instantly.

I started playing at age eleven. There was a cheap hand-me-down department store Stella Harmony Acoustic that belonged to my cool Auntie Sandra.

She was a free-spirit. She was an artist, a teacher, a musician. She even worked in car repo. She loved life, loved to travel, and do things that the rest of our large conservative family didn't understand.

Though, she herself never had children, I was always drawn to her and her spirit.

She died of cancer back in the nineties, and fit a great life into such a short amount of time.

I inherited her guitar. Stella. I wrote my first song on her. Her strings weren't changed for a whole generation. The neck's scale was like a classical guitar. The fretboard was worn down. In my head, I still hear Stella's rusty tuning pegs cranking when I tune the high strings on my newer guitars. (Laughs)

I think about Stella; I think of my Auntie. I hear the guitar now; I think about those humble beginnings.

Maybe that's what it means to *stay in tune*.

Q: Do you still have that guitar?

No. I moved around a lot. It got lost in the whirlwind (of life). In a sense, it served its purpose and I made the best of it.

Plus, what's mind-blowing to me is that Auntie Sandra was like the only Native American woman I ever knew who played guitar back then.

Q: That is mind-blowing. I'm glad you shared that part of your journey with us. So, for the record, you are of Native American ancestry?

Hmm, I guess we SHOULD start at the top. Yes, my name is Azul Morgan. Half-Meskwaki, quarter-Mandan, quarter-Mexican woman. It's what I tell everyone. I always get caught having to explain each part of me to strangers.

I can't just say white or black, ya know, it's always been some big presentation. (Laughs) So many people are confused about Native American history, especially mine.

Q: Meskwaki is a Native American tribe based in Tama, Iowa. Talking earlier, you said they own their own land (in Tama) and it is NOT a reservation.

Yes. They own their own land and it's called the Meskwaki Settlement. We called it, "The Sett," for short. People don't know that. They're taught in school about all Indian tribes being displaced on reservations and forgotten about. Living in tipis and dancing around a fire.

I never gravitated to the Mexican side of me for some reason, even though my name is Spanish. Probably, because I was a skateboarding tom-boy, or I just didn't identify with that culture.

Come to think of it, there wasn't that many Mexican people in Tama when I was going to school, not like there is now.

Q: Where did you get your start?

Marshalltown. Those of us from Tama found out about these punk rock DIY shows from all of these cool-looking flyers all over town. Kids from the surrounding small towns would converge to these shows.

Local bands would sell their CDs on commission at the Sam Goody music store at the M-town Mall. I ended up working there for awhile and met some really cool people.

Just outside the Marshalltown High School was a Hasting's store. We got all our music, magazines, and books there. It was like an oasis of cool in the middle of small town Iowa boredom.

I lived with my mom and baby brother, Zachary. He's half Meskwaki like me, but a little more Mexican than I. We got out of the *Sett*, because the tribe is patriarchal. The system didn't provide financial, housing, or social help to female members unless they remained there or married a tribal member.

Q: Wow!

Right? Some of us had no choice but to leave. The tribe is good at exiling women to fend for themselves in the wild. So, we exiled ourselves. I wanted to go to college. My mom, too. M-town had a good community one. So, the three of us moved there for a fresh start.

After a year of hard times, as a single mom household, we settled on a dead-end street called: Melody Lane. A neighborhood with nothing but cheap box apartments with four units each. There was nothing melodic about it unless you find children screaming and domestic violence easy to sing to. (Laughs) We had some good neighbors and the diversity was as good as you were gonna get in Central Iowa, but it was basically a slumlord's back lot.

So, I set out to find people to start a band.

I was getting frustrated after awhile. I couldn't find a band that would last more than two practice sessions! It was mainly white males in the scene. Not very many girls of color at all. So no one knew what to think of me.

My self-esteem took a beating. I hated my thick, wavy, black hair in the summertime and I wanted to reinvent myself. So, I did the damn thing and chopped it all off. I seriously did the one thing that Native women aren't supposed to do. I wasn't trying to prove I was mourning, or shamed by the tribe. Not everything we do has to mean something. But that gave the tribesfolk something to talk about. I worked out regularly at the Y, started drawing and painting. Then, I got a journal and I began writing some serious songs.

The question to myself was: What do I write about?

I worked at the music store while going to school and bought a new Tascam 4-Track, which was blue, and started making my own home recordings. I loved that thing.

Later, I got a job as a security guard at this big ol' factory in M-town and things really started snowballing creatively after that.

Then, the Twin Towers came down...

The Bastard Chronicle 1: 4-Track Blues

Well. Planes hit the World Trade Center today. Everyone near a communication device is transfixed to this horrible tragedy. It's a hot September. The air conditioner has been running for two days straight.

* * *

This is a small box apartment in Marshalltown, Iowa:

a small town in the heart of Iowa,

a small state in the heart of America,

a large nation that is the broken heart of the entire world.

* * *

The news keeps replaying the images of the burning and crumbling towers. I was up late the night before, recording music on my new blue Tascam

MKII 4-Track recording console until three in the morning. I was woken up at 9AM by Mom, who was FREAKING OUT from the whole crazy media blitz.

* * *

Testing...Testing. This is my new journal BTW. I bought two of these yesterday at Hasting's with a pack of gum and soda for $9.11! No bullshit. Fucking creepy!

* * *

I purchased the Tascam, a Shure SM58 mic, and some cables for a grand total of 565 dollars this summer. I've been making cassettes of my music obsessively.

Sam Goody laid me off. I got a new job as a security guard at Fisher's valve plant. One of M-town's largest employers. I never thought I'd be working a shitty job like this. But here I am!

I'm able to sneak the 4-Track to work! I'm the only guard working in this old building that was once the main plant in the early 20th century. It's located at the mouth of M-town's downtown, and is being renovated into an expanded office HQ. The actual main office HQ right now, is across the street which I can access via a tunnel that runs below. Freaky!

My shift is 4PM to midnight. The cleaning crew and I are the only ones on the premises. I do an hourly patrol for fifteen minutes and go back to my hole (the security station) located in the darkest area of the building. The office is locked with a magnetic badge swipey thing.

So, I lock myself in here, put on my headphones, and escape into Tascam Land!

It's such a cool machine with its orange display lights that dance when the music on the tape rolls. The hissing and clicking of the tape deck relaxes me.

Tonight, I brought my guitar, my cheap Casio keyboard, and harmonica for tracking. I'm amassing a library of cool riffs!

On this night of September 11th, I'm gonna attempt to write a new song about the horrible event; and the fear that is rattling our souls.

All throughout the day in M-town, I saw every gas station lined up with desperate motorists.

"We're going to war with the Middle-East!"

"Oil sales will stop completely!"

"They're gonna bring the draft back to America!"

These were some of the crazy things I heard by M-town's citizens.

I don't know what to call this song. Probably just: 9/11. I got a chord pattern written today.

Songwriting: 9/11 or Magenta?

"Rivets of man's empire, melted with burning fire..." Azul was writing lyrics in her notebook. The 4-Track recorder was placed on her office desk.

"Melted down into our mother earth, behold the fallen empire..." She played an E Major, added a flat fifth, D6 Major, C Sharp Minor, to C Major.

"Hmm. Something. Something. G, maybe?" Her fingers formed a G Major chord, then instinctively went down two frets to F Major.

"I could do a cool chord to end that with. Make it a nice tasty bit. A tail bit. A wagging tail. A lavish tail. A happy dog." She played the chord sequence with some different chord variations added.

"C'mon, think jazzy——" she thought of what John Coltrane would write for piano on *Giant Steps*; her favorite jazz record.

"C Sharp Major Seventh?" She tried the F Major to C Sharp 7 Major, and went back to the original E Major chord.

"Fucking fantastic!" she yelled out and repeated the chord progression until it was memorized enough to record.

She grabbed her microphone on the desk and aimed it at the sound hole of her guitar. She checked to see if her levels were set to record on Track-1, then put her headphones on, strummed and balanced a good sound level that the dancing orange lights were showing levels at -3db, and pushed the red button to record.

She made a mistake, stopped it, rewound the tape to record again until she got it right on the fifth take.

"Good, now I'll play some lead melodies on the second track and try to sing these lyrics over on the third——" she unplugged the mic from Track-1, plugged it into Track-2, turned off the first track and clicked on the second, rewound and repeated the recording until she got all three tracks filled with her new idea.

"Not sure about those lyrics. Too doomy for such a pretty chord progression." Putting her guitar back in its canvas case, she looked at the wall clock above her to see the next patrol round was coming soon on the hour. She jotted more words in her notebook.

She thought about the family pony at Grandma's house in Tama. His name was Magenta. He was a white pony with brown spots. She gave him that name because the sun's reflection on his brown spots gave them a magenta sheen, and she wanted a companion that was named after a color like she was.

Azul hated her name while growing up. Having Magenta around made her feel a kinship to someone else with a color name. Blue and Magenta. Two misfits with color names.

She and her family rarely made it into Tama to visit. Grandma, and her mom Kim, were not on speaking terms. Thinking about that rift between her mothers, she exclaimed, "That's it! I could write the song about that!"

Three loud bursts of force pounded on her office door.

"Jesus Christ! Fuck!" Azul screamed in shock from the sudden sound of fist-on-metal, followed by a beep from the door's magnetic lock. Her fellow co-worker Lisa walked in.

"Hey, what's up! My grandpa was worried about you. He said I can work with you tonight. There's a bunch of lootings and vandalism going on all over town. Ya got your scanner turned on? Oh shit——" Lisa slapped her knee and bent down for a silent laugh, "I'm sorry——Did I scare you?"

"Oh my god! YES!" Azul picked up her microphone and faked a throw at her co-worker, a blond with pink highlights with an Insane Clown Posse Juggalo tattoo on her forearm. She worked at the factory across town. Her grandpa was their boss.

Lisa made a surrender gesture and walked over to rub Azul's shoulder. "Sorry, yo! I didn't mean to. Turn your scanner on. What's all this?" She looked at Azul's 4-Track setup and her guitar case.

Azul looked around and felt embarrassed. She stuttered and explained that she was only working on some songs. "Don't tell your grandpa, okay?"

"Oh, like a rock star? Aww shit! I did hear somewhere that you were a girl guitar player and that you were pretty badass!" She gave Azul a high-five and walked to the back of the office to turn on the police scanner. "Anyway, there's some crazy shit going on, yo! There was just a robbery at the Jiffy Gas Station. Three blocks from here. Did you see anything?"

"No. All the doors are locked. I don't have any monitors in here so I can't really see what's going on outside," Azul answered.

"Let's go check the monitors across the street. I gotta smoke a cigarette. We should go on the roof and look around."

"Awesome! Hey, that's really sweet of your grandpa to have you come over to keep me company, by the way. I was just getting ready to go for my hourly. We can head over there now."

Azul wielded her company-issued Motorola cellphone and *magic scanning stick* that they used to scan small proximity strips on the walls along their patrol rounds.

They walked through the gutted and asbestos-ridden building to the underground tunnel. Lisa, a natural chatterbox, carried on the conversation with nary a recovering breath.

CHAPTER FOUR

"I'm gonna kill that motherfucker! Where is he?! That fuck is on my shit list now! That fag pussy little bitch! He wants to break up MY band! I AM this band!"

In the Empty Caste's rehearsal room, a livid Toby yelled and knocked over the main kick drum piece of a drum kit which crashed into a ride cymbal stand. The noise was followed by the heavy breathing of the 6'6" pasty white skinhead.

"That's fucking uncalled for Toby! That's Rick's shit. We don't go and knock over your shit do we? Calm down, dude!" Jesus yelled.

"Where the fuck is that fag? He's here isn't he? Well, he has to come here for his damn drum kit. He's gonna have to get past me——" Toby cracked the knuckles of his round fists and grunted.

"Is that gonna make you feel better? Break his shit and kick his ass? It's only gonna get you back in jail motherfucker! We talked about leaving after our last show a month ago. We all agreed——

everyone was cool! Even you! And now you wanna throw a fit and pull this bullshit? Who are you?" Jesus yelled and tried to reason with him.

In his peripheral vision he noticed a nearby microphone stand with a steel base that was ready to grab if Toby had the idea to assault him.

"You're gonna run off with that fag? What the fuck are you gonna do? Play pussy music? Is that it? You, of all people, are gonna run off with that fuckin' fag and play fuckin' pussy music together? Well, I'm gonna tell you right now, man, GOOD LUCK with that! We'll find way better guys to replace you and totally lay waste on the two of you AND your pussy music band!"

Jesus laughed and shook his head. "What the fuck are you talking about? All the good times we had? Remember, WE hired you to play bass. We have two bass players, man. Two! And you weren't even the first one we hired! Don't even act like you were King Shit in this band! And quit calling Rick a fag. He gets way more pussy than you ever will in your life, you fucking Eastsider reject!"

Toby growled, then smashed the crash cymbal nearest to him, and rushed to where Jesus stood. Jesus quickly pivoted on the balls of his feet and picked up the mic stand that he eyeballed for his weapon. He swung upward with the ominous iron base and thrust to eye level. The sound of skull-meeting-steel was punctuated by a loud thud on the carpeted floor of the rehearsal room.

A loud, juicy fart and a gravelly, deep groan then receded into a coda of silence after.

Jesus let the weighted mic stand base slam to the floor in front of him. He surveyed the giant's head, which now had a swelling deep cut, and observed that Toby was blissfully unconscious.

He turned and hurried to the outside door. It was 8:00. Their rehearsal room was a walk-in basement that belonged to Toby's mother. They had never met her and often wondered why. Jesus hoped that she wouldn't choose to come down at that inopportune time to introduce herself as he whistled loudly outside the door and signaled for Rick to come into the basement.

Rick, who was waiting in his car, got the signal and rushed out.

"What's up?" he whispered. "What happened?"

"Just come in, dude. Get your shit. Don't worry. Hurry up." Jesus spoke in a calm voice and motioned with his hands to come inside.

"Fuck, man..." Rick followed him in. He gasped at the sight of Toby laid out on their rehearsal room floor with a thick stream of blood running down from his left eyebrow onto the floor that started to pool. "What did you do, man?"

"He'll be fine. He'll wake up from this. Trust me. He deserved it after all the shit he was talking, and he was bent on destroying your drum kit——"

"What?" He looked down at the unconscious Toby and wanted to start kicking.

"Hey man, it's over. He's out cold. Here, give me your bass drum," Jesus said as Rick sighed, went around Toby and picked up the bass drum piece that was laying sideways. He groaned after noticing a scratch on the shell and handed Jesus the piece.

* * *

The two sped out of Toby's mother's house on the east side of Des Moines and met at Jesus's house on the south side.

They sat outside with six-packs of Busch Light for Rick and O'Doul's Non-Alcoholic for Jesus on his plastic lawn chairs in the front yard next to Jesus's small flower garden. It was 9:00.

"Well that wasn't so hard. I didn't need to use my martial arts against him, thank Crom," Jesus, a noted sword collector and Conan The Barbarian fan, was a Judo and Taekwondo expert who used to practice in a Des Moines dojo before he joined the Empty Caste.

"Yeah, no shit. But I was still banking on him taking you down, I'll admit," Rick remarked on their collective size disadvantage to the round, yet muscular physique of the bruising, 400 pound Toby.

Jesus and Rick were both 5'6", and at a combined weight of only 325 pounds.

"Well, I was the one who wanted you to stay out in the car so I could talk him down. It didn't need to go that far! I can't believe how a guy can live like that. Like a big fucking baby!" Jesus put his face in his hands, let out a grunt of frustration, and ran his hands through his long hair.

"Well, he fucking lives with his mom still. He deals drugs out of his mom's basement. She encourages that shit, and there he is now at, what? Thirty years old?! How pathetic can a guy get?"

"He's been in prison. I don't think he can work anywhere. He won't call the cops on me. Or retaliate. At this rate, he'll be back in prison in no time. His reputation is pretty much ruined. No one will jam with him after word of this situation gets around."

"Yeah, he treated everyone like shit. But he had the money," Rick said, as they recalled how Toby got hired on as a second bass player. Their first bass player, Stu, had no problem with sharing the duties of holding down the bottom end with another bass player in a live situation; but Stu was an experienced sound engineer who ran a recording studio in his basement. He knew that having a second bass player was not practical and excessive.

"There was just no sense in talking logically with that dude. None. He kept a nice bankroll, I'll admit. He paid for the party and we had the best gigs for a while," Jesus said while stretching out in his chair.

"Yeah, but we have to think beyond that now. That's how the train rolled off the fucking tracks. He knew he had the money, so he butted in and made himself the 'leader' of the band. He bribed, cajoled, and fucking strong-armed our connections with the scene. Fucked our reputation!"

"A wannabe Suge Knight," Jesus concluded.

"A white, wannabe, mama's boy, Suge Knight." Rick shook his head, and took a sip. Jesus laughed and beatboxed a West Coast rap beat.

"I'll start making calls tomorrow. We gotta get another band rolling," Rick ran his fingers through his short, curly, dyed-blond hair. Jesus agreed. Rick looked at his watch. "Well, shit, I gotta get back to M-town or Mandy's gonna start freaking out; and I don't wanna deal with her being mad for an entire week," Rick rubbed his forehead at the thought of the week-long headaches he would have to endure with his girlfriend if he didn't get back home in time.

"Dude, I thought it was over between you two——"

"I did too, man. I don't know. We're gonna give it another chance. We have too much of a history to let it all go. She called me up crying a few times. Besides, I'm really close to her son. I'm the only one that toddler ever asks for——" Rick answered, and turned his head to the east.

"I hear you. I got pretty close to my first daughter's half-brother. Now I'm fighting with her mother to get a decent visitation for both of them. Crom knows she can't get her shit together and keep a good household for those kids. The guy she's with now is a piece of shit. It's not fair to them," Jesus took a drink.

"Well, with our new fucking band, we'll take over the world; and you and I can have the best lawyers money can buy! All our problems: *Solved!*" Rick thrust his arms out like an umpire at the word solved. The flimsy lawn chair he was sitting on went limp under him as he fell to the grass. Jesus lost all control and rolled in his chair as he shrieked in high-pitched, uncontrollable laughter.

"Jesus! And we'll buy you some new goddamn chairs, too! I'm outta here——" Rick yelled.

CHAPTER FIVE

"Oh shit! It's fucking hot up here, yo! Oh man, it stinks like a motherfucker! You'd figure with all the crazy shit going on in this country they'd shut down the meat-packing plants down for just one night at least! Damn——" Lisa spoke in her machine gun style after opening the door to the roof of the Fisher's main office building. It was an easily accessible walkway from the HVAC room, which was on their patrol round.

"Well, people still gotta eat," Azul followed her out, took a deep breath and was immediately wafted by the stench of the northern Marshalltown slaughterhouse, made worse by the extreme night humidity.

"Yeah, well if there's gonna be a fuckin' war, I hope those Middle-Easterners bomb those damn meat-packing plants to hell. I'd rather smell napalm and tear gas instead of smelly pig factories. Come to think of it, those people don't eat pork right?"

"Mmm. It's an Islam thing. Jewish people, too," Azul said while she took in the M-town skyline that was wholly visible in their slightly askew panoramic vantage point.

"Yeah! Right. So they WOULD bomb those first! To starve our fat asses right out of our houses when we're looking for food and BAM, BAM, BAM, we'd all be fuckin' shot to pieces. Serves us right I guess, for being so damn fat! Want a smoke?" Lisa pulled out two ready menthol cigarettes out of the left breast pocket of her blue, polyester security shirt.

Azul hesitated, then gave in. "Uhh, sure thanks." She had been quitting off-and-on for a year. But it was a strange night like no other. What better reason to light up, she thought.

"Yeah, you shoulda seen the canned food aisle at the grocery! Empty as a motherfucker. Grandpa said to get as much food as we could fit in the cart. My grandma was with me, and we got three-hundred and seventy-six dollars in food! Damn near half of that was baby food! God, but I'm so glad I'm not pregnant now. If it ever comes down to it, I'll fight! Would you?" Lisa lit her cigarette and handed the lighter to Azul.

"Of course I would. Damn! Three-hundred and seventy-six dollars in groceries? You're lucky you have grandparents to help you out like that. Just imagine if you were like, totally alone." Azul lit the cigarette, inhaled deeply, and let the rush of nicotine surge inside her.

"Oh shit, I was! Before I got pregnant I was fuckin' tweaking, like everyday. I hung out with every tweaker in town. Saw a bunch of shit that I don't ever wanna see again. I hope my baby never, ever sees any of that! Remember that one bitch that you trained before I was cleared to come back to work? That one last month?"

"Oh yeah! The one I trained one weekend, and she never showed up for work the next week. Do you know what happened to her?" Azul remembered while keeping up with Lisa's train of thought.

They strolled to the northern edge of the building overlooking the main street where it was still busy for a Tuesday night.

"Look at today's paper! If ya got it. Her AND her piece of shit, fucking man are both in there. Mugshots blowing up that paper, looking tweaked-out as a motherfucker. Both of 'em! Her boyfriend raped and impregnated a thirteen year old girl! She was covering up for him. They got busted on possession charges, too. Crazy. That was the only man her ugly ass could get, AND he was her fucking drug dealer, too. Those are the type of people you don't ever wanna be messing with. Have you ever done that shit?"

A group of Harley riders rode through, the engine sounds canceling out every sound in the area.

"No. I've never tweaked before. NEVER! I DON'T EVER WANNA DO THAT SHIT! EVER! I'VE ALWAYS——" The piercing Harley engine sounds finally drowning out in the distance, "I've always been clean. I wanna keep it that way." She took a deep drag on her cigarette and looked to the east, two blocks away, nestled in the heart of downtown, the illuminated Marshall County Courthouse with its spired clock tower.

"Well, around here it could sneak up on you and take you down to hell with it. I admit it; I didn't listen. I'm here today by the grace of God and my grandparents. My mom and her husband still don't trust me. I don't blame them. But that's okay. I got my little girl with me now, and I'm right where I need to be——" Lisa flicked the ash of her cigarette for emphasis, took a drag, and strode beside Azul who had turned to look to the west.

They noticed a slim figure of a young man walking from a dark alleyway. He met the sidewalk and turned east towards the main street. He had his arms folded tightly. He wore a dark hoodie with a trail of mysterious vapor coming off of his small torso. He appeared to be smoldering.

"What the fuck is that?" Azul tugged on Lisa's shirt, pulling her in until their shoulders bumped.

"What the hell? Is that motherfucker, like, burning? How is he still walking?" They both noticed he was starting to stagger and not able to keep his balance. "Hey you! Are you alright?" Lisa yelled out.

Azul hit Lisa on the bicep repeatedly. "Dude! What if someone torched the dude? Do we wanna get involved?"

"Help! I need to get to the hospital——" the young man's voice bellowed out.

"Hold on! We're Fisher's security! We're coming down to you now! Meet us at the lighted doors in back!" Lisa turned towards the door to the HVAC room and told Azul to come on.

"Holy shit! I guess we're involved now——uhh, where's the fucking first-aid kit, Lisa?!" Azul yelled as they dashed into the building through the HVAC room to the third floor hallway.

"How should I know?" Lisa yelled back.

They reached the stairwell to descend to the street level and exited the back door where they met him in the alley, trying to support himself on the building. They couldn't see what was wrong with him in the darkness but could see that his hoodie was soaked in water. He had an ice pack in his hoodie's right pocket, weighing it down. They could see the mist coming off him in the humid air. When they asked him what was wrong, he warned them not to touch him.

"C'mere hun, get over here in the light. We'll sit you down. We're calling the ambulance right now," Lisa motioned for him to come to the back entrance that was lit.

Azul unclipped the Motorola out of its holder on her belt and dialed 911.

"Oh man, dude, it's a good thing we're so close to the hospital. Just like, three blocks away. The ambulance is gonna be here in no time, hold on——" Azul got through to the 911 dispatch. "Yes, I'm with Fisher's security at the main office HQ, on Center Street and——"

Lisa loudly retched and heaved as the young man, seated on a brick ledge, revealed what he was hiding: A burnt and blistered torso with hanging skin which resembled a steaming meat suit.

Azul's voice trailed off in disbelief, "We have a young man here with a really, really, bad burn."

CHAPTER SIX

"It ain't as bad as it looks," his voice cracking. His head was still under his hood.

Lisa spit out what was left in her mouth and yelled, "Bullshit! How the fuck did this happen? You are not supposed to be walking around like this! I've been burned before, in a cooking accident. There was skin HANGING off my damn arm! I passed out from the pain."

Azul finished her call with 911. "Alright, they're gonna be here any minute! Okay, what happened? We need to make a report," she carried a small notepad in her left breast pocket where her ID badge was clipped on and immediately wrote the time she made the call.

"Don't! We don't have to do that, I was already on my way to the hospital. It was an accident. We don't need to get cops involved——" the burn victim pleaded as he winced from the pain.

Lisa interrupted, "Dude, you are not wasting any more energy on walking. I can tell you're going into shock soon. I can't even begin to imagine what your body is gonna feel after you smack onto the damn concrete! Did someone do this to you?"

Azul repeated the question and started writing.

"Umm, uh——no one did this to me. No one did. I uhh——fucking stupid, really——I accidentally poured lighter fluid on my shirt and got a damn cigarette cherry on there somehow and uhh, fuck this hurts——" his face tightened up, making his pale complexion match his wounded torso.

Lisa came up to Azul's ear and whispered, "This dude's a tweaker. I've seen him around. He's got out-of-state connects. Either someone did this to him, or he really is crazy. We're just gonna play it cool. We don't know this dude——"

"Well, man…I don't know what that all means, but he's on camera, right now!" she pointed at the security camera above them, placed outside of the double glass doors. "We gotta deal with it——"

Suddenly, a slim, dark figure ran toward them from the alleyway.

"Spikey!" It was a pale, long-legged young girl with a shaved head. She wore a black Jack Skellington hoodie, and her physical presence resembled the features of the famous character.

"Uhh——shit. Hey! These ladies are taking me to the hospital. My dad's not with you is he?" He forgot his pain when his attention turned to the bald girl.

"Spike——What did you do?" The bald girl approached the bottom of the small ramp that led up to where the three were gathered in front of the doors. She kept her eye on the hurt boy as he closed his hoodie to hide his torso from her sight.

"Is my dad coming here, too? Is he coming? Answer me! What did he say?" His sudden excitement yielded more shooting pain.

"Hey, how do you know this kid? Do you know who did this?" Lisa yelled at the strange girl.

"It's cool. She had nothing to do with this——My dad must've called her——" He put his hand on Lisa's arm in restraint and turned his attention back to the girl. "Did he? Did he call you?"

The girl's eyes welled with tears and she burst out, "Yes, he called me. Things were getting fucked up at home, and all I wanted was to come be with you. My mom kicked me out. Right when I was packing up a bag to come over, your dad calls and says to me that I need to go over to your apartment and talk some sense into you again! What did you try to do THIS time, Spikey?"

Azul and Lisa both looked at each other with raised eyebrows and back to the girl with looks of concern.

"Uhh, we're not getting into this right here. I need a doctor now. Right now——" His body tightened up more from the pain as the girl drew nearer to him.

"You played with the fire again didn't you?" She choked back her tears and softened her aura as she reached out to touch his hooded head.

"I wouldn't touch his head right now——" Lisa warned.

"It's okay. She's my girlfriend. This is Charlie. Fuck, if she was around in the first place, I prolly wouldn't be in this mess." He exhaled. She slipped off the hood covering his head to reveal that he had a shaved head that matched hers. She bent down and they rubbed their prickly skulls together, creating a sandpaper rhythm. "I really fucked up this time. I mean, really..." He began to sob in her embrace as the two security guards stepped away out of courtesy for their intimate moment. They heard the siren approaching.

* * *

"I've seen you around. I know I have. Did you work at Sam Goody? Or Hastings?" Charlie asked after she took a sip of the grainy hospital vending machine coffee.

"Yeah. I used to work at Sam Goody before this job. I don't think I've seen you around. Are you new in town?" Azul was sitting next to her in the ER waiting room. There was a family waiting in the main part of the room. The young women were seated in the children's area where there were toys still scattered on the floor. Due to the late hour, this area was unlit, except for the luminous 6x3 foot fish tank that was across from them.

"Well, I go to shows a lot; and I go to those music stores all the time. I'm sure you probably saw me——'Cuz I had hair then——" Charlie giggled and rubbed her skull that had a thin prickliness of blond fuzz. "Didn't you have hair then too?

Azul snorted and said she had just shaved her head *for the hell of it*.

"Awesome. You look so cool. Well, bald chicks unite, right?" Charlie raised her hand for a high five and Azul reciprocated.

"You two must be really close. Since you and Spike have, ya know, matching haircuts. You two do look cute together," Azul noticed the UV light from the aquarium reflecting on Charlie's skin. She caught herself staring and glanced over at the people in the main part of the waiting room.

"I love your name. Azul. Ah-Zoo-ell. What does that mean? Is it like, uh, Mexican?"

"How did you know——" She looked down at her left breast pocket and saw her ID badge still attached. She meant to take it off when she volunteered to go with the ambulance to the hospital. "Oh yeah. Whoops! I guess I forgot I had a name badge on. Umm——yeah. It's Spanish for the color blue. My dad was half Mexican. He gave me that name." She pinched on the clip to release it from her left shirt pocket and held it in her hand to look at her picture. She wrinkled her nose for a second and slapped the badge on her lap.

"That's cool——But, if you don't mind me asking about your dad, is he——"

"Not dead. At least I think so. He left my mom pretty early on in my life. Hasn't been around since," Azul interjected and made a forgiving smile.

"Oh, yeah. I know about that shit. Fucking dads right? My mom wanted to name me Angela. A regular, standard girl name. But my dad, at the last minute, named me Charlie. Isn't that some crazy bullshit?" She smiled, and shook her head.

"I do like Charlie though. It's different. Angela is too plain. There's so many Angelas in the world. You stand out. You seem nice, which is why Spike seems to like you so much."

"You like my name? Wow. Man, I wish we had been friends growing up. I grew up in a hick town in northern Iowa. I moved to Des Moines for awhile, moved here, moved to Des Moines again, and now I'm back. I was passed around by my fam. Never got a chance to really settle down and prove myself in order to have a fucking close relationship with any of my relatives. All the men in my family are dickwads. The only one I was ever close with is my brother. We haven't seen each other in a long time though…" Her voice trailed off. The tropical fish inside the tank caught her eye.

"I'm sorry about that. You know——" Azul tried to convey the right words. "Maybe, it's best that you use your experience growing up like that to be a stronger person. It seems to me that whatever Spike is going through, however messed up it may be, is something that will form a closer bond between you two. I mean, from what you two have been saying; and I don't wanna be preachy or nothin', you two need each other now more than ever."

"I know. I mean, he was, and is the only one besides my brother whoever listened to me and talked to me like I wasn't fucking crazy. Ya know? It's like, whatever I was going through, he was going through, and back and forth. I mean, we met right before I had my stillborn. Not even Mom cared enough for me to take me to all of my appointments to see if my baby was okay. It was too late when the fuckin' doctors found out that my baby was dead, and they had to get it out of me."

Azul was shocked and reeling when she heard the word: stillborn, come out of Charlie's mouth, also appalled that she was talking about it as if it was the most casual thing to talk about with someone she had just met.

"Fucking hell. I mean, really? I'm so sorry——" Azul sympathized.

Charlie said it was okay and stated that everyone reacted the same way whenever she revealed her miscarriage, "It was a long time ago."

"I have no words. That's why you and Spike are so close."

"He took me to the doctors and never left my side after that. Anybody else would probably just walk away," Charlie finished. They both looked at the fish tank and watched for a moment.

"Well, I hope he's okay," Azul sighed, after wetting her lips, ridding them of the dryness of being speechless.

"So, do you like your job? Seems to be pretty chill, right? I mean, nothing much happens in M-town besides the occasional tweakers and drunks walking by," Charlie changing the subject.

Azul, looking down at her polyester blue uniform, rubbed some lint off her dark navy blue slacks. "Not even that, really. I play music. I get to sneak in my recording gear and guitar and pretty much record riffs all night long. So I can't complain that it's a chill job."

"Oh wow! That's fucking amazing! You in a band?"

"I was. I did a couple of acoustic gigs at some coffee shops. Nothing much, but yeah, I've been playing with some people. Auditioning——"

"I know some dudes from Des Moines looking for another guitar player. Have you heard of Empty Caste?"

"Yeah, I went to a couple of shows with them on the bill. I've met one of the dudes. He was real drunk though."

"The drummer just moved back to M-town with his girlfriend. He sings while playing drums, too! I've partied with them quite a bit. They're badass! Him and Jesus, the guitar player, are starting another band. You should totally try out for them!" Charlie's enthusiasm grew.

"Hmm. That's interesting. I'll give it a shot. You have their contact info?"

"Just gimme your number! My address book is at Spikey's. I'll give you Rick's number. He's the——"

"Drummer. I remember now. He was the drunk dude I talked to," Azul remembered with a laugh.

"Aww man! He parties hard, but he's a great guy and SUPER-talented. They were tired of playing super-heavy music, and they want to branch out and do something way different! I'll tell him about you saving Spikey's life, too!"

Azul laughed and gave Charlie her number. Charlie said she would give her a call right after getting in touch with Rick.

A nurse approached them; the two young women stood up and acknowledged her. She asked for Charlie to come with her to the ER Triage Unit.

"Is he gonna be okay? I was on my way over to his house. He didn't mean to do what he did. Did he ask for his dad?"

The nurse explained that Spike had just asked for her. He was stable, but had suffered first and second degree burns.

"I better get back to work and write that report. Call Fisher's security. My boss will have anything the cops need. I'm just three blocks away——" Azul headed to the exit.

"I'll call you Azul. I'll tell you how Spike is doing."

Azul sighed and wished her good luck, then headed back out into the humid night.

The Bastard Chronicle 2: A Strange Turn of Events

So, some really interesting things happened at work this week. Lisa and I saved a burning dude's life. I met his girlfriend, who is really sweet. She introduced me to some band guys and now we are meeting up for a jam!

Two things that I've learned:

-I'm never eating pork, or let alone, looking at ham, or bacon EVER again after 9/11!

-Life is strange. You never know who you're going to meet!

The burnt guy, Spike is all I know him as, turns out, is involved with some drug people. I don't really want to know what that's about. My Spidey-Sense tells me that the less I know, the better off I'll be! But he has some issues with his dad.

According to Charlie, Spikey has a hard-on for her, AND fire. A pyromaniac. It's not the first time he has tried to set himself on fire.

But with that image of his fried, pink flesh burned into MY mind?! Now, I'm scarred for life!

Fried white boy. Will I ever eat a decent breakfast ever again?!

Charlie, sweet Charlie… She's a trip. I thought my life was a train wreck. But she is so nice, and I can easily tell she has a big heart. Why she can't get out of the dark alleyways and falling in love with these dumpster-diving Oscars is beyond me!

She called me the very next day, and we had a lot to talk about! (It's strange how you can find someone amid the chaos and just click with that person and feel you've known them your whole life.)

She has these really piercing heterochromia eyes. One eye is brownish-green, the other as blue as my name. Hmm. She's something else.

She pulled through and set up the jam. Turns out, Rick the Drummer, doesn't live too far away from me. Like a mile away! I don't know what to expect.

I looked up the "Empty Caste" website to do my research.

Boom! An announcement read:

We are sad to announce that Rick The Drummer has committed suicide. He was found with a gunshot wound to the head!

WTF!? I looked at their message board and saw there were grieving and distraught fans posting their condolences and stories. I was confused.

So I e-mailed the webmaster to find out what was going on. I got a message back from the webmaster an hour later, and she said that it was all a hoax. They just broke up. There was some band drama, and that the hoax was a bad, bad joke.

She thanked me for e-mailing, and reminding her to take the announcement down. Geez!

I can't believe people can fake their own death online so easily like that! My God! Nothing seems sacred this week!

The webmaster's name is Kitty. Nice. A female webmaster! This could be good. If things work out, I can pick her brain! I've always wanted to learn how to build websites.

Anyways, it's a good thing I knew this because I got a call from Rick. Imagine, if I hadn't heard that his suicide was a hoax…

I didn't bring that up though. We talked about what bands we were into.(They love Mr. Bungle! Extra points for that!)

He told me that their old bassist is an ex-con who is now on the downward spiral. He wants to put a hit out on him and Jesus because Jesus fucked him up with a mic stand. Daaamn. What am I getting myself into?

But, with all of that aside, we're on the same page and want to do something in music that's never been done before. I told him I was on board!

Since Empty Caste was such a macho metal band, they seem really open-minded enough to jam with a girl. After all this time, I'm excited and hopeful that something good will come out of this jam session.

CHAPTER EIGHT

10:15 AM. Azul loaded her gear into her blue Buick LeSabre. It was the first car she ever owned and dubbed it: The Hoopty. She always hummed the Destiny's Child song *"Independent Women"* while admiring it.

She made the one-mile trip to Rick's house, which was on old HWY 30 East. His house was in-between a Mexican restaurant called La Carreta and a cemetery.

The smell of food was in the air as she pulled into the parking lot. The house stood next to the lot on a small hill. A concrete stairway led up to the front. All the windows were open, and it looked like one air-conditioner was in the front window. The entrance was an old aluminum screen door that was left open.

She parked next to Rick's car, an old maroon Geo Metro covered in band stickers. She had noticed it while driving around town and at Empty Caste shows. She wondered outloud how he fit a whole drum kit inside.

A newer, tan Buick LeSabre was parked next to the Metro. This was Jesus's car. It was a marvel of size and capacity. It looked considerably newer than all of the vehicles. Azul never jammed with Jesus, but knew this was his car. At 27 years old, the guy must really have his shit together, she thought.

She unloaded her Fender Twin Reverb Deluxe amp from the trunk. A medium-sized combo amp with two 12" speakers inside. She had her assorted tools, cables, and pedals inside her canvas backpack.

She slung her guitar over her shoulder, a mocha-colored Epiphone Les Paul copy that she affectionately named: Mocha.

Mocha was snug inside her new black nylon gig bag with a comfortable strap. She carried picks, spare guitar strings, and a string-winder tool in the zipped pocket on the face of the bag.

Her amp had small casters to wheel it along, and she carried it up the steps with one arm. It was heavy, but tolerable.

Jamming with males, she often got offers of help to haul her gear; but she always insisted on carrying her own.

She stood at 5' 4" and worked out regularly at the local YMCA *to gain strength to haul gear*, as she would tell others, though she never fully admitted to working out to look good onstage as well.

She got excited as she heard Jesus, already plugged into his amp and riffing out, as she ascended the steps.

She reached the entrance and tapped on the aluminum part of the door, peeked inside, and walked in. The smell of old carpet, cigarettes, and old air-conditioner wafted over her.

She saw Rick setting up his drum kit. Jesus was adjusting his guitar and pedal board set-up along the west wall, oblivious to his surroundings.

"Hey, what's up!" Rick acknowledged after a quick swig of a wet Busch Light can.

"Hey, what's going on guys!" Azul glanced around the room some more.

"Hey Azul, wuzzup——" Jesus awakened from his oblivious guitar player's trance. His brown, waist-length hair was perfectly parted down the middle and draping over his pale English wizard-like features.

"Uh, you could set up your shit over there," Rick pointed towards the wall opposite of where Jesus was. A hallway to the back rooms was beyond that. The drum kit was set up against the south wall in front of the main window. Jesus had the air-conditioner on his side.

"Did we find someone to play bass?" asked Azul as she was setting up her equipment.

"I did! He should be here pretty quick. His name's Chester. He's a cool cat. I ran into him at Sam Goody. We talked a lot about music. He knows his shit! Very cool, and laid back," enthused Rick.

"I know him! I jammed at his house with some dudes about two years ago. I think he was sixteen at the time. He was home-schooled. We jammed on some Snapcase covers and shit. The other guys where all about the punk thing except me and him. He was so young; and his mom came in and gave us all turkey sandwiches, cookies, and milk. It was sweet! I haven't seen him since then," Azul recalled and explained how she felt out of place with the punk scene that she thought was *too cliquey* and sheltered from anything outside white, suburban middle-class culture.

Rick and Jesus were quick to agree. They talked about the different people in the Des Moines music scene and what bands they liked. Azul liked that the guys were from the big city. That's where she wanted to be.

Chester knocked on the door holding a big combo amp and his bass strapped to his shoulder. He was invited in. "Hey all!" he said in a soft-spoken way.

Azul noticed he looked differently than she remembered. Gone were the boyish, clean-cut looks of two years ago as he had grown to be a tall young man. A fully converted Goth, with long black hair, a

Cradle of Filth T-shirt, complete with studded leather on his wrists and neck collar.

"Hello, grown and sexy..." Azul whispered under her breath before he took her hand to be re-acquainted.

"Hey Azul, I do remember you! I'm stoked you're still jamming! You look uhh, awesome!" Chester became flushed-face and stuttered on his words while holding conversation with her and the other two.

He was nervous, but that charm appealed to Azul as she smiled every time he stumbled on certain words.

"Glad you could come over, man! Set up next to me or Jesus. Wherever. Want a beer? Anyone want a beer?" Rick was the host who brought them all together and was holding court. Chester apprehensively shook his head then nodded, "Sure, why not! Heh, heh——Drinking in the morning! Right?" he laughed, as both, Jesus and Azul declined.

Chester was setting up his gear and talked about how his older brother was a singer and guitar player in a pop-punk band called, Jizz-69. This made the two Des Moines guys laugh. Azul noted that the band played M-town and the northern part of the state frequently.

"Well, as Azul probably knows, my parents are pretty religious, and they still don't know that Jizz-69 is a total sexual thing. It's a horrible name! But, funny as hell——" Chester laughed as he turned his amp on, which made the whole house rattle.

"Whoa, dude! That's loud. Turn down a bit, brotha——" Rick cautioned as he started pounding on his drums.

"Volume check!" Jesus yelled, and the four musicians then matched their volumes in relation to Rick's drums.

"Turn the guitar amps toward me and I think I can hear you okay——" Rick ripped into a concentrated blast of beats that put smiles on the others' faces.

Songwriting: Total Sexual Thing

"I got this riff. Goes kinda like this," Jesus fumbled around on his guitar. A clean tone with some doubling effect came out of his 4x12 Marshall amplifier. He owned a prized Digitech multi-effects pedal that he swore by. "It's in the key of A. It's got a swing triplet feel. Bouncy——" he continued.

The rest of the band listened to what he was playing. Chester followed along with his fingering. Azul listened attentively. Rick counted with a head-nod, then played a beat that matched the bouncy triplet feel. He was laying down some snare rolls and rim shots to accent the riff.

"It goes to this after two bars," Jesus transposed the riff. "—— Then up to C!"

Everyone's eyebrows perked up with the key change. The riff sounded menacing.

Rick played a beat on the toms that was in-sync with Jesus's riff. His left foot tapping the straight four-beat on his high-hat pedal. Chester locked in and played a walking bass line. Azul found the rhythm, raking the pick against the guitar strings to find the beat of the riff. Then, she played a single note pattern to compliment the part.

They all found *The Pocket*, nodded their heads with the groove as they jammed on the riff for ten minutes.

"Cool riff," Azul complimented.

"Thanks. I wrote it last week," Jesus said.

"Yeah man! It's cool! Did you all like what I was throwing in on the bass?" Chester asked, with a bit of nervousness in his voice. Everyone else voiced their approval.

"Let's keep jamming on it," suggested Azul, then Rick counted off on his sticks.

They jammed on the riff again and two hours later they had laid out a rough structure of an intro, verse, chorus, verse, chorus, and outro riff. Azul and Jesus each had their own handheld cassette recorders and recorded what they had just written.

"I'm feeling this shit!" Rick said as he started a snare roll and played a percussive section that he was working on in his own time.

"I like that! That'd be sick if we did like a percussion jam where we each grab a drum!" Azul exclaimed.

"Yeah that'd be cool! I got some percussion instruments at home. I'll bring them in next time!" Jesus added.

Chester started a bass line on top of Rick's beat. They all played along. The cohesion fell apart soon after. Everyone laughed. They took a break and felt at ease knowing that they could play well together with enough practice.

* * *

The four sat outside on the concrete steps and talked about what they had just created.

"So, are we really gonna call this song: *Total Sexual Thing?*" Azul asked the guys. After a resounding yes, they laughed and joked about it some more.

Rick asked everyone if they wanted to get together a few hours earlier next week. He said he would get his PA system out of storage so they could use his microphones and start singing.

With collective nods of approval, they all agreed to meet again.

A man dressed in white walked up to them.

"Hello, I'm the manager from the restaurant next door. How you guys and girl doing?" They were all surprised at his sudden presence and greeted him. "Hey, you guys think you could turn it down? Maybe, stop playing? The music is really loud, and we are busy with lots of customers, man——" he gestured to the full parking lot, and to the restaurant that was filled with guests.

"Oh wow! Uh, well, I think we can quit for today. Sorry if we're being too loud, brotha. I'm Rick, your new neighbor, by the way," Rick extended to shake the manager's hand. He explained that they had just started a new band that day, and they would try their best to compromise as neighbors. "How 'bout we start earlier next week, like eight or nine?" he asked his new bandmates who all said 9:00 was good, as it gave plenty of time for Jesus to drive the hour-long journey from Des Moines.

"Oh man, we're too loud," Azul smiled to Jesus and Chester. "Chester, your bass, man! We told you to turn down——" she nudged his arm.

"I did! I hope we didn't piss him off too bad. I can ask my parents, ya know, if we could just jam there if it doesn't work out here. We have a nice setup," Chester offered. He explained that it was out in the country, just five miles from Rick's house. Jesus said to just wait and see what would materialize next week.

Azul, Jesus, and Chester packed their gear into their cars as Rick was raving about ideas for the band and what they needed to do.

"Whoa! One thing at a time, dude!" Jesus said, laughing while quelling Rick's excitement. Everyone said their goodbyes for the week, and left excited for what the future held for them.

CHAPTER TEN

The band reconvened at Rick's house at 9:00 AM. The humidity was worse than the week before. The musicians were eager to start. Rick had a friend waiting with him as they loaded their gear in.

"Hey guys! You ready? I'm excited. This is Mick. I've known him for fuckin' years, and he's gonna be our new percussionist. He's got another band he sings for called: Resonating Wire. I'm hoping we could have him do vocals as well," Rick had his arm around the young musician whose look resembled a punk-rock nerd with dyed-blue hair.

"Hey everybody! I know Azul," He raised his hand to her in a high-five, and she reciprocated. "Glad to see you! Looking forward to playing with you. All of you guys——"

"Damn! You already know each other?" Rick was surprised how she both knew Chester and now Mick.

"We used to work at Sam Goody together! He used to go play gigs with his band, Safe Seconds, and I'd have to cover the register," Azul laughed. "It's been awhile Mick. How's the music retail business treating you?"

"Swell! I backed off on hours when school started. Just been doing my thing. You still going full-time? I've seen you in the halls every now and then."

"Yep! Doing that, working my security guard thing, and this band. Small world. I hope we can get you to sing with us."

"Yeah, Rick has been saying you guys have been working on some great stuff! I can't wait to hear it," Mick said in his soft-spoken way as he met Jesus and Chester for the first time and helped with the rest of the gear.

Azul and Jesus brought some percussion instruments for *Total Sexual Thing*; a set of bongos, two congas, tambourines, chimes, and bells.

The restaurant was not open yet, so they were looking forward to making some noise.

Songwriting: The House by the Cemetery

"I'm feeling this great energy. This percussive vibe. I'll get my PA set up. I got a couple of mics. We can do a percussion song with a great bass line and some vocal harmonies!" Rick started tapping a rhythm he had been working on with his sticks on the kitchen table. The musicians listened. Azul caught on and pulled the set of bongos near her area and jammed along with that same rhythm as Rick went to turn on his PA head next to his drum kit and to find his microphones, cables, and stands.

"I got these lyrics. I wrote them when I was waiting for my girlfriend to get out of classes at MCC last week. I'll say these lyrics like protest-style, with a megaphone or something, over percussion. Kinda like a reggae thing," Rick was excited as he was setting up the vocal microphone stand that he planned to sing into.

"Yeah that'd be fucking sweet! I got a bass line," Chester played a simple line as Jesus started playing a blues-based riff. Azul and Mick were finding *the pocket* and built a good rhythmic foundation.

Two hours later, the band had another rough outline of a song.

* * *

"How 'bout we call this song *The House by the Cemetery?* Ya know. Being as this house, our jam spot, is by a cemetery," Azul said while they were taking a break outside.

Jesus laughed, "Yeah, what about *The House Next to the Restaurant!*"

"The lyrics and singing parts you were coming up with are awesome!" Mick complemented Rick's performance of the vocals while playing drums. "It's inhuman how you can do that at the same time!"

"Thanks, my fucking voice is already shot. But this song is like a three-parter. With the U.S. going to war, I figure we could sing about that. I mean, the first part is like a protest. My lyrics go: *We kill and die for oil, and they label it glory, we sell our policies to the rich, and they label it choice.* We could do that first part as a call-to-arms protest, the second part being the brutal riot of the storm, and maybe some sort of sick resolution to it all——"

Azul got excited, "Yeah! The title! It could be allegorical, like the WHITE HOUSE by the cemetery. Ya know, I've always had an idea for a title: *Cemetery on the Hill.* I dreamed about this. I mean, the White House is literally surrounded by cemeteries. We could work on that being the subject. The music will embody that idea."

The rest thought about it with raised eyebrows.

"That's a fucking awesome idea! Fuckin' aye! Let's do it!" Rick exclaimed.

An old and rusty red Toyota Camry pulled into the full parking lot in a hurry. There were no spaces to be had, so the car parked horizontally behind Rick's car and Azul's. A young blond woman got out and unstrapped a little boy out of the toddler seat in the back. She had two sacks of groceries with her. She stormed up the concrete steps to where the band was sitting, the boy was following slowly behind.

Rick began to introduce her to the band. "Hey, guys this is Mandy. This is the new band. Chester, Mick, Azu——"

"Can I talk to you inside?" Mandy's sharp, husky voice cut Rick off, changing the mood instantly.

Rick followed Mandy inside. Yelling ensued, then the crashing of a cymbal, and the incessant crying of the toddler

"Uh, guys——I think practice is done for today. Let's kinda stay behind and wait to get our things until she's out of the room," Jesus told the rest as the yelling intensified. "That's Mandy."

The Bastard Chronicle 3: Second Week

Awkward, meet Volatile!

It didn't quite get down to "M-town White Trash Bash! Hosted by: Jerry Springer" between me and Mandy, but it could have!

I mean, the bitch did block my car in. Rick had to move it out of the way in order for me to get off the property…

The boys and I were getting some good work done, and we were on another plane, man. Then it was interrupted by her, with her jealous ways.

* * *

Well, it IS her place. We're making a bunch of noise in there on a Sunday morning. Mick overheard her yelling about having orgies in the living room. That was funny.

Jesus said that this type of thing happened all of the time in the past. He can only count a couple of times when he's seen her be nice to people. I feel bad for her kid having to see all of that.

What's Rick thinking? Can he juggle domesticity and whatever we're trying to do?

* * *

Next week, we're meeting at Chester's place. I was there already, two years before. I wonder if his mom will bring us sandwiches, cookies, and milk this time? The antithesis of Mandy. That should be interesting. With Rick being a wild guy, downing beers on a Sunday morn', I wonder how that's gonna work out?

I hope Mandy is cooled down by then, lest she find out that the orgy has moved to another, more "Christian" location.

And, in other news, Chester asked me out, and we're going on an official date! Mmm-hmm. I had some thoughts on mixing business with pleasure, but that long black hair, those leather cuffs and studded collar were too much for me.

* * *

I wonder if he likes to be pulled on all fours like a dog in that collar? (Oops!)

* * *

Anyways, we are going bowling at the Chippewa on Saturday, the night before practice. I'm looking forward to it! I haven't had a decent night out in this town in forever. School and work is a drag.

Hmm. Drag. That'd be hot... (Whoa!)

CHAPTER THIRTEEN

"I've always wanted to come here. I love seeing that big ol' white bowling pin on the outside of this place whenever I drive by," Azul said as she and Chester stood gazing at the giant 30 foot bowling pin near the entrance of the *Chippewa Lanes* bowling alley.

The pin was erected in the mid-twentieth century. Along with the speakeasy 1920's-style neon sign next door for, *Jax Steakhouse*, it was a remnant of a bygone era of famous roadside statues along the old Lincoln Highway.

"Me too! Ever since me and my family moved to M-town I always wanted to come here," Chester slapped the concrete mold.

"Yeah, this pin, it's been here forever. Before my mom's time, even."

"Whoa! When was your mom born?"

"Early 60's. What was that for? 'Whoa!' She's not that old. What, are you gonna call ME old now?" Azul furrowed her brow to him.

"Oh. I wasn't saying y'all were old. Umm. We're talking about this statue here——" Chester was tripping on his words.

"I'm just playing. Hey, if we're gonna be in a band together you're gonna have to learn to know when I'm giving ya shit," Azul laughed and pulled him by his black silk shirt towards the entrance.

"Oh! Um. Allow me!" He hurried ahead of her and she watched him open the door for her.

"Aww! I thought chivalry was dead for metal dudes."

"We're the most chivalrous of all, my dear," Chester exhaled a breath of confidence as they entered.

* * *

The bowling alley had a throwback early 1980's feel. The carpet's color was faded blue. The upholstery, the equipment, the decor all looked totally unchanged since that time. Streams of pastel and neon colors were awash in the smoke-faded ceiling lights. The bar ran the length of the wall adjacent with the main entrance. The service desk protruded from the bar wall and it was stocked with varieties of different bowling balls in front. There were two pinball machines next to the desk, and the eight bowling lanes were easily accessible.

"Well, from what I've heard about this place is that one, the bowling lanes are crooked; two; the balls are total shit; and three, this place can get pretty damn rowdy," Azul said as they walked over to the service desk.

An obese, middle-aged, bleached-blond woman greeted them. She was wearing a faded, pastel pink, vintage Spuds McKenzie beach shirt, and was propped at the cash register, smoking a cigarette.

"Best three-out-of-five, hun?" Azul asked Chester as he got his chain wallet out of his black slacks.

"Sure that'll be fine," Chester pulled out a 20 dollar bill and went to the lady. "Five games for two please."

"I'll pay my half. Don't worry about it. How much ma'am?" Azul asked the woman.

"At eight o'clock, Cosmic Bowling starts. It's ten dollars each. All-you-can-bowl. It's almost that time, I'll give it to you two since you're so cute together. Shoe size?" she let out a husky phlegm-soaked laugh as the two smiled. They told her their sizes, and she got off her steel perch and hobbled behind the desk to look for their shoes hidden behind.

"It's alright Azul. I got this. I mean. This is a date. Right?" Chester with apprehension in his voice.

"Well, how 'bout this, you pay for the bowling; and I'll get the drinks. Fair enough?" Azul put her hand on his shoulder, putting him at ease as he agreed.

The customers were coming in as they got their shoes and picked out their bowling balls. There were two lanes already taken by two large families with small children. They chose the lane farthest away from the crowd.

"It'd be rad to play a place like this. I know there's a place in Chicago that has all the punk bands playing. The Fireside Bowl, I think. Yeah! The Ranch Bowl in Omaha is one venue, too! God, I've seen a few kick-ass shows there," Azul mused as Chester was getting his shoes on.

"Oh yeah. That'd be neat. Umm. Here comes the lady. You like popcorn? I'll take a Coke," The waitress walked up to their lane to take their orders. As Chester reached for his chain wallet, Azul brusquely stopped his hand from entering his pocket, and she started ordering in between playful touching. They both saw Rick walk in the front doors with a group of friends and Mandy, who was smiling and looked to be in good spirits.

They both tightened up their playful demeanors to finish their order. They both looked at each other, and Azul murmured an *Uh-oh*. "Should we say, what's up, or wait for them to see us?" Azul pulled Chester close and whispered.

He looked to their proximity to the bar, "Too late. Hey! How's it going," he shifted from whisper to a shout-out to Rick, whose arms were outstretched and he quickly approached their lane.

"Yo! My band! What's up motherfuckers! My fucking band is here!" Rick yelled at the top of his lungs. Some ladies from one of the family lanes glared at Rick for cursing so loudly in the presence of their children. They shook their heads and watched as Rick ran towards Azul and Chester's lane to give them ecstatic hugs.

"Whoa! Hey. Careful, man! Your knockin' people over here——" Azul said, as a result of Rick's overbearing hugs that sent both of them off-balance.

"Sorry! I just get so excited from seeing my brothas and sistas and shit! Gotta keep the family together, yo! You know what I'm saying?" Rick mimed in a husky hip-hop voice. "So, whatcha guys doing? It's too bad we didn't have our fucking instruments here. We could totally do an impromptu practice and just call it our first gig!" Rick laughed.

"Yeah! You know, we could. It might take some coaxing," Azul looked toward the bar where Mandy and her group of friends were socializing. "Besides, we only have what——two songs?"

"——not finished yet!" Chester added, with a chuckle.

"That's right," Rick laughed and took his voice down to a softer tone. "Hey look man, sorry about last practice. Again, it was just a small thing. Blown out of proportion. I got this under control alright? Mandy's cool. We're out having a good time tonight. It's her birthday. We're having some cocktails." He raised his hand for both of them to high-five, in which they reciprocated.

"Sweet!" Chester said, slightly taken aback by Rick's obvious intoxication.

"Yeah, man. Knock yourself out," Azul stated.

"Fuckin' come on up and join us. We can do some shots. Band shots! Novel idea——I don't wanna be hanging out with Mandy's lame-ass friends all night," Rick tried to get them both to come to the bar with him, but the two insisted on going about their night.

"Alright——I see," Rick threw his hands up in the air. "Well, don't be rock stars and leave me hanging. I'll be at the bar talking about big trucks and football with Mandy's friends. Feel free, my friends. Feel free…" He made a playful bow of adieu and whisked back to the bar. His voice returned to the loud gregarious tone that cut through the bowling alley crowd noise as he could be heard calling for shots to Mandy's social circle which included her sister, her sister's boyfriend, and three of their friends.

"Well, in a public setting, he is quite the natural frontman. Don't ya think?" Azul shrugged.

"He's a character alright," Chester agreed.

* * *

The bowling alley lights were shut off, and the black lights were turned on for Cosmic Bowling. Chester and Azul were having a good time. The bowling area and bar was packed, and the TV's were airing CNN and Fox News telecasts.

"Man, it seems to be getting worse in this country. All of the TV news shows are just relentless! Watch, I bet there's gonna be some idiot yelling, U-S-A, and is gonna start some shit with someone at the bar," Azul observed the drunken crowd.

"I never watch that stuff. It's forbidden at my parents' house. We don't even have a TV," Chester said.

"Whoa! Really?! That's probably a real blessing. Ya know, if you have people brainwashed by this shit twenty-four seven, the damage would be irreversible. Imagine in twenty years, someone raised by the O'Reilly Factor could do some real damage to this country."

"Oh yeah, by then, some stupid reality show TV star could be president by then——" Chester laughed while watching a news show graphic cut to a U.S. Army recruitment commercial.

"That bitch is down there! I see her! What the fuck is she doing down there with HIM? I can't believe you're into that shit Rick! You, and your FUCK buddies! You guys are having orgies where my kid sleeps?!" Mandy was yelling and could be heard above the crowd noise. She was marching towards Azul and Chester's lane as Rick was desperately trying to hold her back to keep her away from his new bandmates.

"Yeah, bitch! I'm talking to you! You fucking slut! You let all these guys fuck your body all over my house! You're trash! You're fucking trash! Get outta my town! Get outta my bowling alley!" Mandy's harshness had everyone's attention.

"Stop it! Stop it! We're leaving! We're leaving!" Rick was heard saying over, and over. His trademark loud voice was being overpowered by her demonic roar.

"Hey! Is there a problem? Take it outside! Better yet, leave!" a booming baritone voice cut through the commotion. A tall, husky man with dark features and long black hair confronted them and told them to leave his bowling alley.

Azul remembered him as the new owner. She had read about him in the newspaper and discovered he was a real member of the Chippewa tribe.

Chester put his arm around Azul. "Don't worry, I got you——" Azul rubbed his hand to acknowledge his gesture.

"Well, I guess you fucking Indians stick up for one another! Goddamn it! They're takin' over my town. This is MY bowling alley! Whores! Fucking whores! What the fuck are YOU looking at?!" Mandy snapped at a random onlooker.

Rick brought her to her sister's circle of friends. They got the intoxicated blond to not struggle, and they turned around to walk her out as she was still yelling.

That bitch is fucking guys all over my house, was the last thing that Azul and Chester could hear as they went over to the bar area to see Rick, who was pacing back and forth, muttering incoherently, and punching the air in anger.

Chester turned to Azul to console her as she bit her lip and shook her head while staring at the front entrance.

"Don't believe anything that crazy woman is saying. You're a true, one-of-a-kind person Azul," Chester tried to hug her, yet she was rigid as steel against his teddy bear-like embrace.

"...and I thought I was having a good week. Excuse me," She broke away from Chester and marched to Rick who was still pacing where he stood.

"Hey, uhh...goddamnit," Rick murmured.

"What does she know about me? I've never even met her, and this is how she talks to total strangers? And what are you doing about it? I'm nobody's fucking punching bag!" Azul was about to say more until Rick stopped her.

"Hey, hey, hey——I'm sorry. She doesn't know a damn thing about what we do. What any of us do! We've been off and on for a reason. I just...I-I'm done with this bitch! I'm gonna get my shit and leave. Tonight! I can't fucking put up with her any longer. We're gonna fucking practice tomorrow at Chester's! Chester?" Rick turned to Chester.

"Umm——yeah, man. For sure. We planned on it. Anything you want. You need help with anything tonight? I can come over——" Chester responded in his soft-spoken way, but Rick interrupted.

"Naw man! Naw man——I got it tonight. I'll call Jesus later."

"Okay. Okay, Rick——" Chester nodded.

"Damn it Azul...I'm sorry I had to put you through this. There's nothing more that I want and NEED right now is to make music and I wanna make music with you! If we can get this behind us, we won't have to worry about Mandy ever again. I just——fuckin' forgive me. I'll make it up to you," Rick was on the verge of tears.

Azul sighed and nodded. "Man. Okay. I'll see you tomorrow. I'll stop by your place at the same time to make sure everything is cool. I'll just wait in the parking lot. You and Jesus and Mick, too, can follow me to Chester's. I know the way."

Rick sighed in relief, and hugged her. He started to sob. "Thank you. You're a brave woman for doing this, ya know——" Azul let her steely guard down and returned the embrace. She gave him an assuring pat on the back.

"Please be careful. Don't do anything stupid," Azul said to him, hoping it would resonate.

* * *

Azul and Chester returned their shoes and balls to the service desk. They went outside in silence by the big statue and were reeling from what transpired in the bowling alley.

"Now I'm having second thoughts," Azul said.

"Umm, about what?"

"About jamming with Rick and his whole world of unnecessary drama. I've looked all over to find a band to be in and this whole thing with Mandy is getting in the way. I swear, if Rick just ends up staying with her tonight, it's over for me."

Chester sighed, and spoke. "Maybe it'll be like he said. Just a minor thing. He'll break up with her tonight. We'll meet at my place, and it'll all be good."

"Nothing is ever that simple, Chester. Women will complicate things. It always happens in relationships," Azul crossed her arms and looked at the hazy sky, where no star was visible.

Chester nodded in agreement, looked down at the patterns of cracks on the concrete, and sighed again. "Well, I'd better get home and clean up the space. I gotta move the drums and amps around down there. My car's all the way across the lot. Umm, great time, right?" Chester added with a laugh. Azul pulled him in to give him a kiss. Their size difference made it so Chester lost his balance. He almost fell toward her, catching himself in time. They both laughed, then kissed once more.

"It's been weird. But really interesting. This part especially," Azul assured him.

"Wow! Well...I will see you tomorrow then! My place. Bye."
Chester parted with a blushing smile.

The parking lot was full. Azul had parked in the closest space next
to the bowling pin. Azul was looking for her keys in her hemp purse
when the owner walked out of the front doors, lit a cigarette, then
greeted her in Meskwaki.

"*Hoat!* You're Native right?" His booming baritone endearing her
with a certain familiarity of the Native men in her life back in Tama.

"Yeah. I noticed you were, too. I uh, saw your thing in the
paper about you taking ownership of this place," Azul smiled and
instinctively used her *Rez-style* head and lip pointing gestures.

"Yeah! It's a good investment. The family likes it here. We're from
Minnesota originally. Way up there. Fond du Lac. So, are those your
friends?" he pointed his head down the road, as if pointing to Rick
and Mandy's circle of friends that were, most likely, far across town.

Azul shook her head and chuckled. "Not really. The crazy
one's boyfriend is a friend of mine. We play in a band. She thinks
something else is going on. I don't know her at all."

"Oh really...hmm." He took another drag. "Well, be careful. Those
Mookoman ladies will do some crazy shit. *Enit?*"

Azul laughed, and nodded. "Yup. True dat."

CHAPTER FOURTEEN

Rick was in a faraway state of despair when he was found by himself in the humid dawn, sitting on a marble bench in the cemetery by his house. He had a deep swelling cut on his right temple with dried blood encrusted over his face like a grisly crimson mask.

"What the hell did you do, man?" Jesus asked Rick who was still in his clothes from the night before: a white cotton "wifebeater," with an unbuttoned and hot-colored Hawaiian shirt, ripped jeans, and his gray skateboarding shoes, all stained in dried blood.

Rick took a swig of a half-full bottle of Jack Daniels, winced at the sting as it burned down his throat. "Fuck all, man. I'm alright. *(Cough)* She's alright. I uhh…shit, I busted a beer bottle over my head. Put my head through the mirror of the medicine cabinet. Twin Peaks-style." He revealed both of his knuckles were wounded, too.

"She wouldn't shut up. She practically begged for me to hit her. So, I just exploded on myself, instead of her. She uhh...yeah..." he hawked up a loogie, spit on the grass before him, and cracked his neck.

"Can you forgive yourself for putting yourself through this?" Jesus asked and he offered his bandana from his shorts pocket for Rick to clean his face.

Rick looked at the bandana. He smirked. "Is that some shit that they teach at the AA? One of the stairs to ascend into the heavens of his majesty? Do I have to forgive myself to sit next to him on his throne?" Rick took the bandana to his eyes.

"Well, the blood is your own. It's in you. Now it's out of you. I guess...I guess we can thank someone for intervening on your behalf," Jesus looked above him and stared at a looming marble statue of the Christ, with arms outstretched, staring down upon them. "Who THAT is, isn't OUR place to know. But I guess, the point is that some of that bloodletting had to happen in order for something to stay in balance. Sometimes, I understand it. Sometimes, I don't. But all I can do is offer you my hand, man..."

"I love her, man..." Rick shook his head and trembled as he inhaled and exhaled. "I'd never hurt her like that. But, man——her words are like...anchors gouging through my limbs. When I get that way, all I see is red. Red. Then, it's over and it's always me that's taking the damage. Or, uh...damages." He looked at his scarred hands, hawked a blood clot loogie, and spit. They stayed silent for awhile.

"You got some shit? We can——" Rick started.

Jesus interrupted. "No, I don't got any shit. That's the last thing you need. What we need is to get you out of that house. Come and stay with me for awhile. Don't get too comfortable, but we'll get to your next move, quick."

"Yeah. You know, I was just coming here. I come here a lot actually——" Rick took another swig and wiped his mouth. "This is the place where we all end up. I think about it. Especially, when I'm by myself——" he wiped his face with the handkerchief again. "Well, I figured if I had died last night; I wouldn't have too far to go."

"Did you come here to die? Is that what was going through your head?" Jesus shook his head, then stared at him.

Rick just stared in front. In a state of looking at nothing and everything all at once. "I figured I'd just bleed out with a bottle of fuckin' whiskey in my hand. But before that...I called you. So, I guess in reality, I wanted to be stopped. Turns out, I got you to count on, man. That's the beautiful thing in all this bullshit," he took another swig. "Besides, I told you that's how my dad went. Alone. Bleeding out, with a bottle of whiskey in HIS hand," he paused and looked to the east. "I don't wanna end up like that..."

CHAPTER FIFTEEN

Azul pulled into the parking lot at 9:00 to find that Jesus was already there and parked alongside Rick's car, helping him load his drum kit and his personal belongings into both cars. She groaned, rolled down her window to ask what was going on.

Jesus walked up to her and explained that Rick and Mandy got in a huge argument, he beat himself up really bad, and that he was *leaving today*.

"Beat HIMSELF up? Oh my god——I know they were arguing last night. I was there when the shit went down. Chester and I saw her at the bowling alley freaking out on me and creating a damn scene. He said he was leaving——"

Jesus interrupted her. "Wait, you saw them? You and Chester? Out at the bowling alley? He failed to relay that part——" he explained that he got a message late last night and came to Marshalltown as soon as he could.

"Is she here? Well, I guess I should be asking is she and the boy okay?"

"As far as I know. He said he never touched her. The boy is living with the dad somewhere here in Marshalltown. She was gone when I got here. He left a written message on the front door that he was gonna be under the Jesus statue in the cemetery on the hill"

"Oh my god...Well, what about practice? Does Mick know? Chester is still expecting us."

"I know. We'll wait for Mick to show, and we'll follow you out to Chester's. We're still gonna do practice. But Rick is still out of it. I don't think his condition is going to send any great first impressions. You know what I'm saying? Chester still lives with his parents, right?"

Azul sighed. "Yes."

* * *

"I'm making a fresh batch of cookies if you kids are wondering what that wonderful smell is! I'm pleased to meet all of you. The friends that Chester brings to the house all seem to be such talented and nice people. Chester has been talking a lot about your band, and hey, maybe we can invite some people over, we can all have a listen to your guys' music! Wouldn't that be great?" Chester's mom, Pam, cheerfully greeted them all. Her silver hair tied back. Her hands clasped on her black and white checkered baking apron that fit her petite frame like the world's most recognizable family TV cook.

"Thank you Mrs——" the band, sans Chester, collectively resounded.

"Pam! Just call me Pam! And don't call me missus. I'm not that old, ya know! Haha! I play in a band, too, with my husband and some of our church friends. Maybe, you've seen us before. We've played Oktemberfest every year since we've moved here. Now, which one of you is from Marshalltown? Or, is everyone here from Des Moines?"

"I live in Marshalltown!" Azul raised her hand like she was back in grade school.

"Me too!" Mick answered, with a child-like hand raise of his own.

They engaged in small talk as Rick was uncharacteristically keeping a low profile in the back of the group. He hid under a baseball cap, and green hoodie, and was looking down the entire time.

"Well, we should get started guys. Mom, if you wouldn't mind——" Chester chuckling, and obviously embarrassed by the doting mother routine.

"Oh, well——Here I go! Being a chatterbox. This basement is soundproofed so play as loud as you want! Chester's brother has a band that practices here, too, and they get pretty loud and raucous. They're a punk band. They're called Jizz-69, if you've heard of them. The cookies should be ready by the time you guys finish. Ooh, and I'm making finger sandwiches! Hope you guys will enjoy! Buh-bye——" she slammed the soundproofed door shut, abruptly canceling out all sound.

"Dawg...that was a trip!" Azul whispered in astonishment to Mick, nudging his arm.

"She's so sweet, I don't know what came over me when I raised my hand like that——" Mick laughed.

Songwriting: Anchor

"Sorry, if I'm dragging today, guys. I tried everything in my body and mind to be here in the practice room. To be of sound mind, I guess. I'm all messed up. This is the lowest you'll ever see me. I'm leaving that house and leaving Mandy for good. I'm not going back there after this. I want to continue doing this band. I want nothing more than to be here, creating music with you guys. I have some issues that I need to take care of. But that's not gonna affect my playing ability and commitment," Rick said while sitting slouched on his drum stool, looking haggard. He was still wearing his hoodie to deliberately sweat out the alcohol.

"What happened?" Chester asked.

Rick explained what happened the night before. He briefly forayed into his history with Mandy. He warned them that his temper could match hers, but he wouldn't dare show that side of him to his bandmates, who he considered like brothers.

"——And sisters, too. Azul. Sorry about everything again. I know I'm being redundant on that. But it's already behind us now. Look at us. I mean, we're all here now. We're pushing ahead already——"

Jesus started playing a psychedelic guitar line. They all fumbled around on their guitar necks. The weight of Rick's ordeal was heavy on the mood. No one was saying much.

Rick finally caught onto a groove that followed Jesus's line. Azul joined in with a lower octave riff. Chester was *walking* around on the bass than decided to just play in-unison with Azul. She switched keys and Chester followed her. Mick locked into a polyrhythm that complimented Rick's drums, all the elements coalesced into something that made sense.

"That part should be the verse," Azul commented after they stopped for a minute. "If Jesus wants to keep doing that riff, I can do this different chord progression to make it sound darker and more ominous. I got this riff that would make a good chorus after that." She showed them the latter riff. They jammed on that awhile, and everyone liked it.

"Let's keep going on that cycle. Repeat those in sequence, over and over——" Rick said, regaining cognizance and focus. They jammed away for an hour, and he started doing vocal lines as he was drumming. They took a break, and Chester rushed to give Rick a microphone behind his drumkit.

"That's really starting to feel good. I've never heard anything that sounds like that. It almost could be like an unreleased Doors song or something!" Jesus said.

"Yeah, man, I was channeling Jim a little. You guys like it?" Rick adjusted the microphone stand to his liking behind his kit. Everyone agreed, and started throwing in their opinions and ideas. Rick, in the middle of the conversation, grabbed his pen and notebook from his drumstick bag and started writing lyrics.

"She throws anchors that gouge my skin, All I see is red, she begs for me to release, seducing me to the jail bed," Rick was thinking outloud.

After a few minutes, Jesus asked Rick if the creative outburst felt good.

"Yeah, man! This is just what I needed," Rick answered while scribbling down more thoughts into his notebook.

The band jammed on the new tune and got a rough structure down. There was a sense of accomplishment that they chiseled out a solid tune as a result of Rick's struggle. Nobody was more relieved than Rick as he named the song: *Anchor*.

"I'm glad we pushed through and did this. I'm really digging this song, man!" Jesus said with celebratory praise that was cut short by an irritating, sharp pain in his left hand. "Ah! Fuck, my hand's cramping up. Let's quit, man," he stretched his hand and winced from the pain.

"Well, we have to get it down on the tape recorder. Can we run through it again? Ya know, so we have something to listen to for the week?" Azul asked with some disappointment in her voice. Rick concurred. The other two just listened.

"I have to work tonight! I don't wanna be dealing with maximum fuckin' pain for the rest of the day! I need rest!" Jesus snapped. Once again, creating a certain tension in the room.

Rick sighed, "Well, that's fine. We can remember what we got until next time we get together." He put his sticks back in his bag. Everyone else nodded and started to break down their equipment.

After a few minutes of uncomfortable silence, Jesus apologized to everyone and revealed he had Chronic Carpal Tunnel Syndrome in both of his hands.

He explained for the past year he tried to work around the pain, day-to-day, so as not to risk permanent injury. His retail job wasn't helping in his healing and he vowed to never quit playing guitar.

"I'm burning the candle at both ends, but I'm doing the best I can to stay healthy."

"Well, man, just let us know when we need to stop playing when your hands start hurting," Azul assured Jesus.

"Oh man, I'm not gonna be a whiny little bitch about it. You don't have to worry about that. I mean, but hopefully, with some care, I'll be able to go for a long time," Jesus answered like a burden was finally lifted from his shoulders.

The door swung open as Pam entered with a large silver tray of snacks that was half the size of her body. "Hello, hello! Snack time is here, guys! ...AND girl!" Her jubilation was exclaimed by a sing-songy hum and giggle.

"Hmm. I could get used to this," Azul said to Jesus as he tied his hair back.

"Oh man, it'll be the best meal I've gotten all week," he replied in absolute surety of gorging himself with the tray's contents, which had the freshly-baked cookies and finger sandwiches Pam promised. Also, with crackers, cheese, celery, blue cheese, and pâté.

The Bastard Chronicle IV: A New Hope

And so it goes, our heroes are woodshedding and crafting their repertoire into battle hymns and great American standards that will stand the test of time. At least, we hope.

The songwriting has been going super-duper well! I never say: super-duper. That's some real white people verbiage going on right there. They're rubbing off on me, dammit!

It's probably just Chester's mom that's rubbing off on me. It's ehh, eye-opening to see Chester interact at home. It's cute, though.

Mick's fam is pretty well put-together, the common, good ol' American nuclear family.

I've always wondered how people like these see a single-mother family household like mine. Fascination or pity? A little bit of both maybe?

That reminds me: Mom has been sober for two years now! I'm proud of her. It'd be great if she were like Pam, commandeering a nice house with a soundproofed basement hidden in the outskirts of town with a prize-winning husband. Alas, my mama is raising two kids on her own, works and is trying to get her degree. Poor brown people problems. There's not enough time in the day to be the doting, mother-goose, "Suzy Homemaker" type. Especially living on Melody Lane. The social inertia is too great. (Sigh...)

Another reminder: I'm about due to leave the nest aren't I?

But, I'm learning a lot by seeing this whole 'nother side of life on the other side of town.

Rick and Jesus were both raised in a single-mom situation, too. Which is probably a huge reason why we are clicking so well. I feel accepted. It's cool that being a girl in a boys' club isn't raising any issues internally, yet. But externally...

We haven't heard about Mandy in awhile. It sounds like it is truly over. Rick's mood has improved. He's now staying in town with one of his buddies.

I still find myself looking over my shoulder around town. I still have that visual of her being the "Drunken Accuser" at Cosmic Bowling. She goes to the same school I go to, so that's a thing. I'm guessing I'm known as "Queen Orgy" in her clique...

* * *

The band took a photo session, too! I can't forget that. We went to Des Moines at the state capital building and got some great shots.

The two Empty Caste dudes got their webmaster Kitty to do the photos! It was good to finally meet her as she is a fellow brown chick. Yes! I'm not alone after all. We had some good laughs. Turns out, she does a few other bands' websites, too.

She expressed the apprehension she felt about putting up Rick's "suicide note" on their web page. Toby, their second bassist threatened her to put it on there.

He sounds like a real piece of work. Threatening a nice girl like that? But it sounds like he's a violent one. Jesus said he got lucky he didn't get mauled by him. They expect him to retaliate. It's making Rick and Jesus look over their shoulders, too. A "White, Mama's Boy, Wannabe Suge Knight" is what Rick calls him. I hope we never have to deal with him.

I hope Charlie and Spike are doing okay. I haven't heard from them since she hooked the band up. I haven't formally thanked her for that yet. I'm especially hoping she talks to her family again. She needs all the support she can get.

I started writing some riffs inspired by her heterochromia eyes. (Heart flutter!)

But, things for us are turning out really good. I haven't been this excited since the fam and I moved to M-town. New beginnings!

I can't wait for the next practice session!

PT II

CHAPTER EIGHTEEN

I guess in hindsight, since I haven't talked about it for so long, the main reason I cut my hair was shedding off the old *Me*. Peeling away old skin. In a sense, I was in a transitional phase and acclimating to this new thing.

As a patrilineal culture, the Meskwaki way wasn't conducive to what I wanted to do. You know, I wanted to find a band and be the next big thing.

I should point out, though I grew up there, I wasn't a tribal member. That's two different things that I always have to explain to people.

Anyways, back in the beginning, when I played guitar in my cousin's band with my friend Marlin, it started out being fun, and we were jamming on covers. More of the metal shit. Which was great!

Then I started writing my own riffs and songs; and let me tell you, it's not as awesome as you see in the movies like *The Doors,* or that Johnny Cash flick, or *Ray.*

Q: Dewey Cox? (Laughs)

Yeah! That one was good. Where the riff comes up and the band comes together and the song is finished right then and everyone is dancing. (Laughs)

I use to present a riff, or an idea, and then the other "creative partners" in the band would laugh at it, or wouldn't respond. It's a total beat-down of your ego and confidence when that happens!

Add the chauvinist, macho upbringing of these Meskwaki guys saying to me that "Girls shouldn't be writing songs——" or "Eee! You must be a witch!" or just flat-out saying my ideas sucked, it really brought me down. Yeah.

I made a five-song demo tape. They heard it. Laughed in my face. Shot it down. That's when I was like, well, maybe you can do better? Show me master! Please, show me how it's done! (Laughs)

Then, nothing. The band disintegrated. Marlin became really good at quitting all the time. My cousin turned out to be a pathological liar. Blah, blah, blah. That was that——

Q: You were looking for a band, having no luck, yet, this bizarre circumstance with people you just met in a dark alley throws you an opportunity to meet the right people. I can imagine that was great for you.

For sure. We took the ball and ran with it!

Q: It also was an exciting time in the music scene amid the post-911 era. What was that like?

It was awesome! Bands were playing out all the time. No one knew what was gonna happen. We heard about record labels coming out and scouting the scene. It was the next Seattle and we were in the thick of it. We learned a lot of new skills really quick, and we got to know hard work, real fast.

CHAPTER NINETEEN

The band started a regular practice schedule at Jesus's house in Des Moines.

Chester canceled practice for two weekends in a row for different reasons. By the third week, he stopped answering his phone.

Jesus rented a house with his wife Amy. She was four months pregnant when the band loaded their gear into the musty basement that had an aluminum storm shelter two-panel door with a precariously jagged concrete stairwell going down. There was no soundproofing at all.

"Is Amy gonna mind the noise, dude?" Rick asked.

"We talked about it. She doesn't mind, just as long as we always have a set time to start and quit. I talked to the neighbors, and everyone is totally cool. We lucked out, man!" Jesus answered.

The house was on the south side of Des Moines. A small white rental on a corner. A typical working-class family lived next door to them. The father was a middle-aged, leather-skinned, overweight man who introduced himself right away to the motley crew of musicians on their first day of loading in. His name was Jim, and he became their first fan.

"What type of music you guys play?" asked Jim with a beer in hand, speaking in a slight southern drawl.

Jesus answered, "It's got a little bit of everything. Rock, punk, blues, freaky circus stuff. Country."

"Country! Hell, I love country! You know any Haggard? Judds? We'll get along just fine if you play some David Alan Coe!" Jim took a swig, wiped his mouth, and scratched his full keg of a beer gut.

Jesus laughed, "No nothing like that. But you never know, man!"

Jim turned to Azul, "Get on him about that. I'm sure with a pretty voice like yours, you could sing some Judds! D'you sing?"

Azul coyly responded, "Sure. I try. You must really like the Judds, Jim."

"Oh man! I do. We need some good healin' music around here. None of that rap crap or that heavy metal——" Jim did a rock pose and head-banged in place, almost spilling his beer.

Everyone laughed. Rick responded, "We'll do what we can brotha. We're just writing more songs. Feel free to come down anytime and listen to us jam!"

"Oh shit! I will. I will, anytime my ol' lady gets on my fuckin' case I'll just come down here and drink a cold one and watch you play! Y'all drink wine? I got a wine cellar in my basement. I make the shit! If you know anyone that wants some good homemade wine I'll sell it cheap!" He toasted to the band and took his exit.

"When did we start writing country songs?" Azul asked Jesus.

"I've been working on it." He put his long hair in a pony tail and turned on his amp.

Azul snorted and replied, "Well, we'll push it to the bottom of the list..."

Songwriting: Hunting The Pig

"This next song I wrote is about hunting and killing my ex's lover, who she was cheating on me with," Jesus said.

"Dude, are you saying you actually killed someone?" Azul furrowed her brow at him.

"No! No——" Jesus laughed, "This is totally fictional. I caught them in bed after I took our daughter to the hospital for an ear infection. Did I tell you this story?" Jesus was sitting cross-legged at his pedal board during a break. Rick and Mick were smoking outside. Azul was seated on the haphazardly placed couch having a beer.

"Damn——I didn't know. Sorry you had to go through that. Didn't you write a song like that before? It was on your old band's CD? That was pretty brutal."

"Yeah——Brutal in what way?" Jesus took a drink of his soda.

"Heavy. I remember seeing you guys play, and you introduced that song before you played it. You went off on unfaithful, greedy, irresponsible whores, and started a, 'You Fucking Whore' chant," Azul recalled.

Jesus laughed at the memory. "Yeah that must've been at the old rock bar and strip club by the airport. It used to be called, The Runway."

"I think it was still The Runway before it shut down. Your bass player was all drunk. He could barely stand."

"Yeah, we started doing that chant for the next few gigs. We had to stop because the other guys didn't want me doing it anymore."

"It was cool! I mean it left an impression on the crowd and made your band stand out," Azul picked up her guitar from the stand next to her amp, flicked the *On* switch, and took it back with her to the couch.

"Yeah, but I was partying pretty damn hard. I used to drink all day. Everyday, back in those days. On show days I would rage hard and get rowdy. Destructive, man. That's why I quit drinking," Jesus got up to strap on his guitar and turned on his amp.

"Is it hard to fight the urge? I mean, Rick, it seems like he's always got a beer in his hand. I figured you'd think twice about starting another band with him."

"Well, he's a good dude. Crazy. But we've been through a lot. The dude can fucking play. I could never play drums AND do vocals at the same time. Great lyric writer, too!"

"Yeah true. I was super stoked that he called me. I almost quit trying to look for people to play music with."

"Oh yeah? I remember feeling that way, too. I used to live in Earlham. A small hick town on the west side of the state. Not much to do except get fucked up and get in trouble. I got my first guitar from a small town yard sale, where everyone in the whole town had something for sale. Everyone looked forward to that every year. You can find some cool things at those big bazaars." Jesus fumbled around on a lick, turned on his tuner pedal, and started tuning.

"Yeah, I know exactly how that small town shit is. So, whatever happened to your bass player that was too drunk to stand at your show that night?" asked Azul, as she raked her strings to hear if her amp was on.

"He didn't last very long. Uhh, where's our bass player we're supposed to have now?" Jesus responded, as he looked toward the unused bass amplifier in the corner which he bought used for 300 dollars so that Chester didn't have to haul his rig from Marshalltown for every practice.

"Chester hasn't been answering. We don't know what his deal is," Azul looked toward the storm door to see if the two smokers were still outside. "I hope he doesn't quit. We got a good thing going with him."

"How's it going with you two? Did things get weird between you?"

"Honestly, probably. Most of all for him. Looking back on it now, maybe he really wanted one thing and I wanted another. Maybe, I wanted everything. Ya know, friend with benefits——boyfriend with benefits, sort of thing. I'd like it all, but I guess that's too much to ask of a person. Especially a young guy like him——"

"I see what you're saying. It's a crazy deal to get into that situation. Personally, I could see having a relationship with a bandmate being no problem at all. But I've been wrong before," Jesus strummed an E power chord to A sharp power chord. "But if he has a problem, he should straight-up answer the phone and talk about it; instead of leaving us all hanging. You know what I'm saying?"

The others were coming down the jagged stairwell. Azul watched them and sighed. "Yeah. You're totally right about that. We can't get nothing done if someone doesn't want to be here."

"What are you guys talking about? Chester? Fuck him. Sorry, I know you two were getting sweet and all; but we got a good thing going. We need a kick-ass bassist who wants to be here. Anyone got any ideas? We're gonna have shows coming up," Rick walked behind his kit. Mick remained silent.

Azul got perturbed by the *sweet* comment. "It's none of your business if we were getting sweet as you call it. Thank you very much. But we were talking about him not being here, and yes, we do agree."

Rick put his palms up in a calming gesture. "I'm just saying. No hard feelings. We gotta start calling or e-mailing people." He reached into his shorts pocket to get his keys, which had his drumhead tuning key attached and started tuning his snare.

Azul sighed and thought for a bit. "Well, shit. I know a guy..." Azul bit her bottom lip and chugged a tremolo rhythm on her guitar.

"Can you get him here by next practice?" Rick finished tuning his snare and hit it two times.

CHAPTER TWENTY-ONE

"This is where you guys practice?" Marlin remarked with a smile, and an air of ridicule in his baritone voice.

"Yes. This is actually our third practice space since we started," she parked The Hoopty in front of Jesus's house. "We don't have to tear down our gear this time. Which is nice for a change."

"Damn! You leave your stuff here? In Des Moines?" his voice in disbelief. "I wouldn't trust anyone to leave my gear here in this neighborhood!" He looked around at the quiet southside Des Moines block, let out a tisk, and shook his head. Some sparrows chirped nearby.

"Well, don't worry about an amp. We got one here for you," Azul sighed as she put the car in park.

"Fuck, man——Remember your cousin's house? We could make all the noise we wanted. No neighbors. Play ball during breaks. No one bothered us," Marlin reminisced.

"That was a long time ago. We got everything we need here. You'll like the guys. Everyone's nothing but cool here, man." She started to get out of the car.

"Hey, hey. Do you wanna hit this pipe before we go in? New situations make me nervous. Besides, it's not like we're drinking yet." He took out a small velvet sash and revealed a brand new glass pipe and a small plastic bag of weed. "It'll relax you. I got this pipe brand new in Iowa City. This weed is from Colorado. Cost me a grip, but I was like, fuck it! Per-cap is coming up next week anyway. My cousin, Lou, remember him? He just graduated. He got his big money. He owes me some of that, too."

"Uhh, no. I can't play like that. Did you really spend the rest of your money on weed, and a pipe? God, I could think of so many better ways to spend my money."

"Hey, it'll make you play better. Remember we got high down in Tama? And we walked around downtown, and almost got our asses kicked by the cholos and gangster wannabes? We wrote a song about it later that night. I still got that tape somewhere..." He started packing the bowl of his pipe to full capacity.

Azul snorted. "I bet you're still listening to that tape everyday. Shit, I tried smoking later on and tried to write some songs to see if the myths where true, that getting high will make you *more creative*," she shook her head. "Total bullshit. I just ended up really paranoid and sought food for comfort and pigged out."

"*Sah!* Your doing it wrong den. Here, let's hit this," he handed the pipe to Azul, who just got out and slammed the door.

"Go ahead. No one's stopping you. Hurry up. We'll grab your bass, and we'll get your sound dialed in," Azul said. She looked around the neighborhood to see if anyone was watching. Then she heard Marlin take his first hit. Loud coughing ensued. She shook her head and went to the trunk to get his bass.

      * * *

"It's sounding good, dude!" Jesus complimented Marlin's performance.

"Thanks, man. I'm just learning this stuff now. The songs sound pretty good," Marlin nodded and stretched his arms overhead, accidentally knocking a wooden beam just above him. His towering 6'2" frame didn't make it easy for him to move around in Jesus's subterranean dwelling.

Jesus laughed. "It's okay dude. Sorry for the meager accommodations. All I used this basement for was storage. You're a big dude. Here, let me get you a chair to sit on as we're playing."

"It's alright. Hey, Az, remember the basement at your place we used to practice in? That was worse, enit——"

"Oh yeah. It was like this, but about half a foot lower. That place was awful!" Azul remembered as they both told the story of their first jam spot at Azul's house in Tama back in their high school days.

"Yeah, at least at your place, you had two stories, enit?" Marlin remarked to Azul.

Azul unstrapped her guitar to go outside for break with the others. "Yeah, that was a long time ago," she said as she arched her eyebrow, gave a sigh, and asked him if he wanted to come and hang with them. He declined.

She got upstairs and the rest of the band were taking a cigarette break and in good spirits.

"Hey Azul, I'm waiting on a call from the guy who's promoting a Winter Ball at Mega Toad's. You've been there right?" Rick boomed in his animated style.

"Yeah, I saw a New Year's Eve gig there. What's up?" Azul asked.

"Well, we know the guy from the Empty Caste days and I told him we got a new project in the works. He says he can get us on the gig! It'd be a huge opportunity for us!" Rick's enthusiasm, though infectious didn't resonate well in Azul's skeptic ears.

"Yeah, well we barely have five songs ready, and we're teaching Marlin to play bass on them right now. Will we be ready? I don't think so," Azul crossed her arms, as if to convey the point.

"Fuckin' aye we'll be ready. It's a little more than two months away as long as we don't skip a practice," Rick said while both Jesus and Mick agreed.

Azul looked down at the basement steps, grimaced, and nodded. "Well, I guess we'll make it work." It was settled and the three were in good spirits, Azul said to the group before heading back downstairs, "I'll tell Marlin." She mouthed to herself while in the crawlspace, *Well, I guess Marlin's in the band now...*

Azul visibly had her doubts as she went down to tell Marlin. He just took a drag and was coughing from his pipe when she told him about the upcoming gig. He nodded his head and spoke nonchalantly, "That's cool."

The Bastard Chronicle 5: WIP's

We haven't decided on a band name, yet. We need a new one for the show coming up.

Rick brought a stack of flyers one day at practice, and they billed us as the Empty Caste. Definitely annoying...

So, we all tried to come up with names. Ohh man, we laughed so hard at some of the names we were coming up with!

"Chester's Rejects"

"The Chippewa Sirens"

"The Psycho Ex's"

"Open Mic Nite At Toby's"

"Mama's Boy"

"Panic And Murder" (Acronym: PAM)

"Riot of Chimpanzees"

"Yard Sale Prostitute"

"Spunk Ugly"

We ALMOST chose "Jesus in Drag" because Jesus is gonna dress in drag at the show. It was a part of their act in the Empty Caste to piss off Toby, since he's a big homophobe. I'm all about it, so I don't have to be the only girl that has to worry about wardrobe malfunctions while onstage!

I brought up "Vultures, Bastards, and Thieves" It was an idea I got from something Grandma had said at Aunt Sandra's funeral. It was a warning to watch over and protect the body while it was being transported from the wake to be laid to rest in the cemetery.

"There are always vultures, bastards, and thieves wanting to desecrate bodies before they enter the spirit world," she used to say.

That stuck with me. I guess it did for a reason. VBT, man! I hope the name sticks!

We've got a five-song setlist:

Hunting the Pig

Total Sexual Thing

Anchor

The House by the Cemetery

9/11

The latter was the acoustic song I was working on the night I met Spike and Charlie. I like the other guys' input and it sounds a bit too moody for a rock show, but we're gonna try it. I hope it works because it's nice and with the name: 9/11, there is no one that's gonna have the balls to write a song after such a tragedy!

* * *

I've been putting tons of miles on The Hoopty, as of late. Driving to Tama to pick up Marlin, to practice in Des Moines and back is taxing. We've been able to get in two, sometimes three practices a week now. I barely have time at all. A new semester is here. My job is getting in the way. But I need that paycheck.

I'm making $6.50 an hour on my night shift. With all the miles I'm putting in, it's just not cutting it. I need a day job soon. With better pay, hopefully, after graduation. I need my nights totally free since we'll be playing shows now.

As far as Marlin being in the band, in my mind, it's only temporary. At least until this first gig. After that, we'll see. I don't tell the other guys that. If he had his driver's license, it wouldn't be so bad because I wouldn't have to pick him up.

But then again, at least, since I've been giving him rides every week, we can count on him being there.

He gets about $3000 in his Per-Cap check every month and can't even drive his brand new Escalade that's just sitting there in his parents' garage.

He's on his third Operating While Intoxicated charge. He has to serve prison time in the upcoming year. (Sigh)

It's depressing because that is the norm for a Meskwaki dude that gets Per-Cap. They get all that money after high school, spend a few months ballin', get a couple of nice rides, and then the offenses start piling up. Then they score prison time, wreck their cars, and get barred from driving by age 24.

The cops are shaking their heads, "Y'all should've never gave them NDN's money!"

Well, at least NDN's are giving them job security, right? The cycle continues...

But, as much as I don't admit it outright, I hope he gets his head out of his ass and gets his life back together. He's a talented cat. He can play anything. I'm doing my part to show him the world. I like to see my brotha's levitated.

But we'll see how long I can carry on this highway zealotry.

CHAPTER TWENTY-THREE

"Have we decided on a name?" Azul asked, as she arrived at Jesus's basement as the band, sans Marlin, was packing up their gear.

"Hey, what's up! We can decide that now. I've just been so busy. I haven't got around to brainstorming any serious names," answered Jesus, as he was unplugging his amp and effects pedal board.

"Today's the day, right? Yeah, man. I'm still loving *Spunk Ugly*. I don't know about you guys. I'm sticking to it 'till I die!" Rick declared as he was putting his cymbals in his cymbal bag. Azul and Jesus just looked at each other and smirked.

"Where's the homeboy? Marlin? He showing up, man?" asked Jesus.

"He said his cousin was picking him up, and was gonna leave the same time I was leaving M-town. In theory, he should be here a few minutes after me," Azul answered with concern in her voice.

"Ah! Well, we got time. It's two o'clock now. Load-in is at four. Mega Toad is just a couple of miles east of here," Jesus said. He looked at his watch. "That reminds me, I gotta take my girl clothes out of the washer and dry them now."

"Yes! You're doing it! Now, what am I gonna wear?" Rick said with excitement.

"Ah shit! So, are you gonna be the prettiest one on stage tonight?" Azul arched her eyebrow at Jesus.

"Don't worry! I look pretty damn horrendous in drag! It'll be great!" Jesus said as he whisked up the basement stairs to be met by Marlin coming down the steps. "Oh hey! What's up dude!"

"Hey, what's going on...uhh." Marlin couldn't remember his name.

"Jesus. Uhh, excuse me guys. I gotta get upstairs. Thanks."

Marlin had a crew of three guys with him. They let Jesus through the staircase. Azul had recognized them. Rick and Mick were taken aback by the surprise visitors.

"Hey guys. Had a helluva time finding the place on my own. Traffic was kinda crazy. Oh yeah, these are my cousins," Marlin was mumbling slowly and monotonously. His eyes were glassy, and he looked lethargic. Everyone politely exchanged their greetings.

"What's up Drew. 'Sup Cyrus. Hey Lou! Haven't seen you in a grip!" Azul went to school with both Drew and Cyrus, two years in descending age behind her. Lou, the smallest, both in size and age, was in middle school the last time she saw him.

Lou put his hands in his pockets, nodded his head. "Yeah... Damn, man——"

"'Sup! We gon' party or what? I ain't never been to this place. I hope it's good! I wanna get to drinkin'. Maybe scrap, later——" Drew, who was the same size as Marlin except 100 pounds heavier, threw his hands up like a boxer, and was dodging imaginary punches as he threw some pretend hooks.

Azul just rolled her eyes. "Yeah. The party should be pretty ill. Well, glad you all came. Marlin. Your cab——" she pointed to the bass amp and motioned for him to load out.

Marlin shuffled over to the amp when Drew opened his mouth again. "Fuck, are they gonna have the fights going on when the bands are playing? That'd be sick! Maybe you guys can play me a ring entrance theme. Something real badass and heavy. Not some weak shit! Oh shit! Ring girls, too! I forgot about the ring girls! Daaamnn——" he shoved the middle cousin on the shoulder, and they both started laughing.

"Whose vehicle did you bring? Hey Drew. Did you bring your vehicle? Maybe you could fit some of our equipment on yours!" Azul hastily asked.

"Yeah. My new Escalade. I don't want no one else's shit in my ride, though! Just Marlin's is okay. Word?" Drew puffed out his chest and fished for a cigarette in his pocket.

"That's fine. Whatever. Hey Marlin, you got it?" she saw that Marlin was struggling with the amp.

"Damn, man. I can't figure this shit out——"

"It's still plugged in!" Azul rushed to unplug it from the wall as Marlin lumbered forward, almost falling over from the weight of the huge speaker. "You gonna be alright?!"

"We'll see——" uncharacteristically, Marlin started cackling.

The band looked at each other with worry. Jesus got back downstairs to see Drew had lit up his cigarette and was smoking.

"Hey! Be cool and not smoke in my basement. Other people I care about live here!" Jesus pointed at him sternly and motioned for him to take it outside.

Drew started laughing. Took a drag, blew smoke, and nodded. Fake laughing all the way up the staircase.

Jesus shook his head and looked at Azul and the rest of the band in disbelief.

Azul just sighed loudly. "Here we go..."

CHAPTER TWENTY-FOUR

The band pulled up to the venue. The marquee read *Mega Toads* in red neon lights.It resembled an over-sized aluminum, tin shack on the outskirts of the city. A seedy porn shop was across the street.

The building was surrounded by gravel for parking. It was a remnant of the American Roadhouse with its notorious atmosphere for rowdiness.

Mega Toad was the latest incarnation and had a few big shows come through. But recently, they had started the Mega Toad Fight Club nights, where amateurs could get inside the venue's own makeshift octagon and fight each other for a small purse. These nights became a media sensation.

The Winter Ball was once one of the biggest draws for the venue, but the promotion for the event that night seemed secondary to the fights, as ultimate fighters, and the ring girls were booked to appear for autograph signings.

The venue staff told them to unload their gear next to the stage. There were three bands already unloaded and milling about. Some of the bands looked fatigued from the weekend, as it was a Sunday afternoon show. Jesus looked for the soundman to get the soundcheck information and set times squared away.

"Uhh, our band name is *Vultures, Bastards, & Thieves*," Jesus said.

"What?" asked the soundman. He was a small, weathered, pale man in his 50's. He scribbled away with a sharpie on a legal pad.

"*Vultures, Bastards, & Thieves* is our band name. We went by our old name for this show: *Empty Caste*."

"Ohh. Jesus! You just change your name or something?" asked the soundman as he scribbled away.

"Yeah, just today. Like an hour ago," Jesus told him with a bit of apprehension.

"Well, that's a pretty cool name. I'll just take the *Vultures* outta there. I can't fit the whole name on the paper. *Bastards & Thieves*. Eh, are you guys really bastards and thieves?" the soundman raised an eyebrow and took a drink of his Bud Light.

"It ain't literal. Don't worry, we're not gonna jack anyone's shit!" Jesus laughed.

"Hope not. There's six of ya. Bands that is. I want a good clean show with no fuckery, man."

Jesus told the soundman what was needed to mic the band. "We have two guitar amps, a bass amp, and we need three mics for vocals. We have a standard drum kit, and a percussionist rig."

"That's a lot of mics for the bands that usually play here. But I should have you covered. No backlining for anyone, except the last band. You guys are on fourth. Fifteen minutes to soundcheck. So be ready." The soundman finished and went back to setting up his mixing desk for the night.

* * *

The band had opened a bar tab and watched the other bands play. Rick and Jesus knew a lot of the people attending and were mingling as Azul and Mick mainly stayed at their table.

Jesus was adamant about not drinking, but he had a friend who had offered him some weed outside so he took a trip to the parking lot as their set time approached.

He then went to the bathroom and changed into his black fishnets, mini-skirt, and bare midriff blouse as promised. He even put on rouge, eyeliner, and fixed his hair in pigtails to complete the look, visibly making Marlin and his cousins uneasy when he walked out in full costume. The reaction from the rest of the band was positive.

The cousins had opened their own bar tab and had a case of recreational Whippits that they purchased at the porn store across the street. The nitrous oxide gas concoction was a treat for the out-of-towners. The party had approached another level and everyone was in different stages of intoxication as soon as it was the band's turn to take the stage.

Azul carried her amp to stage right. She noticed the stage seemed to stretch out in size from her vantage point. She looked out at the dark dance floor that was filled with people.

"Fuck, man——I think I did too many Whippits, man! I don't think I can remember the songs——" Marlin was cackling in falsetto, which was too unlike his normal stoic, reserved behavior.

"Really? Have you guys been doing them this whole time?" Azul yelled.

"I don't think I can do it, man! Help me Az! Help me!" Marlin impersonated the voice of a screaming child, cackled again as he drooled on himself.

"I told you to just take a few hits! I took a couple with you. I wasn't phased. Just...just concentrate dude——" Azul gave him a bottled water and returned to setting up her gear.

As everyone had their instruments set and amps turned on, Jesus, Azul, and Marlin turned up and immediately started playing at full volume as the soundman was scurrying about, trying to get the microphones in place. Rick blasted through some warmups on the drums that made the irate soundman livid.

"SHUT THE FUCK UP!!! Everybody! Shut the fuck up——" the soundman screamed at everyone onstage, with veins popping, and face bright red. Everyone laughed uncontrollably at the man's tirade.

Rick tried to apologize. "Alright, sorry 'bout that, man! I know you've been at it all day, brother! This is our first sh——"

"I DON'T GIVE A FUCK!!! Just, just let me do my job! Everyone! Turn your amps, the fuck, down!" the soundman yelled, looking especially at the guitar players, Jesus and Azul.

Thus, it was their first lesson in soundcheck etiquette. They all turned their amps down, stopped playing, and stood impatiently as the soundman and his young assistant were scrambling on the stage to get the microphones in their right places for their unconventional ensemble.

* * *

The band was in a state of confusion during their set. The monitors were not loud enough. The musicians could hear nothing but drums and feedback. Azul, Jesus, and Mick tried to rock out and put on a show but would lose their place in the song and have to look at each other to lock in. Rick was missing his cues because he couldn't hear either of them. Marlin just sat down on the bass amp with head down and played.

The lack of sound reinforcement in the old aluminum and concrete building made the sound muddy and indecipherable to the crowd, whose response was confusion turned to apathy.

* * *

The set was over in 35 minutes. The band was underwhelmed as the crowd had herded to the autograph-signing table away from the stage where the ring girls and fighters were making their grand appearance.

Rick was fuming that the sound was so bad as he kept repeating, "——the sound guy screwed us." They got their equipment off the stage as fast as they could.

Azul almost fell after setting her amp down. From the sudden change of being under hot stage lights to the cool and dark backstage area, she realized she was really buzzed and told the others. Mick nodded and began taking the conga set apart. Rick went to the bar. Marlin went to be with his cousins. Jesus was starting to pack his gear.

"Well, that was the first show. How do you feel about it?" Jesus, curious to know what Azul thought.

"I'm glad it's over. I don't feel we've done anything real special. I thought it'd be a huge thing. We'd all be in a huddle, sweaty with victory. Champagne guzzling——*We are the Champions* bullshit. But, no. I'm just glad it's over," Azul shrugged, smiled at Jesus, walked over, and tugged on his pigtails.

"It'll get better. We did our job. Trust me. This place is a shithole," Jesus gave her a hug, and they both continued to pack their gear.

Rick came back with a beer for Azul and Mick. He toasted them and started laying out the next plan.

The newly christened, *Bastards & Thieves* had no CDs or merchandise to sell, were not on the flyer, and had a disheartening crowd response.

Rick had an idea to book an appointment with their old bass player, Stu, who had a basement studio in his house. They could pay to record a demo there on a weekend, depending on how much money they made that night.

"We get percentage of the door, right?" Jesus asked.

"Yeah, I closed the band bar tab so we won't accrue any more cost. Y'all are paying for your own drinks from here on out," Rick chuckled, and toasted the three drinkers and acknowledged Jesus.

"Hey, I'll take a beer. Fuck it! Tonight's a celebration!" Jesus grabbed Rick's beer out of his hand and made a hearty celebratory swig. They were all surprised at his sudden revelry. They teased him a bit and spirits were high again.

* * *

"Fuck! What the fuck did we come up here for? There were hardly any bitches up in here to fuck! The bands are all whack. Where the bitches at man!?" Drew was getting riled up, standing with the cousins at the neon-lit bar.

Azul, seated next to them at the bar, just shook her head and rolled her eyes at Drew. She remarked, "Well, get in the octagon then!" She pointed to the fully-lit, empty octagon ring that was off-set from the dance floor.

"Shit, naw man. I might embarrass the challengers. And besides, I'm boozing tonight! Aye——" Drew laughed and took another swig.

"It's pretty good, man..." chuckled Cyrus, his demeanor was considerably mellow compared to his older cousin.

"Damn, man...heh, heh——" was the only thing the little cousin, Lou, could say the entire night.

"I heard some people up front saying we sucked. Did you hear them?" Marlin asked Azul.

"I couldn't hear a thing onstage. I'm just glad it's over. You didn't fuck up. So, that's good——" Azul answered.

Marlin interjected, "Naw man, I mean we probably sucked because of the other fucking guys, man. We should just kick 'em all out, man. Let's quit this bullshit and get the old band back together."

"Wait, kick them out or quit? Which one are you suggesting? I think we did okay, Marlin. Are you thinking about quitting? Again?" Azul shook her head.

Marlin snickered, shrugged, and scratched his medium-length hair.

"I don't know man. Maybe I'm just not feeling it. You sure you wanna keep jamming with these guys? We should go back to playing heavy shit with your cousin, like the old days."

"Fuck that!" In annoyance, Azul took a swig of her beer.

A moment of uncomfortable silence was between them as the last band was soundchecking before their set.

Marlin finally spoke. "Alright then. I'm just gonna call it a day then. We're gonna take off. The cousins wanna hit the strip club. It's better than being here…"

Azul took another drink, bit her lip, and slapped her hand on the bar table and waved him away. "Well if that's what you wanna do! Get out of here then. No one's stopping you."

Marlin hiccuped and asked her. "You gonna be alright?"

"Don't worry about me," she responded in a cold way that made Marlin back off. Rick and Jesus came up to them in a jovial mood.

"What the fuck is up guys? We pulled it off. What's next? We're all gonna stick around for the last band right? Don't be rock stars!" Rick had his arm around Jesus who was smiling away in his glassy-eyed state.

Azul got up from her seat to join her happy friends. "Of course! It's what we came here for."

"Alright!" Rick just glanced at Marlin who was sulking where he stood. He turned and walked away toward his cousins who were hanging out at the pool tables by then.

Azul hugged the two, and they were joined in a trio huddle. "Love ya guys. We gotta find another bass player."

The two jovial guys laughed. "What? We were just talking about that!" Rick said as they parted their embrace.

"Yeah man! Fuck 'em if they don't wanna be here. I had a great time guys! We can find someone else," Jesus affirmed.

"Okay. Let's do a shot and watch the next band!" Azul and company went to the bar.

Marlin and his cousins stood around the pool table and left after a few minutes. As they were walking out the door, Drew shouted loud enough to be heard from the bar in his slurring baritone, "Man! Fucking weak! Fuck these bands! Fuck this place! Ain't no bitches up in here anyway!"

CHAPTER TWENTY-FIVE

Marlin shivered and looked up at the moon. His eyes stung from the focusing. The moon shone with a pallid halo of frigid light.

He was seeing double. He clenched his eyelids and re-opened them only to see the moon blurring and splitting into threes.

He asked the moon why she was dancing.

His nose was filled with dried blood and frozen nose hairs, also with the smell of tobacco and alcohol from his upper lip. He felt the sensation of being punched. The nerve endings still feeling the blow.

The cold air was enough to frostbite within minutes. He knew this as he put his hands up to warm his afflicted face. He couldn't feel his right hand.

His left hand felt like when he used to jam it into the car door when he was in a rush to get to school. He didn't know his own strength at his size. He wanted to move like a point guard but was a defensive lineman.

So long ago, he thought. He hadn't needed to rush to get anywhere since then.

He looked at his right hand to see a bone sticking out of his wrist. Blood had soaked through his flannel. He looked at the protruding abnormality and studied it.

"Fuck man, it looks real fake..." he said outloud. He tasted some loose enamel with an iron-tasting hole in his top gum.

"Shi..." His tongue needed a drink of water badly.

He looked before him and noticed the twinkle of the snow crystals on the flat fields were making it look like a dream.

His alcoholic breath was getting in his eyes. He shut them again, turned around to where the others were.

The white Escalade was completely turned over in the ditch. If he was driving, he wondered how he ended up on the edge of the open field, and his three cousins were in the ditch.

He staggered to the black road. He could see a car coming from the south where they had just come from Des Moines.

He then remembered they were about to turnoff on HWY 30 which led them straight home.

He thought he had seen an owl. In Meskwaki, called a *Witiko*. He was always told that they don't like Indians. He pushed hard on the brake. They slid and hit something that rocked their entire world and spun out of control, like he was in a laundromat dryer, like the one he used to ride in as a kid.

That was all he could remember.

From the approaching car lights, he saw another dark mass upon the cold, highway they had been on moments ago. The closer he got, the pieces became more elaborate and spread out, like dark pebbles on black asphalt.

His eyes adjusted as the approaching car's headlights made a wash of light, enough to light up the dark pieces on the black road.

They were tattered clothes, and body parts. He noticed a small reflective glass shining near him and made out the glasses of his youngest cousin, Lou.

The Bastard Chronicle 6: Another Cousin

Lou, Marlin's youngest cousin, died in a car crash right outside M-town.

It turns out they were driving in the Escalade on the way home from Des Moines at 4:00 in the morning. Marlin was driving, lost control, and ended up in the ditch.

They had alcohol and drug paraphernalia inside. Of course, the newspapers felt compelled to report that important tidbit...

I still haven't talked to Marlin yet. I'm pretty sure he is sitting in jail now, reliving that horrible night over and over.

Perhaps, he's blaming me...

* * *

Wasn't sure what to call this journal. I did a lot of sitting and thinking, not much writing.

But with the events that have surfaced back home in Tama, it just seemed a fitting title. It pretty much sums up why I'm so guarded of my feelings and have always kept my affection for people I grew up with so limited.

Ever since my cousin, who I was very close to, died when I was a teenager, it's been happening on the regular since then. All the cousins are dying... from stupidity. It isn't fair that people so young and full of life are the ones that get plucked out of the mortal bingo ball chute. The old ancestors in the bingo hall of death are calling their cards and yelling bingo when one of our cousins gets picked. Another young cousin is dead, one of our old ancestors scored a bingo...

It's not like I was really close to this guy. Guy. More like—kid.

I use to see him tagging along with somebody else at powwows, at the store, on the school bus. Just some kid.

It was only much later that Marlin said that he had a crush on me and told me all about him. I was flattered. But I didn't think of him that way. I don't think of any of those guys that way.

When you have bad experiences with guys from Tama, you tend to throw all those bad eggs into the basket of shame. Even cousins of my own. That stuff tends to follow you around, and you try to get as far away from it as you can.

But, he had likes, needs, and goals, too. Growing up, we just never give some people the chance...

I read in his obit, that he liked drawing, fishing, playing basketball, and wanted to become a beta-tester for a huge video game company. That's wild, man. I just think about that, smile, and get a fucked-up feeling inside.

Nowhere in his obit did it say that he liked to drink all the alcohol he could get his hands on. Take any drug that was given to him. That he was depressed. Mentally abused. Peer-pressured to do things he wouldn't normally do...

* * *

He liked me. Could I have possibly done something? Is it fair to my well-being? Should I have reached out to him? Should I have asked him to stay and ride with me?

Is this how it's gonna be until no cousins are left? Are the brothers, sisters, lovers, and friends next?

Then we end up as elders who are on this other side of the bingo hall. Waiting to be called...

R.I.P Lou. Say "Hi" to all my cousins for me in the great beyond.

CHAPTER TWENTY-SEVEN

"Jesus, can you guys go outside to smoke?! It's getting into the control room! My eyes are stinging, and everyone's coughing their damn lungs out! Especially me. I ain't fucking around. I don't need this shit——" Rick was waving smoke away while sitting next to Stu. The namesake of Stu's Studio. An impressive 16-Track DIY recording studio built in the basement of his modest house on the east side of Des Moines.

"I wasn't going to say anything, but, yeah. Go outside you two." Stu, a laid back middle-aged man who was a carpenter by trade, part-time sound engineer, and former Empty Caste bass player, backed up Rick's admonishment of Azul and Jesus as they were celebrating by drinking beers, chain-smoking, and being brats in the lounge.

"Sorry——We'll go outside next time. You got any fans in here? We'll help set 'em up," Jesus took another sip of beer. Azul looked him over and laughed.

"Well, guess you're off the wagon now. Officially——"

Jesus laughed. "I'll be fine. Just gotta maintain is all. We got our recording shit done. Done! It feels good! Wooo!" They both high-fived and talked about the road to their first demo.

"We don't need a bass player. Me and you got this shit down!" Azul wiped her eyes and finally realized how smoky it really was.

"Well, for playing live we do. Yes. You got any worthy candidates in mind?"

"Ohh, fuck. I don't even wanna think about that right now. I'm just enjoying the moment. How's your carpal tunnel now? I know it was hurting you earlier," Azul looked at her own heavily-calloused fingers.

"Still hurts. But we're working on medicating that right now." Jesus tipped his beer bottle to her, and she returned the toast.

"It's six o'clock now. We got a little time. Do you guys wanna squeeze in another song before we tear down the drums?" Rick walked in the lounge and asked the two.

"Ugh——Hell no. Jesus's hands are crippled. My callouses are near broken. Bloods gonna start gushing out. This is a triage unit, man. We're on medication now——" she laughed. "Besides, Mick's not here to record his parts."

"Hmm. Yeah, he did bail on us pretty quick right after we got done with the songs. I was hoping he'd stick around," Jesus said, with slight disappointment. "But, I think we have enough, man. Three songs. Boom! Let's work on getting a killer mix for the rest of the time. How's it sounding in there? You likin' the vocals?"

"It's sounding good. My voice is shot, so it's probably a good thing we stop. Maybe I can come back another day and do more takes later on." Rick wiped the sweat on his forehead with his t-shirt.

"Sixty bucks a day, man. That reminds me," Jesus took his wallet out of his camouflage pants. "Here ya go Stu! Thanks for this. It means a lot!"

"Ah yeah! Thank you. I'm telling you, you guys got some weird stuff. I can't quite put a finger on what it sounds like, but I like it," Stu took the 60 dollars from Jesus.

"That's all our show money, man. Seventy bucks from the Mega Toad gig. We just spent the remaining ten on the booze!" Azul laughed.

"That's actually pretty good. I'm telling you, the real money is in the cover band circuit," Stu told them how he was able to sustain a good living by playing in a cover band that gigged all over the Midwest. "All my recording equipment is directly funded from that."

Azul sat down next to Stu and was admiring his recording console. "This is one of those new Korg D1600 hard drive recorders isn't it? Is it hard to mix stuff down on it?"

"It's not too hard to figure out. I have some discs, if you don't——" Stu pointed at the stack of blank CD-Rs on the shelf next to the console.

"I have a Tascam 4-Track at home. I burn tracks onto a CD-Burner with RCA jacks. Ghetto style! This is totally, a step up. Walk me through it, I could figure this out——"

       * * *

"...and one for you, my cross-dressing man!" Azul handed Jesus one of the roughly-mixed CD-Rs she made for each of the three remaining members.

"Cool, we can sit and listen to this all week, come back, and fix what we want and do a final mix. Stu, you down with us coming in next weekend?" Jesus asked Stu, who said he would leave his schedule open as he turned off the power to his gear in the control room.

"Have you talked to Marlin at all?" Rick asked Azul.

"No, I haven't. But, I did get this really damning message from his mom. She told me to stay away from her family and to stop with my witchcraft."

Both Rick and Jesus exclaimed, "What?"

"His family is real traditional. Marlin isn't, but that kind of thinking is instilled, though he never practices the culture and religion of the tribe." She put her CD-R into her backpack and took a look around the studio to see if there were still things left to pack. "The funeral was a few days ago. I was told by my mom to stay away. There's been rumors going around that I had used bad medicine on him. Ya know, which is absolutely ridiculous," she sighed and took a drink of water.

"Wow, I didn't realize. The one that died, was that the big one who was talking shit all night?" Rick asked.

"No, that guy...I don't know why Marlin brought him along. He has no interest in anything except getting fucked up all the time. No, it was the real quiet one. The little guy."

"Oh, man. Did you know him real well?" Rick sat down.

"I've just seen him here and there. As a boy..." she caught herself and hesitated telling them about his attraction to her. "He was kind of a tag-along. But, he just graduated and got his big per-cap trust fund; so all of the broke cousins, friends, aunties, uncles, broke second-cousins and their mommas all came out of the woodwork to hit him up. That's the kind of thing that happens out there when the high school graduates get their big money."

"Whoa! How much did he have?" Rick again.

"In the high six-figures, man. It's absolutely crazy!" Azul shook her head.

"Crom! All of that money. I take it those guys were using him weren't they?" Jesus said and Azul thought so, too.

"——and they are accusing me of casting bad medicine on those guys that were too fucked up to drive. You've seen them right? They went to the strip club after our show. Man, I don't know if any of this is supposed to make sense. I've been thinking about it, and now I have to look over my shoulder for this now. All this talk of death and witchcraft has got me kind of creeped out now…" she sighed and looked at her bandmates.

"Well, don't worry. We got your back. We got our first demo done and things will be better for us. I'll start calling around and put up a classified online for managers. What do you guys think about that? Having a manager would be a huge boost, don't ya guys think?" Rick ramping up the excitement.

"I'm down!" Jesus lifted up his beer for a toasting gesture.

"Yeah, man. That's a silver lining," Azul sighed in relief and looked toward the drum room and saw the sliding glass door shut by itself. She blinked her eyes to focus more clearly on what she had just seen, looked to Stu, who gave her a mischievous grin and motioned at his switching panel on the wall that controlled the automatic sliding doors in the whole studio.

CHAPTER TWENTY-EIGHT

"Hey guys!" Barry greeted in a raspy, drawn-out, cool surfer-dude way.

He was a short, handsome man with Pacific Island ancestry, with carefully trimmed facial hair, and his thick black mane tied back. He walked into Jesus's basement as they were in the middle of writing a new song they were planning to debut at one of their upcoming shows in Des Moines. The band acknowledged him, finished playing, and introduced themselves.

"Barry, thanks for coming! Umm. Well, it worked!" Rick laughed in reference to the classified ad he put on the popular Central Iowa Music Scene Message Board web page: *Newly formed, innovative, and genre-defying band BASTARDS & THIEVES looking for Next Legendary Manager!*

"It did! I'm here, and I wanna thank you for letting me in your digs to see where the magic happens," Barry scanned the room, genuinely enthused at the meager accommodations. Though clad in a treated leather coat and wool scarf, his Pacific Islander aura set a warm summertime presence in the cold underground dwelling.

"It's my basement. It ain't the best in the world, but we can get stuff done here," Jesus apologized for the mess.

"Oh no, it's totally rockin'! It's got a great vibe, and hey; great art comes from pain, right?" Barry, with his palms turned up in a congenial gesture, let out a boisterous laugh.

The band relaxed and put down their instruments.

Rick walked out from behind his kit and took hold of the conversation with Barry and started in his inimitable style.

"So, what we want is a manager because we feel we have something wholly different than what the scene has. Our music is diverse. We are diverse. We're a collection of the most talented musicians in the area. And we want to push an image where we can stick out like sore thumbs, but this sore thumb is like the 'The Kid'——ya know. 'The Son of a Bitch!' The mean 'Bastard' that you don't wanna mess with because we'll steal your fans and your hearts, man! See, that's where the——"

"——*Thieves*, comes in!" Barry finished his sentence and started in his own exaggerated showman-like way. "Yeah, man! I'm definitely feeling your vibe! From what I've just heard in your practice space was a kind of sound that you could only dream of hearing being played in the streets of Des Moines. Or LA! A kind of band that could only be put together in such strange and unusual circumstances. You all just wrote that, I'm assuming?" he asked the band and they confirmed it was a new song. "I'm telling you guys, man, I was excited! My palms were sweating. I was getting goosebumps from what I was hearing! Then, to come down into this basement and see what was making all of that great noise, this band that has all these percussive elements, y'all are young and beautiful, AND hip!" The band smiled at each other. "Man, I'm a big Jane's Addiction fan, and it's the same feeling I got when I was listening to you guys outside! So, yeah, I am in one-hundred percent! I'm thanking you right now! Let's do this. What do you want me to do?" His heavy use of emotive hand gestures further accentuated his enthusiasm, and the band was responding positively to his good vibes.

They played him some songs and were flattered at his glowing appraisal of their work. They were relieved that he was a family man, had a normal job as an IT Tech, and was not a drug dealer. He was a lifelong music fan and had been attending shows around the Des Moines scene since the 90's.

The brainstorming began. They started planning out promotion, website ideas, and where to get shows. Barry was new to management, too, and welcomed whatever challenges that came with the job.

They were all on the same page that no one was going to get paid for their services right away, and that this team was working for the greater advancement of Bastards & Thieves. Everyone was excited about the new partnership, despite their bass player vacancy.

The Bastard Chronicle 7: New Friend

We have a new manager in Barry. He's smart, cool, and has enthusiasm. He says he's been "in the scene" for years. Though, I've never seen him around. He's a pretty stand-out guy to have in the Iowa scene. He's got the Hawaiian Punch surfer dude thing going on. Which is great, I mean, we are gaining ground, and have a diverse team on board.

Let's get some Hip-Hop dudes to guest on some tracks, and we could have all the bases covered. No country music though! Absolutely, no country music!

I talked with Lisa on the phone today. I told her I have to find a new job because I can't do the hours, and the pay is just not right. She understands. She has been nothing but helpful in covering for me when I needed my nights free. I just hate to tell her grandpa I'll be leaving. Oh man…

But, I'll be job-searching first thing tomorrow. New beginnings!

Rick and I have been carpooling to Jesus's place for practice every week. We're talking about getting an apartment together along with another friend of his. I think it's time I move out of Mom's place. I'm hardly ever there it seems. Zach is gonna be in eighth grade soon. Mom seems to be holding it down well. It's definitely time.

I suggested we move down to Des Moines, but Rick is sure he wants to stay in M-town, which I can understand as he's afraid of retaliation from Toby.

But, what about the psycho-ex, Mandy? I'm not so sure she's out of the picture yet. 'Cause remember, I'm looking over my shoulder for that hag, too!

But the pros are outweighing the cons. We're looking for places now.

That would be ideal to find a place where we can practice, too! That could be the new Bastards & Thieves Hideout! Our own crash headquarters! The possibilities are endless.

Jesus' wife is due any day now. We would have to move the practice space soon anyways. So yeah, dilemmas.

We are still looking for bass players. We've just been writing songs with no bass parts. I've been trying to hold the bottom end down with rhythm parts. It's great and all, but I like throwing in some upper mid-range parts and leads, too. Jesus has been hogging all the leads, dammit! I hope we find the right guy.

Speaking of the right guy,(Heh!) I heard Chester joined another band in M-town as a guitar player. I haven't talked to him since our last practice with him last fall. I hope he's doing well.

We've got a REALLY busy schedule coming up as the spring finally approaches. This winter has been memorable, let's hope the next season is full of greatest hits.

CHAPTER THIRTY

The View, was the newest venue to feature live music on Des Moines' south side. It was a two-story building built into the slope of a great riverside bluff which faced the downtown skyline, hence, The View moniker.

The venue kicked off its booking for the spring by hosting a Monday Night Battle of the Bands. Three bands would compete by playing a set every Monday night and the winner was declared by the loudest crowd response measured by the PA decibel meter at the end of the night. The winning band in the first round won 200 dollars, with prizes "to-be-announced" at a later date.

The Bastards had entered the first round and were poised to make an impact as the night was turning out to be the beginning of their live show Renaissance.

"Oh hey! How's it going stranger? Seen any good shows lately?" the soundman laughed and greeted Jesus.

"Hey, you're working this club, too, huh?" Jesus shook his hand. It was the same soundman that did their first show at Mega Toads.

"Yeah! This new place is keeping me busy. They've been putting on weekend shows for the last month. It's steady work for me. The space is small enough that I don't need to bring my big setup," the soundman was in a better mood than the band's last encounter with him.

"Sweet! Hey man, sorry about the noise we were making during soundcheck. It was our first show, and we were all a bit nervous. Tonight, we'll know what to expect and we've gotten better since then, I hope——" Jesus earnestly apologized regarding their last discordant exchange.

"Ah man. Forget about it! I forgot about it until you just said something. You got your percussionist still? I have some better clip-on mics for those drums."

"Yeah. Unfortunately, it's his last show with us. So, if you could make him sound good on his last run, I'm sure he'd appreciate it," Jesus revealed.

"Oh really? Well, that's a bummer. Those drums definitely add something to your guys' sound. I'll give you some phone numbers of some guys I know that might try out for you," the sound man suggested.

"That'd be great man! Thanks for that Mr..."

"Skully! The name's Skully," he extended his hand to Jesus, and they shook on it.

* * *

"I'm glad you guys understand. I'm just not good at keeping priorities intact. Man, with school, work, my other band, traveling to Des Moines all the time is something I can't do anymore," Mick was apologetic in his reveal to the band as they met outside the venue. Everyone understood and wished him well.

Azul put her hand on his shoulder and they looked to the north where the skyscrapers of downtown Des Moines shimmered from the setting sun. "We understand, man. I'm bummed, for sure, but I'm grateful that we got to jam finally."

"For sure, I've learned a lot in this time," he explained that he was transferring to the University of Northern Iowa, located in Cedar Falls, after finishing his Associate's degree from Marshalltown.

"That's great, Mick. I'm really happy for you. That sounds like quite an adventure, man. Well, consider this great skyline of downtown as a parting gift for your last show," Azul and Mick basked in the view which, in front of the venue, a busy intersection teed to a bridge that crossed the Raccoon River into the heart of downtown.

"Yeah, we don't have any views like this in M-town. It's great here," Mick exclaimed.

* * *

The Battle started with a metal band called File 9, to be followed by the Bastards, and a rock band called SL8. The bands were all hoping to upstage each other, but stood in good camaraderie because it provided good exposure for the scene as a whole. Each band had brought their respective crowds to attend the show and the Bastards were no exception.

Mick brought his longtime girlfriend.

Jesus' mom, his brother and sister made a first-time appearance to see his new band.

Azul's mom and little brother finally got the opportunity to see her play since it was an all-ages show, though minors had to leave the venue at 9 PM.

Because he had no family in the central Iowa area, Rick brought some of his rowdiest friends to the gig to act as bodyguards for the band.

"Watch the front doors for Toby! Word is that he's coming out to the show tonight to start some shit. I already gave the door guy a heads-up that he might come in with a group of people, but we need to be ready——" Rick warned everyone as the band was waiting with their gear while the first band was playing the last few minutes of their set.

"I've been keeping a lookout, but I don't think he has anyone to back him up anymore. Man, why does he have to be here tonight? All our families are here. This wouldn't be a good look, especially for me, since I'm dressed in my miniskirt and fishnets; but I'm the guy that took him down! He'll definitely go for me first," Jesus said.

"I know, which is why I brought my man, Meatballs, from Job Corps. He's back from the Army now. He'll be the guy smashing beer cans over his head and deadlifting me in a few hours. Believe me, he's a good guy, and he won't let anything happen to us," Rick said. He greeted Barry who walked up to the band with digital camera in hand and was ready to take some good photos for their upcoming website.

File 9's lead singer was introducing the band's last song for their set. "This next song is called *9/11*! This will be on our upcoming CD! It's about time for us Americans to rise up against the goddamn terrorists and never back down our rights as citizens to bear arms and kick ass the American Way!" Then, the band counted in. The sound exploded into a barrage of 80's-style thrash beats with down-tuned guitar rhythms as the singer screamed out vitriol which culminated in a chant-like chorus of *Nine-Eleven*.

Azul and band were taken by surprise at first, then laughed at the irony of them having a song with the same title, the same subject matter, but entirely different styles.

"How many bands do you think wrote a *9/11* song besides us?" Azul asked Rick.

"Well, they're an underground band like us so we just gotta beat their version, but when country singers start doing 'em, it'll be time to stop——" Rick answered as File 9 stopped abruptly and said, "Good night."

"That was fast!" Jesus laughed, as the band started unplugging all of their gear onstage.

"See, that was it. Only one minute! Ours is like five. Don't worry," Rick smiled.

Azul sighed. "I got this feeling that every single band in the whole country wrote their own little *9/11* song..."

         * * *

They started the set flawlessly. The sound was exponentially better than the Mega Toad gig as they could hear each other in the onstage monitors. The energy was high, as the crowd was getting into their unique sound. The Bastards were rejuvenated and playing with refreshing fervor onstage, and being that it was Mick's third and final performance with the band, it gave their set the extra special ingredient it needed.

The band finished a song and the crowd cheered. Jesus looked to see if his family was still sitting next to the front windows that were lit with neon beer signs. They were still there, along with Azul's family and Mick's girlfriend.

The next song began with a brief guitar solo by Jesus. The rest of the band kicked in as Jesus looked to the crowd again and a feeling of dread came over him as he saw a large figure walk through the front door. The bright stage lights shined in his eyes as he squinted more to focus and then recognized who it was. He hurried over to Rick's drum kit, he gave him a series of nods and signals to get his attention, and swayed his chin towards the crowd to signal that Toby had arrived.

"Shit——" Rick muttered as he came upon the next verse in the song where he had to lean toward the mic in front of him to sing.

Rick tried to signal to Meatballs and his other friends who were at the bar that was located near stage right but couldn't get their attention through the dense crowd.

Mick and Azul were on their percussion parts and engrossed in the music, totally oblivious to the situation that Jesus and Rick were preoccupied with.

A song later, Jesus looked up from retuning his guitar in between songs to see that the pale and imposing figure of Toby was working his way through the crowd to the front of the stage. Jesus's eyes got big and he bent his knees into a fighting stance. He was ready to spring into action and use his guitar as a weapon.

Rick was watching Toby move through the crowd. He was poised to announce the next song, which as luck would have it, was an old Empty Caste song that they used to play with Toby before they quit, called "*Smegma*."

It was a heavy, uptempo song that they were debuting that night. They refined it to make it tighter and more expansive than the old version. Rick licked his lips at the taste of the creative insult he was about to unleash on his former bandmate.

"Hey, I wanna thank everyone for coming out tonight. I especially wanna dedicate this next song to our old buddy Toby. Hey! Everyone give good ol' Toby a fucking hand, man!" A few claps of indifferent applause followed. "This next song is a brand new version of an old song we used to play with this cat a lifetime ago. It's a love song about fat, piece of shit drug dealers trying to masturbate while their mother is in the next room! It's entitled: Smegma!" Jesus played the opening riff, and the band let loose.

Azul and Mick were rocking out and still oblivious to what was going on despite Rick's insult. Jesus was laughing from Rick's scathing banter, having fun and headbanging away. Rick finally managed to get Meatballs's attention and pointed to where Toby was glaring at them.

The band got to the part of the song where the tempo kicked into high gear in a relentless frenzy of blast beats and triplets when Toby began to spit continuously at Jesus. Jesus himself didn't notice until the third gob landed on his face. He was livid and sprayed right back at Toby.

Azul looked over and saw the last saliva exchange, looked at the human powder keg standing in front of Jesus and put it together in her mind that he was, no doubt, their irate former bass player.

She took a step back. Right after she did, she heard Rick yell, "Meatballs! Kill!" Then, Rick's beer-guzzling friend jumped onto stage-right, where Azul was once standing, and made a linebacker charge into the spitting monster in the front of the stage, kicking over a front-wedge stage monitor on the way.

The rest of Rick's friends came from behind the beast and pummeled away.

The band were still holding the music together despite the chaos. Azul saw that Barry and Kitty were snapping away on their cameras. There was a younger blond man videotaping the show and was capturing everything.

The gauntlet of fists, with Toby at the center, moved away from the stage. Two staffed men muscled through the crowd, grabbed Toby, led him out the glass door, and gave him a final shove out into the cool, downtown-lit night.

"Don't come back motherfucker! We're calling the cops if you do," yelled the door man as he stood outside the door.

Toby spat blood from his mouth, took off his ripped T-shirt to wipe his bloody face to reveal a tattoo of a swastika and a *White Power* slogan on his piggish, pink torso. "Fuck you all, man! Fuck you all!" He limped to the gravel parking lot to his pickup truck and sped off.

* * *

"Are you alright?" Kim asked Azul.

"I'm fine. We got all of that shit on film and it looks badass! Our new manager Barry, Kitty, our photographer, and this new blond dude named Travis, he's a videographer, got all this awesome footage and we're gonna use it on our new website——"

"Hold on now, are YOU alright? Are you in danger? That doesn't happen every night, right?" Kim sternly refocusing on her daughter's well-being.

"Oh, sorry. No, that fool had it coming. He's barred from every venue in town, now. So, I'm not too worried about it. I feel safe with the guys. I do, Mom——You don't have to worry. I actually feel accepted. More accepted than with my *own* people back in Tama. Ya know what I mean?"

"You're not gonna drink anymore tonight are you?" Kim watched her take a shot at the bar with the entire Bastards crew before she came over to talk with her and Zach.

"It was Mick's last show, so we had a shot for him and took a group photo. Yeah, it's kinda Rick's thing, ya know——He calls everybody in the band to do a shot of Jäger. Band shots. It's like our new tradition now."

"Oh really? Tradition? Is that what we're calling it now? Be careful how you use that word. We're NDN Women remember——Ya can't be saying to everyone, 'My tradition is downing shots of Jäger on Monday nights!'"

Azul sighed and repeated, "I know, I know——" she turned her attention to Zach and ran her fingers through her brother's near-identical black wavy hair. "Hey little monster, what'd ya think of the show?"

Zach said, "It was good——" his shy demeanor turned to nervousness as he was distracted by a group of drunk women flashing their bras and taking photos with a digital camera.

Azul noticed what caught his eye and laughed. "Uh oh...the ladies are getting sauced up. It's becoming R-rated territory up in here."

Skully announced on the PA that it was 8:55 and minors had to leave the building in the next five minutes.

Azul put Zach's zip-up hoodie on for him by habit and they got up to exit the bar.

"Just be careful. No more tradition tonight, you hear? You don't need to do everything those guys tell you. Bad things happen at night, you should know that. You know that alcoholism is in our family. You need to keep your head on straight, AND over your shoulder, do you understand?"

Azul sighed and repeated, "I know, I know."

The Bastard Chronicle 8: Guerrilla Radio

We won $200 at the Battle of the Bands! That's going to the pressing of our demo, which we'll have ready to sell by the second round Battle, which will be in a month or two from now. The winners are supposed to get paid double at that show. The final will be this summer, TBA, and the grand prize is $1000!

* * *

The website is under construction and I can't wait to see it! Barry, Kitty, and new guy Travis have been working on getting the footage on there. We already have such a great crew!

* * *

We will miss Mick. He brought a positive energy to the band and he is such a talented artist as well as a musician. Maybe we can go visit him if we ever make it to Cedar Falls.

* * *

We did an interview AND played an acoustic
set on the Local Lix Radio Show in Des Moines.
Broadcast all over Iowa! Talk about nervous energy.
The three of us only had a little bit of time
to prepare at Jesus's house and rushed to the
downtown studio.

As nervous as I was, I was most worried about
Rick and I staying in key for our vocal harmonies.
We don't put too much emphasis on practicing our
harmonies like we should. Because playing acoustic,
on-air in a studio, it's a totally different
experience because you can hear every little
fuck-up and bad note as clear as day. Oh my god!
I hate the way my voice sounds, and man, we hit
some BAD notes!

C-Bone, the on-air DJ who does the Local Lix
show, recorded it and burned it on CD-R for us to
have. I just made copies for everyone in the band.
I had to mix it down and hear it over and over.
I wish we could do another take. And another.
And another…

* * *

Update: I just got a new job at the Meskwaki
Casino as a Valet driver! I'm officially working for
tips now, honey! My cousin, who just got some new
PA gear and a new Harley Davidson, hired me, so I
got the hookup.

I only have a few weeks left of college. Things
are getting so busy, I'm glad that will be out
of the way. I don't know if I'm gonna pursue
anything after. I've been doing the acting and
Theater Production thing on top of that, and my
grades this year have suffered. My G.P.A is now in
the 2.0 range. Blecch…My chips are on the band
at the moment.

Double Update: At the time of this writing,
Jesus dropped the inevitable. Amy popped the

kid out. A healthy baby girl named Amelia! Wow! That's so cool!

But, to be honest, I'm worried about the future of our band. Can he continue with that burden? Those 6 pounds and few ounces are gonna be HEAVY! He already has his daughter from his previous marriage, AND he's drinking again. Seems like a lot to me.

But, Rick and I are gonna do a shot for him and his new daughter, because the "Bastards and Thieves" are just getting started!

The Thieves' Conundrum Compendium 1

"Let Freedom Ring With a Shotgun Blast" That line from that one song. By that one band. On that one CD.

Fuck! I wish I had written that one. Except, I would change the context into something more meaningful.

I would write it about us, my friend. Fuck that Dave Koresh bullshit.

Sometimes. I wish I had a shotgun. How it could solve a bunch of problems in one powerful blast. The sound wouldn't reverberate outside. Only in my ears. The last minutes of endless chirping, BLAST, and a ringing tone. Until blackness.

Were your last minutes like that my friend? When you were watching the sunrise...when you were coiled up in the darkness for so long?

The fucking pigs surrounding you in that alleyway! Trying to talk you down...make you understand...you need to talk them down...make THEM understand!

It's hard, brotha. It's hard to know that you're gone with that shotgun blast.

You're free from the pigs' squeal...the whore's throat...

Your martyrdom has played out at 24 years old. I try to understand.

You left a little girl behind. How I wish I could take your child in and put her on my tour bus with the rest of us and raise her how guys like you and me are supposed to be raised. Wild and free!

Like all the times we used to talk about on those late nights. We'd want to skip town and fuck it all! No consequence!

But I'm pouring you a glass tonight...

* * *

I just moved into a new place with my chick guitar player and buddy Nate the Cook. You'd like it here. It's an apartment up above a Sign Shop, across the street from Chippewa Lanes, the place we used to booze alot at brotha! We'd have such a good time!

You'd like Nate. He's okay. He's a cook at the bar I work at. He's crashing out on the "Nomad's Couch" in the living room. He'd be cooking food while we booze, brotha...

But I'd tell you to not fuck my guitar player, Azul! Hands off! She's something else; but knowing you, you would've found your way into her panties. Your pierced, swinging cock is still a legend here, man! Everyone talks about it...still.

We're talking about setting up the jam spot up in the attic. We want to set up the Bastards & Thieves headquarters here.

You would be our mascot. You and me would be having them lined up. We would be banging chicks together...side-by-side...oh how cruel God can be...I miss you.

...and the final question I have for you brother: Is freedom still ringing for you?

PT III

CHAPTER THIRTY-THREE

Q: Tell me a little bit about the Iowa live music scene back then and how you fit into it.

Well, in such a conservative, boring state like Iowa, the swell of scene activity was all underground. But, it was at its most prominent because of our one big signed band that was killing it in the majors. We (bands) were all making noise, and kids were coming out to see shows.

We would play gigs in peoples' houses and rent VFW halls. The M-town Coliseum was host to some legendary shows, as well. Any bar that was willing to let us plug our amps into their wall, we would all show up with our friends and jam.

I collected flyers from that time, and it's a trip to look back on them now and see where some of those bands went with their careers.

It was a huge deal for me when we started making flyers of our own. We definitely put our own unique flavor with the Bastards and Thieves imagery. We became known for being crazy and unpredictable live, so we had to have images that were equally as crazy and, to be honest, obnoxious! (Laughs)

Rick and I would spend days out on the street hanging up flyers and tagging all of these cities and small towns with our stickers; it became a part of our routine. Looking back, it's something we have kind of lost with the advent of social media and bands just don't do that anymore. I could write whole books on our flyering adventures alone! (Laughs)

Q: So, it was a tight-knit community of music lovers finding each other in a scene spread out in these small communities, not central to any one major city. That's really interesting!

Oh man, we met SO MANY people that are still friends to this day. Some of them, not so much! (Laughs)

CHAPTER THIRTY-FOUR

The band were still having practice sessions at Jesus's house, despite the baby being born. The weather was getting warm again as the second Battle Show was approaching.

By that time, they had auditioned seven people for several different instruments in the band, but for various reasons, none of them worked out.

The search for the important bass player role had only yielded one audition in Travis, the videographer, who struggled with their material. The Bastards broke the news to him that they weren't interested due to his lack of skill. Travis assured them that his feelings weren't hurt and he would continue to film their shows and work with Barry, who was still coming to practice to update the band on what he was working on.

Trying to find a new bassist was wearing down on their morale as they were torn between auditioning new members and writing new songs.

After practice one night, both Azul and Rick decided to have a drink at The View before they made the hour-long trip back home to their new apartment in M-town, when they met an easygoing guy and his girlfriend that were attending a show there. Rick and Azul had seen them around the bar scene back in M-town and told them that it was great to see some familiar faces in Des Moines.

The guy's name was Jordan but went by the nickname "Squash." His longtime girlfriend was named Reagan. They both lived in Ames, which was 30 miles north of Des Moines. Azul and Rick had hit if off with both of them.

By night's end, Squash was excited to be trying out for the band as a bassist that Saturday.

     * * *

"Thanks for loaning me the bass, Az! It's got really good action, and it feels right on me. How much you want for it?" Squash was gushing over the coffee-brown Fender P-Bass that Azul had inherited from one of her uncles who didn't play much. It was practically brand new.

"Well, if you're serious, two hundred bucks would do just fine. It certainly does look good on you, dude——" Azul, surprised by the offer, picked the number value at the top of her head.

"That's cool! I don't have any cash on me or anything right now. I'm getting a Hartke cab and Ampeg head real soon. I'm in between jobs right now. I was thinking of selling my guitar for a cheap bass, but if you're willing to sell it——"

"Dude, take it home with you. You need something to practice on. It's nothing! We know where you live——" Azul laughed.

"With the show coming up, we'll just have you come up and play the songs you do know. Matter of fact, let's just do the three songs on the demo. You learn those, and we'll play those last in the set and have you come up to finish it with us! Is that cool?" Rick asked as he was doing his arm stretches behind the drum kit.

Squash immediately laughed in his easygoing way and said he would try his hardest.

This was the first time that Jesus had met him, and they immediately bonded. They were both weed smokers, and after that first practice they became known as: The Fellowship of the Leaf.

The Bastard Chronicle 9: Round Two! Fight!

We spent the last month-and-a-half auditioning new people. Those people just did not GET us. All due respect to Travis for trying out on bass, but man, I started thinking that maybe there's something wrong with us.

But now I'm convinced there's something wrong with them! Okay, check this out…

We had one douchebag who came to try out for percussion, but insisted on being THE drummer and move Rick over to percussion and vocals.

Which, kudos to Rick, he gave it a shot and still toys with the idea of just being the frontman. I'd support that, given we have the right drummer to do it.

But the guy was an arrogant prick that brought his tattooed groupie with him. We'd try to teach him the song, but he'd go off on a tangent, totally not doing what the song called for.

We told him, "The next part goes there!"

He would whine, "No, that's not what I wanna do! You should be following me!"

Then his tattooed groupie with her shrill, nasally voice repeats, "Yeah, you should be following him!"

Grr! I wanted to pull that bitch's hair out so bad! I'd never been so pissed off at a band practice!

* * *

Another time, we got this other chick from M-town to try out for keyboards. Which, I was all hopeful she would work out. I love bands with keyboards!

Turns out, she was more interested in talking about drugs and most of all: tweaking.

Rick was very adamant about not having her in the band after she kept going on and on about it, having his own issues with meth addiction and talking to her must've made his mouth water for a hit.

When we dropped her off at the end of the night at her place, she showed her true colors and straight up asked if we knew any dealers that could hook her up.

Plus, she was only 16. THAT would've been a huge problem.

We had a few more experiences, but they didn't quite work out. Short story is, our morale needed a boost.

We met Squash and his girlfriend, Reagan at The View. We got to hanging, and he is 100% in!

He's been looking for a band to be in for awhile. He's going to school right now. He's a tech genius and a good musician. Right place, right time. Turns out, we know the same people in M-town and Des Moines. BOOM!

* * *

Fast-forward to The Battle at The View: Round Two! We slayed!

We were up against a band called Trailer Trash, and one of my favorite bands, Retrograde. It was great, because they both have chick singers, and there's me and my cross-dressing lead guitar player guy. Females repping the scene, baby!

There was a music critic from the Des Moines Register whose review was so glowing that it should help propel us into major players!

Squash did great, and we fucking WON! $500 this time!

We also sold 20 CDs of our demo, which gave us our first real taste of the merch life! Everyone was happy, and we are stoked for the future!

…now, about a percussionist.

Songwriting: Un-Sleeping Village

"You know that really small town outside M-town? It's a creepy town on a hill with nothing but a church, a hidden cemetery, and a closed-down gas station?" Rick asked Squash, the M-town native.

"You described every town around there. I'd call them villages," Squash answered as he sat down on his speaker cab.

"LaMoille! That's the town! I was talking with our roommate. Recently, some tweaker had an all-night standoff with the police. He had been up for days, locked himself in his house, and started sniping the town!"

"Oh yeah! I heard about that! I went to school with that guy! He used to work at the porn shop in M-town. He was a dealer and a prostitute——"

"Daaaamn..." the band collectively exclaimed as he continued talking about the man.

"No shit! The word is, he had some powerful clientele coming to the shop. Lines of dudes would be there on the weekends going into the red-light arcade in the back, and he'd be working the glory hole!" Squash said, the guys laughed in disbelief as Azul asked what a glory hole was.

"An anonymous hole in the wall to fulfill one's sexual needs, in that case, many, if you know what I mean——" Jesus explained to Azul as she grimaced at the mental picture he just painted in her psyche.

"That was happening at the porn shop down the street from my old place by the cemetery? I didn't realize, man——" Rick shook his head in disbelief.

"Yeah, all of that was going on while that dude worked there. He was a cool guy, too. I mean——he skateboarded, played sports, played guitar, good artist, everyone seemed to like him. His parents were great——they were a typical church-going farm family. His life just spiraled out of control and he dropped out of high school. But he was at all the parties, went to all the shows, and had a hot girlfriend who stripped at the Tiger's Den strip club in M-town. He just snapped one day and started sniping."

"Fuckin' aye. There's something fucked up about that town and the people that live there. I went to this house party on the edge of that town a while ago and remember tripping out because it seemed like the whole town was there in this crazy white trash circus. What really stuck with me is that kids were walking around. Toddler age kids, too! It was insane. What really pissed me off is that a porno was playing on the TV in the living room, and the kids were watching the thing with the adults! Everyone was doing lines, needles, drinking..." Rick recalled.

"That's wrong, man——What did you do after that?" Azul asked.

"I honestly don't remember. There were so many people there. Not my proudest moment. We should write a song about that, we'll call it *Un-Sleeping Village*——" Rick thought at the top of his head.

"Like the Black Sabbath song, *Sleeping Village?*" Jesus remarked with a laugh.

"Yeah——except they're still awake. Boozing. Fucking. Tweaking. Watching pornos with children——" Rick's tone went from conversational to morose; he cracked open a beer.

"So, was anyone hurt? What happened with that tweaking sniper?" Azul asked.

Rick took a long swig and cleared his throat. "No one was hurt, except him——He lived. They arrested him..." he started to play a swinging John Densmore of The Doors-style drum beat. The others, bewildered by his short answer, joined in and started putting together improvisational ideas to the song.

They worked on it for the rest of the night, with the zombified imagery of entire villages addicted to meth going through their heads.

The Thieves' Conundrum Compendium 2

I've been running up and down the list of my connects all over the state. Our demo sounds like shit, still. But people are responding to it. It feels good to be back in the game.

Seeing fat fuck Toby getting pummeled by Meatballs and crew should be the album cover. I can't get enough of looking at that picture! I'm cracking a cold one to that!

I thought of booking a show back home. I miss the Mississippi River. I miss my people.

Central Iowa, there's not enough water. The tributaries aren't to my liking. But I now have my people here, and I'm floored how far we've come.

* * *

Oh shit! I gotta e-mail Barry these bookings I've got coming up. I can see us butting heads on some of these. We'll see how it plays out. Truth is, we may not even need a manager.

* * *

Damn, I met this fine tattooed senorita at work. She's a new girl that's working as a waitress.

Her name's Rosita, and she is half-Hispanic. She's from Chicago! She moved in with her aunt to get away from the streets. She has a daughter back there. I can feel where she's coming from.

Me and Nate the Cook where placing bets on who fucks her first. He got to her before I did. But she kept asking about me. After that, he tried his best to cockblock me! But that motherfucker isn't a rockstar. I am!

("You're just a Cook!"———that dude from the OG Texas Chainsaw Massacre)

I invited her out to our next show! We're gonna get together before then, though. Nate is a sport and a gentleman about it. I said to him that maybe he could cook our dinner! Ouch! Naw, it's a good thing he's taking it so well because he makes way more money than I do, and we got rent to pay! Haha!

She may be the answer I need to finally move on from Mandy. I've spent alot of years going through the same bullshit. But now, with a new band, a new woman, new shows, new music, life is getting more eXciting! I'm kinda nervous how I can contain myself with all of this energy.

Well, I shouldn't have anything to worry about. I can do anything!

The Bastard Chronicle 10: Last Battle

Wow! So, The Battle: Round Three came and went.
We threw everything we had into the music and performance side. But it turned out we had to throw everything we had into the production and advertisement side, as well. We basically had to pull rabbits out of our asses for the promoters!
First, they asked us to create and hand out the flyers.
Okay, I just so happen to be in Computer Graphics Design class in this last semester of school, so I was happy to do so. I worked hard on that shit, man!
We all pounded the pavement around town and flyered everywhere we could. Everywhere! Rick and I

were usually listening to Henry Rollins' "Get In The Van" CD to keep us motivated as we spent many hot days handing out flyers to strangers and hitting every streetlight pole, gas station, bulletin board imaginable. Exhausting, but if we could flyer at that rate regularly, we'd be unstoppable!

We need to start a mailing list. I'm putting that on my "Things-To-Do."

The View lost Skully as the sound man for the show. The word was that the venue didn't want to pay him X-amount of dollars to do it.

So at the eleventh hour, the booker asked us if we knew a soundman to work The Battle.

Turns out, I did know someone.

I called my cousin from Tama to see if he could do it. I didn't want to because I knew he didn't have that much experience doing sound professionally besides my high school metal band and a couple of birthdays.

He gets per-cap from the tribe and is loaded with great sounding gear, so, in desperation, I called him to see if he wanted to do it. He said "Hell yeah!"

So, we secured a soundman and got the flyers out. We did our part. Right? Whew!

My fears came to fruition as my cousin was totally overwhelmed by the task at hand!

The last battle had SIX BANDS on the bill! Why there were so many bands at the last show of this contest is beyond me. The point of these gladiator events is to whittle down the competitors to the top two, right?

Does greed have something to do with it?

The gear he was using wasn't quite figured out yet and the first band didn't go on 'till 7PM for a targeted start time of 5PM sharp. The minors had to leave at 8:45. The bar was packed with kids to support their favorite band.

One of our friend bands from M-town, Two Words, had 95% of their crowd leave before their set.

People were pissed off! The kids were chanting "Two Words," "Fuck The View," and throwing stuff. One of their biggest fans, a big, bear-sized, beer-swilling, sandy blond afro-guy named Skinny was leading the charge! (The party ALWAYS gets started every time that dude's around!) But, the bouncer threatened to call the cops if they didn't disperse. Damn! I wish I had a video camera because I was right there and saw the whole thing!

We were the "headlining band" and didn't get to go on until midnight. The crowd looked tired and the night was over for most of them.

Rick was fucking sloshed by then…

The sound was shit, and the monitors were feedbacking the whole time.

Rick, at one point, flubbed the intro to one of our songs, and we had to start over.

Jesus had transformed his patented drag costume to "Queen Status" as he was THE best dressed fool in this whole lot! He was glittering and so radiant, which made it look like he was in the wrong band, hell, the wrong event entirely!

I was a mess just from being so tired.

…AND THEN RICK SMASHES A BOTTLE OVER HIS HEAD! During one of the percussion bits in the set, he comes up to the front of the stage, and on beat, he smashes a half-full beer bottle on the right side of his forehead!

The booker rushed him off the stage a few seconds after the blood started pouring. We still had a song to do, but we just cut it off to end this fuck-all marathon mercifully.

Back to the subject of a video camera, Travis had indeed captured our set entirely with his trusty device complete with the bottle-smashing and the painfully, bloody aftermath.

Rick's blood/alcohol content was so high, that the bleeding on his head didn't stop. It was like red Kool-aid.

Rosita, Rick's new chick had to take him to the hospital where he got stitched up. They just met; now they're bonded by blood. She'll be a keeper after this, I'm sure.

So, we are using the still image of his skull/bottle-breaking incident as our intro page to our website and a T-Shirt. The image, with the band name, looks like a top seller.

Bastards & Thieves! Guy smashing a bottle over his head! Fuck yeah! I'd buy those panties!

* * *

We ended up not winning The Battle...after all that hard work. Some 90's Hits cover band from Iowa State University won when they brought their frat boy and sorority girlfriends from Ames to watch their set, to act like elitist douchebags, to drink, to vote, and to leave.

It's like the quickest and most vile diarrhea virus that hits you for the shortest time, and then you're fine the next day. That's what that was...

So, I hope that cover band spends their $600 winnings on some original tunes.

(The View ended up not making good on the $1000 prize either... We're starting to see a trend here, yes?)

CHAPTER THIRTY-NINE

"Hey guys, got a show. It's gonna be at the House of Bricks!"
Barry came down for practice and handed a stack of flyers for the
upcoming show. His cool, emphatic demeanor was on full display.
"It's a 21-&-over gig. I'm working with the owner, JC, on getting a
huge all-ages show mapped out! Seems we've hit a brick wall, no pun
intended, as they're not used to having all-ages shows happening on
a regular basis. But this is prime real estate. If we can establish a run
of shows where we can draw insane amounts of kids out, we would
own it!"

   "Awesome! It sounds good," Rick looked at the flyer and noticed
one of the bands was from a small town up north. "Wait, I think
I've seen these guys at a small town show, and they're still in high
school. That might be a problem with it being a 21-&-over gig,
man!" he laughed.

Barry assured all was *copacetic*, and he went over the logistics of the show.

Rick, then laid out his booking plans for the upcoming months.

"I see! You've been putting in work, too. Well, I would suggest we all get on the same page and continue these meetings so we don't have a scheduling conflict arise," Barry warned. He then revealed that he had set up a recording studio in his basement. He asked the band if they were interested in recording a new demo.

"I don't see why not. I mean, the demo we have now is pretty sub-par. If we can get better tones and have more time to mix, I'm all in," Azul agreed, and the band discussed which songs they would record.

"Alright, alright! Lastly, if you guys got internet access, I have a special surprise. Here is our link to our new site! It's live now. We got a few pictures up from the last show; and since we've confirmed it, this next show will be up in the *Shows* section of our site! Dig it——" Barry handed out printed sheets with the link of the website for each member of the band to have.

"Hmm, suiteberryrecords.com/bastardsandthieves——that's the website? What does Kitty have to say about that?" Rick looked concerned at the domain name, "Suite Berry Records," being listed before their band name.

"Well, ehh, unfortunately there was a breakdown in communication about the site. She wanted to have complete control. I didn't see it that way. See, we're an organization that is trying to build something this world's never seen or heard before. The domain name is, umm, temporary. I admit, it's my baby that I've been nursing for quite some time. It's called Suite Berry Records! I own the name and I have a dedicated server. Plus, I live right in town, and I have all of our interests at heart, man! At least, this way we have something for now. Further down the way we can see how it goes," Barry reasoned, and tried to get around any concerns that the band may have felt.

"I'll talk to Kitty and see what's up. Well, man, it sounds good. Umm, guys? Shall we? From the top?" Rick changed the subject, and the band went back to work as Barry sat down at the couch to hear them play with a six-pack of beer by his side.

The Bastard Chronicle 11: Second Demo

We are getting a second demo made at Barry's studio. It's not as sophisticated as Stu's. I was skeptical because there was no soundproofing or reinforcement at all. He's got a few foam walls for sound partitions, but that's it. He says it's all "in the box" and "within the software." I don't know about all that, but we're all set up down there so we are gonna make the best of it.

It's a slow-going process. He seems to have to reboot his computer after only a couple of takes. With Rick's drums, it was taking forever!

Everyone was getting frustrated, but we finally got the basic rhythm tracks down, all we need is lead guitars, and vocals. The last demo took a weekend, so at least for this one we are blessed with time. I just hope Barry doesn't pull the money card and starts charging us for HIS time. That would be fucked up if we had to pay…

Which brings me to the issue at hand. He gave us a fully drafted contract for us to sign to his label: Suite Berry Records! It came out of nowhere.

We were all drinking beers after a recording session at a bar on Linn Avenue, which is his neighborhood on the north side of Des Moines, and he offered us this "Recording Contract" that we said we would look at.

Rick and I haven't looked at it since. Jesus has it at his house, and he is straight-up saying that we shouldn't sign a damn thing. It has a clause in there that WE have to front all the cost for recording and mixing, which HE is providing. The only cost he is fronting is sending it off to CD Baby to get it pressed which could be a measly cost compared to what he might spring on us after this is all over. Jesus is afraid he might hold us up and lock our gear that's in HIS "studio" when he hands us a bill out of nowhere.

And, we only get 30% of CD sales. I don't know what the industry standard is nowadays, but we're a local band. We need profits!

Barry is so damn likable, and he's got a great wife and kid at his nice home on the north side. I wouldn't think he'd do something like that. We all genuinely like him and trust him; but with this contract, I know Jesus isn't sure he's all he makes out to be…

Songwriting: WOMD!

"We need another song!" exclaimed Rick. "Something to really kick up the crowd!"

The string players started playing different licks on their guitars until Jesus blurted out, "There's that country song I've been writing...".

"Oh gawd! Really? Jesus——" Azul shook her head and sighed.

"Hold on. I got it..." His voice trailed off as he let his fingers do the riffing in the key of D. It was a twangy sounding piece with fingerpicking-style, double eighth notes with hammer-on pull-offs at the tail end of the lick, sounding like comical musical exclamation points.

Azul winced at the sound of it, but it won her over and made her smile.

Rick thought it was hilarious; he then chugged out a standard uptempo bluegrass beat, sped it up and locked in with Jesus's flying fingers. Squash listened for a few seconds, and started a moving bassline that established the foundation.

Azul started chording in D-major and embellishing with single note runs. She happened to be in drop-D tuning, so she did some heavy palm mutes on the thick strings to give the riff some heaviness.

"That riff is the embodiment of: Silly!" Rick laughed. Rick started yelling and even yodeled. "The yodel is gonna be the chorus part!"

Rick got his notebook out and wrote the lyrics about having sex with the lunch lady at school.

They brainstormed what to call it, and Azul yelled it was a "Fucking *Weapon of Mass Destruction*!" They all burst out in laughter and agreed that was going to be the song title.

They started rehearsing the song and Jim, the next door neighbor and their first fan, came dancing into the basement. He was holding his trademark homemade wine concoction bottled inside an old 80's Budweiser 40-ounce. His demeanor, pure joy from the music and his grin was ear-to-ear.

As soon as the band watched him bouncing away with the beat of the song they couldn't stop laughing.

"Look at that! If Jim loves it, we might have something here!" Rick boomed in the mic and yodeled some more.

In the space of five minutes, they had written a two-and-a-half minute punk-bluegrass joke. They rehearsed it late into the night and laughed every single time they played it.

The Thieves' Conundrum Compendium

I think I'm in love! I'm going south of the border in no particular order! Mamacitas por vida! Mi amor!

Yes. I'm learning Spanish. White boy Spanish! I'm feeling cheesy. This Rosita chick is rocking my white-boy world!

She fucks like a beast AND cooks me breakfast! I'm definitely moved on! Mandy who? Don't care!

Nate the Cook is acting kinda bitter about it now since she's been coming over after work. I can see how being at work with us and walking home together everyday, has him feeling like a third wheel. I felt bad for him and I said to him, brother, just hook up with Azul! He's like, I don't think she likes me. I said he was absolutely right! Haha! She definitely doesn't! But, start hanging out with her more often. It's a small world in M-town for thick swinging cocks to be ignored. I just draw the line if he breaks her heart. Fuck that shit! But she's tough. I think she can fend for herself. Life is interesting like that!

         * * *

We got a bunch of shows coming up, and we are stoked! I've been talking to a percussionist guy in Des Moines. He says he'll check out practice next week.

         * * *

Squash has been talking about buying a lighting rig that he can control from his pedal board! I wouldn't be surprised if he brings that shit into the next few practices!

He and Reagan are coming over and partying with us alot more than just at practice. We're all thinking of holding weekly BBQ parties! We invite everyone we know, and our house could be party-fucking-central!

Well, Rosita is calling, she'll be over in a few. We're probably gonna need new roommates after this next round of wild fucking!

WASP: Fuck Like a Beast! Hahaha!

The Bastard Chronicle 12: House of Bricks

This place is really cool! The stage is only a foot-and-a-half high, but it's quite spacious. The club is in the back of a little strip mall across a really big mall. It's kinda hard to find from the main street, but there is plenty of parking, and the face of the club is a fortress of red brick. It's got a cool vibe and lots of potential!

We played with a couple of the veteran bands of the scene, so they brought the crowd, a Des Moines metal crowd. So, it was a bit intimidating as we don't really fit into that scene.

When someone asks me what Bastards and Thieves sounds like, I can never find the right words. It's hard to explain. We just sound like us! Come on out and see for yourself.

* * *

Rick had a guy named Ben come to the show, who is trying out for percussion. I didn't really hang out with him. He's just a normal white dude. Clean cut. Blond. But he works at Rieman Music. (Sweet! Maybe he can hook it up with some deals!) He didn't really say much either. He'll be coming to practice next week.

We sold a few more CDs. I can't wait till we finish the new one. Barry was surprisingly absent from the show. He had something to do with his family. That's understandable, but you'd think he'd make an effort to at least make an appearance at the show since it was his baby.

The staff were really cool at the club. Everything was nice and clean. It had a lot of space to hang out. Pool tables, darts, arcade machines. I like this place!

The soundguy was a trip. He's around Skully's age. Tall, rugged-looking, tattooed, light-skinned black dude. He was a bit of a grouch when we met him. Fast-talking. Kinda harsh.

After we played though, he turned around and said he loved our band! Awesome! We got another good soundman on our side. He made me laugh! We hung out, and we slammed some Jäger shots.

Jimi Strychnine is his name. He's like the cool, long-lost, rocker uncle that I've never had!

The Thieves' Conundrum Compendium Cuatro

We got a new percussionist! He's a great dude. Really chill. Like REALLY. He can slam shots with the best of 'em. He is gonna invest in a full percussion rig at the music shop he works at! I just called Barry to update the site and announce him as a new member.

Squash, that badass motherfucker invested in a lighting system that he wired himself! He can control the shit via foot pedal next to his bass pedal board! He's a genius and we are lucky to have him in our band!

We played a couple of shows with the system, and they are TRIPPY! If anyone coming out to the show doesn't remember anything else, they'll remember our awesome light show!

***

Kirk from fellow M-town band, "Dirtnapp," has been running a DIY screenprinting business out of his basement. He's been making t-shirts for us!

We had a fan of ours from M-town draw a really great design. We have a couple of other designs that we made up, too. You can pretty much do any design and put the name, "Bastards & Thieves," on it, and it will look killer.

* * *

I'm gonna cover the ENTIRE APARTMENT in photos and our flyers! I've always wanted a house with my band's escapades and good times on the walls as reminders of what I'm here for.

We've been having people come over alot now. Fans that we have met. Someone's partying somewhere, all the time!

We've got a vid cam and have been taping all kinds of funny shit with these people as well as all the videos of our live shows and appearances. We got loads of titties! Gobs of 'em! It would be great for our DVD in the future!

* * *

I'm getting sick of Nate the Cook! Fuck that guy! I'm sick of seeing him in our living room snoring and farting on the Nomad's Couch. I'm quitting the bar and finding another job.

* * *

Rosita is moving in! We're both gonna get bartending gigs.

She's got a girlfriend named Annie from Chicago moving here. She's looking for a fresh start, too. I said she could stay with us. I don't know where she's gonna sleep, but we'll take her. I wonder if she's hot? Threesome?!

My buddy, Will, who's getting discharged from the Navy is moving back home. He needs a place to stay, too! We have to lay out the red carpet for our fucking troops! He doesn't have any family to come home to. I'm the only family he's got. So he's moving in!

* * *

Nate..."Just-A-Cook Nate,"I don't even wanna walk in any room and see that motherfucker! Ima tell him to move out this week. Good fucking riddance! Go get cooked. Beer drinking time!!!

* * *

Re-dun-dant! Re-dun-dant! Re-dun-dant! Re-dun-dant! Re-dun-dant! Re-dun-dant! Re-dun-dant! Re-dun-dant! Re-dun-dant! Re-dun-dant! Re-dun-dant! Re-dun-dant! Re-dun-dant! Re-dun-dant! Re-dun-dant! Re-dun-dant!

Re-dun-dant! Re-dun-dant! Re-dun-dant! Re-dun-dant! Re-dun-dant! Re-dun-dant! Re-dun-dant! Re-dun-dant! Re-dun-dant! Re-dun-dant! Re-dun-dant! Re-dun-dant! Re-dun-dant!

...I have hair in my mouth...

The Bastard Chronicle 13: Iowa Barn Burner

We debuted our stupid bluegrass song at this show. It was booked by our friends in Drax, our State Center band brethren.

State Center is a "village" literally in the center of the state, in the middle of cornfields. Self-explanatory.

A few weeks ago, we played its annual Rose Festival on a flatbed stage on the main street in front of a steakhouse called, I'm not shitting you, "Steak Center." We gained some fans from that gig and drank one-dollar draws and ate one-dollar hamburgers, afterwards. It was great!

BUT, this show I'm writing about NOW, took place in a barn in the "center" of nowhere, basically.

Three bands. All ages. One keg. Even though the keg wasn't advertised on the flyer, the word gets around pretty easily in the metropolis of State Center.

* * *

The first band played at about 6:00. There was about 100 people there. The first band was about 20 minutes into their set, and the cops busted it. Oh man, the kids scattered.

The band was playing Judas Priest's "Breaking the Law," as it happened. Classic!

We still had two bands left to play the gig. So, just like in the movie, "Dazed & Confused," (Alright, alright, alright!) we spread the word, got another keg, and the party was moved to a more remote location in the backroads of my old stomping grounds: Tama County, at my pal Justin's house, which had a huge barn. (I've known Justin since third grade and Rick knows him from Job Corps! Total coincidence!)

* * *

We got there as the sun was setting on the clear sky. It was a perfect Iowa evening to rumble the earth with our noise!

Rick, with Rosita in tow, was already hammered and woo-hooing around like a drunk white person. We had to tell him to slow down on the booze.

Jesus was keeping it chill, so that was good. He had to leave right after the gig to be with his wife and kid.

Squash and Reagan were in high spirits. They're always fun to have around.

Ben was kinda just there. He hadn't bought his percussion set, yet. We told him to just be in rhythm with the band on our percussion gear, and he'd be fine. It's just a barn gig, man.

* * *

After all that trouble, we played our set, and we debuted "Weapons Of Mass Destruction," and we melted faces! The kids ate it up! There was dancing, a pit, and there wasn't a body NOT moving inside that barn. It really was a surreal experience. The weather started getting chilly and all of those sweaty bodies created a cloud of evil mist in the night.

I think we are on to something!

The Thieves' Conundrum Compendium
Five Finger Club

We got a fucking van! We're calling it: The Burnt Burrito. It's a '89 Ford Econoline. It's got cargo space. No seats. We called it the Burnt Burrito because the exterior looks exactly like a burnt tortilla on the outside. White, with rusty spots all over! I love it and now we got a vehicle to haul gear in!

"The Bastards are coming to your town in a Burnt Burrito!"

* * *

We just had our first practice here!

We're practicing in the attic. It took awhile to get it ready. It's a haul to go up a flight of steps, through our kitchen, and up another staircase to get there. It's hot as fuck, but that's conducive to great art, man!

* * *

Nate the Cook has moved out! Fuck that fucker! He can go fart on someone else's couch! I hope his whole family gets fucked!

          ★ ★ ★

Rosita, Mi Amor, is all moved in!

Her homegirl from Chicago, Annie, is coming in a couple of weeks. She IS kinda hot! Threesome is on the table?!

Will the Patriot, finally back from overseas, has come home! He's living on the "Nomad's Couch" where Nate was sleeping. Better company, and it's awesome to hear his military stories!

Bomb all those fucking Towelheads, man! REMEMBER 9/11!

          ★ ★ ★

We're getting a big stage backdrop made for us from the Sign Shop guys below our apartment. They are cool dudes! They come up on Fridays on their time off and party with us.

It turns out, the landlord that owns this building is Spike's dad! Fucking small world man! Spike himself came over, and we partied. I haven't seen that little fucker since the "Empty Caste" days!

Rosita and I are working separate bars now. We're making decent money. Azul's working at the Casino. Will is living off of his GI bill for awhile. We're doing alright man! I'm gonna call everyone for another get-together at The Compound tonight!

We're gonna start calling our fans: The Little Bastards!

CHAPTER FORTY-SEVEN

The band played Marshallfest, an annual festival organized by *Delusions*, a popular local tattoo and piercing shop. The bands played in the parking lot outside the shop with a who's who roster of bands from all over the Midwest.

It was on that crowded lot that they met a metal trio of high school graduates called, Infant Dust, from Cedar Falls, which was an hour-drive north of M-town.

The Bastards approved of Infant Dust's approach to playing live, which was like being caught in a whirlwind of guitars, bodies, and violence. Their music was nearly indecipherable as they performed with such reckless abandon which sufficiently made up for their lack of musicianship.

Infant Dust was promoting a DIY gig two weeks later at a riverside park in Cedar Falls, just north of the famous College Hill area. The venue was a rental hall beside the Cedar River.

Infant Dust's lead singer/guitarist, John, offered them a slot on the bill and was excited about the Bastards accepting their invitation.

"Fucking, Cedar Falls is gonna freak out once they see you guys play!" he exclaimed. His bandmates voiced the same enthusiasm as they made the date official.

* * *

The Bastards entourage arrived just before they were scheduled to play their set on the floor of the rental hall that was packed with over 60 people. There were rigged stage lights on the floor that shared the same power supply that the bands used for their amps. Extension cords and guitar pedals slid around the beer and sweat-soaked floor. The crowd loved the Bastards' unorthodox sound and went crazy for *Weapons of Mass Destruction*, which by popular demand, they played twice.

Kitty relished the opportunity to take some punk-style photos of the band. She even got into the mosh pit as she kept snapping away.

A touring band from California named, Horse the Band, was next. Their sound was a mash-up up metalcore and 8-Bit video game sounds. The Bastards were inspired by their creativity and energy.

After that set, Rick and Barry held court in the back of the venue with the video camera. They were filming an impromptu contest with crowd participation. Rick brought together a young man and a set of two young girls. The prize was a Bastards CD to whoever received the loudest crowd response.

The young man said he would chug a tall-can of beer for the CD, and the other contestants, the two girls, said they would "make out with each other."

The man began chugging the beer, and the two girls immediately embraced and locked lips. One pulled off the other's shirt and started devouring her breasts, upstaging the man's futile efforts to win the Bastards CD. The crowd lost their minds as the two carnal exhibitionists won the contest.

Azul shook her head and said to Jesus, "Well, that was the stupidest thing I've ever seen. I guess the two girls have to share that one CD now, don't they?"

Infant Dust played a loud, scream-filled show that left the crowd drenched in beer and sweat as the sun went down. Barry congratulated the band and offered to book some shows for them in Des Moines.

Infant Dust accepted, as Barry planned for them and the Bastards to meet at his house for a meeting a week later.

* * *

"Well, since I got everyone here I wanna say congrats to all! We've had a run of some successful shows. That shit in Cedar Falls was the bomb! I got it all on video. 'specially those tittays——" Barry's whole body choked and sputtered into a sleazy, cackling machine at full roar, making the group uneasy. "But hey, uh——sorry for the ladies in attendance——" he regained composure and motioned toward Azul who just crossed her arms at the acknowledgment. "Seriously, we got some great connects, and you guys made a great impression that the kids in Cedar Falls are gonna remember for a long time."

Barry, then gleefully announced that Infant Dust had just signed exclusively to his managerial outfit: Suite Berry Management.

Travis, the Bastards' videographer, unofficial roadie, and friend was announced as a partner in the new agency as well.

But, that wasn't all he had up his sleeve in this slew of announcements. He also signed Infant Dust to an exclusive recording contract with Suite Berry Records, and that they were to start recording in his basement studio that month.

* * *

After the meeting, the Bastards convened in the yard outside. The group was quiet until Jesus spoke up, "I don't know man, do you guys feel used? Nowhere did Barry say he was gonna sign another band to a management AND label deal!"

"Remember, we haven't signed anything yet; I dunno, maybe it's just his way of getting us to sign," Rick said.

"But WE are still recording here, and it's taking fuckin' forever to get it done. How is he gonna record and mix two bands at once?" Azul looked at Infant Dust's van parked in the driveway, which was much nicer than the Burnt Burrito parked in the street.

Squash and Ben left after a few minutes, leaving the three original Bastards. They talked more and could foresee a conflict of interest happening.

"Yeah, I mean, we do need a new demo; but we're still not signing anything," Rick affirmed.

Jesus thought to himself and spoke up, "Hmm, ya know, to be honest, their great dudes and everything, but Infant Dust fucking sucks..."

The Bastard Chronicle 14: Refugees

The Sign Shop downstairs fashioned us a banner for our stage show. Hmm...yeah.

I fucking hate it! It looks like a bad 1980's beer bash or monster truck rally banner! But our landlord made it, and that's Spike's dad. I guess we can just keep forgetting to pack it when we load up the van to go to shows. (Whoops, forgot the banner again! Oh well!)

*   *   *

The machine has been chugging along, and it's getting harder and harder to keep a journal.

I actually tried to do some shopping for myself the other day at the M-town Mall and got stopped by fans. (I guess we're calling the fans, Little Bastards, now.) They were some high school kids. We just ended up hanging out. I got out of there an hour later and didn't get myself anything...

(Oh well. Fame, right?)

*   * * **

I've been getting uncomfortable with all of the EXTRA fucking bodies at the Compound. Rick keeps having people come over ALL the time. I long for a simple home with decent roommates that keep to themselves after working so hard everyday.

This blond chick from Chicago named Annie moved in. Rosita's friend. It's strange; she kinda reminds me of Charlie…with hair. She has Heterochromia, too. (Why do these beautiful creatures keep coming into my life…) She's sleeping on a mattress where our practice space is in the attic. That's some tough shit, man. She wants a fresh start from her choppy future in Chicago, much like Rosita.

Sounds desperate. I sympathize, I guess. Though, I never signed up to be a fucking Mother Teresa to all the displaced souls in the Midwest.

Rick has his friend from the Navy living with us, who is a decent guy. He can cook, and he watches movies all the time. He's sweet to talk to. He farts really loud.

Rosita is cool for about the first three minutes of conversation; then I gotta get the fuck outta there. She's, at most times, not worth the extra toilet paper we have to buy all the time. I don't know how much air is in that cute little chickenhead, but there's probably enough to fill every single tire in town.

(Too mean? …sorry.)

(Alright, alright. I'll say something nice…"I wish I had her hair." I'll give her an Air-Chuck for Christmas…)

*   * * **

I mainly miss hanging out with Zach. After hanging out with those Little Bastards at the mall, I called home. He's growing up so fast. He'll be in high school soon. So, when all of the white people start to make me grind my teeth after not shutting the fuck up and getting out of my room, I'll just head back home and camp out there. They have internet, and I can do a lot of the band's stuff there. (I've been doing the mailing list and keeping up with the artwork!)

The Thieves' Conundrum Compendium 6: Denison

The band just got back from playing at Iowa Job Corps. My old home in Denison! That's where I met Will, Meatballs, Justin, and Mandy. Oh fuck, I worked hard to book this show without Barry's or anyone's help. It was one of my bucket list items for sure. When I ran from home, away from the Mississippi River, this was the destination for every fucked up and fatherless kid in Iowa, man!

It's a hidden fortress on this big hill, surrounded by trees with a beautiful lake hidden in the back trails.

I showed the guys the lake.

I almost proposed to Rosita. It was so nice! Haha!

The Missouri River is not far from there. It all lies on the outskirts of that old hick town Denison. So many times, we snuck out and fucking partied.

Me and Will would hitchhike to town, sneak into all the bars, get our beers, score our drugs, and get lost.

I fucked Mandy at the Wally-world parking lot, the elementary school playground, shit, everywhere! I truly fuckin' miss those long gone dayz...

I booked a couple of M-town bands, Us, and a hip-hop group from Des Moines to headline!

A band shell was constructed on the yard of the school. We played as the sun was setting. The weather was perfect. It was beautiful!

The fucking kids went insane! We tore it up and blew the other bands away! Every kid wanted an autograph from us after the gig.

We couldn't sell any merch because of the agreement with the Corps, though that didn't stop the hip-hop guys from trying. They managed to sneak weed onto the premises, and we could smell it when it became close to their set.

I wasn't too pissed. Mr. C, the coordinator for the event never found out, or he just let it slide. Of course, he and I were pretty tight back in the day. He let my no-good shit slide all the time!

It was a moment. Mr. C used to say he'd adopt me if he could which was pretty rad because he was a 40 year-old black man, and I was this skinny fuckin' white kid from the country.

I only got through Job Corps to be good enough to cook toast with a culinary certificate, but the experience of being there is one of my cherished memories and made me into the pussy-pounding rockstar I am today! Mr. C's encouragement to chase my dream got me started working odd jobs and selling dope to get my first drum kit after I got out of there.

       * * *

Azul turned me onto the new "Mars Volta" full-length CD. Fuck, it is sooo good. We were blasting it on the way up. I'll remember this day whenever I hear that album now.

The Bastard Chronicle 15: Gabe's Oasis

I got a new car! A Mitsubishi Diamante. Quite the upgrade from The Hoopty. But she had to retire. The Diamante is a college graduation "present" from my fam! (I gotta take over the remaining payments, of course.) This thing gets up to 90 MPH in like, a couple of heartbeats. But, DAMN, college came and went and now I'm driving like a Michelle Rodriguez!

* * *

Gabe's Oasis is one of those venues where, if you start a band in Iowa, you definitely want to play there. They have an unrivaled legacy of great gigs. Ascending the fabled staircase of death up to the stage where a lot of my heroes and storytellers have performed was a definite bucket list item; checked!

Unfortunately, it was a Thursday night show and we knew nobody in town. The gig was a tough sell, and I was the only one from the band who was able to come over and flyer.

So, I pulled Zach to come with me to do the damn thing and we spent the whole day together in my new car. Going to all of the great record stores, book stores, skate shops, and everything in between! I LOVE Iowa City and actually wish we were based there.

* * *

On the bill, we were playing with an indie band and a punk band. We were the ones to "headline," which meant we played dead-last at midnight. We brought as many M-town people as we could get to fill the club.

Squash and Reagan had just split. Bummer. But he brought his new girlfriend, a blond chick that he just met at a Long John Silver's. (I can't keep track of all these girls…nor, do I remember their names. Long John Silver's Girl it is…)

* * *

Annie rode up with me. She likes to share stories of her past drug use, about her old boyfriend in Chicago, and about even MORE drug use. It pisses me off after awhile, because these drug people seem to talk down to others who haven't done any of that. Like I'm some prude!

I'm sure it's great for you, babe. Keep doing what you're doing. Ima pray for ya, dawg!

Yeah, I got a tall-can of beer at one of the gas stations along the interstate to cope. She did get lovely after a few swigs. I remember asking about her Heterochromia eyes. She calls them her "Heroine" eyes, with an "E." I told her the band has been writing a song which has the working title: Heroin Eyes.

She tisked and said, "Y'all don't know nothin' 'bout REAL heroin eyes!" I asked her to elaborate, and she said, "Let's score some drugs in Iowa City, and I'll show you."

I just dismissed it and told her straight up that I don't do that shit and that I don't waste my precious time with that stuff.

We didn't score anything, much to her disappointment, but she had me get her on the band drink discount at the bar. I told the bartender that Annie was the backup singer. Was I used?

* * *

Post-show thoughts: We played OK. But, Spike got so trashed he was moshing by himself during our set and he threw up all over the floor, then took off his shirt (revealing his BURN SCARS!!!) and rolled around in it. We got that on film...

The staff wasn't too pleased with us after that. They will probably think twice about booking us M-town bands for awhile...

The Thieves' Conundrum Compendium 7

We lost our damn percussionist this week!

Ben was being a jackass, drank whiskey with his friends one night and cut his hand wide-open by smashing the damn bottle against the wall while still holding it. He took pictures of it and e-mailed them to me. He ripped up his tendons, he was bleeding all over the place, and everything.

Was he trying to be like me? Doesn't he know you're supposed to do that onstage?!

He won't be able to pound out jungle beats anymore while we're playing.

He was totally worthless anyway. He started out really cool. Bought a set of congas, roto-toms, chimes, and a triangle! A FUCKING TRIANGLE!

We managed to get a few deals out of him from the music store he worked at. Still, it didn't fucking justify him being an extra body to worry about. There were definitely times where none of us even noticed he was there!

We started having him control the lights while we played so Squash could concentrate on his bass-playing. We filmed some of the shows, and his lighting cues were completely off! Total darkness on the heavy parts, full bombast and strobes for the quiet parts. That motherfucker!

We took him off the website as a full-on member, and I'm pretty sure his "music career" is over.

           ✶ ✶ ✶

Speaking of www.suiteberryrecords.com/bands/bastardsandthieves

We're getting pretty fucking fed up with Barry. I've been booking all the shows. He's been doing the teenage boy band thing and their little friends. That makes me think he has a thing for really young boys, that 30 year-old prick!

We told him we are fed up with the fucking slow progress on our CD! He said that maybe we shouldn't bring beer to our sessions anymore! ...Fuck him.

Maybe I'm just drunk. Either way, we got more awesome shows to play! See ya.

           ✶ ✶ ✶

C-C-C Conundrum
C-C-C Conundrum
C-C-C Conundrum
C-C-C Conundrum
C-C-C Conundrum
C-C-C Conundrum
C-C-C Conundrum
C-C-C Conundrum
C-C-C Conundrum
C-C-C Conundrum
C-C-C Conundrum
C-C-C Conundrum
C-C-C Conundrum

The Bastard Chronicle 16: Hairy Mary's

Damn. I will say this about Rick. He is a handful.
Like, all the time now. We almost get into it
nightly, since we live together AND work together.
But, he has been booking us some really great shows
and is getting some credibility as a mouthpiece
and a booker.

* * *

A national grindcore band out of Denver called,
Cephalic Carnage, came into town. Rick booked two
of our friends' bands, us, and them headlining at
the legendary Hairy Mary's in Des Moines!

This place is a hole in the wall, piece of shit
venue; but is so gnarly, and like Gabe's in IC,
has a fabled history within its four walls! It's a
goddamn hall of fame of punk-rock and metal glory!

I've seen so many shows here! (AND, its other claim to fame is having the nastiest bathrooms this side of CBGB's…so I've heard!)

We brought the majority of our crowd, which along with Cephalic Carnage's draw, we packed the small, black, obscenity scrawled, 300-capacity room adorned with gore-soaked artwork on the walls. It was a success!

Cephalic Carnage is our first truly national and signed band we opened for. It's hard to believe that we shared a stage with a band of that caliber as they sounded so tight and massive! We felt amateurish, and Rick said that their drummer was seen mocking us and dancing, in ridicule, at our stuff.

That sucks. I'm glad I didn't see THAT, but we made the best of it as we watched them show us how it was done!

* * *

The bartender was a full-on prick that almost ruined my night. He's a big 400 pound dude named Gabe, (not related to Gabe's in IC) who looked Native American. I asked him if he was, and what tribe he was from. Right away, he said, "Tribes are for pussies!"

Of all of the things to say, especially, to a Native Woman? WTF, dude! Rick was there, too, and we were confused; but we just shrugged, turned our backs to him and drank our dollar Schlitzes (I shit you not! One dollar Schlitzes! The shittiest beer imaginable.)

But, all night, he was making snide remarks and tearing down the local bands.

For Cephalic though, he treated like royalty. Even taking the bass out of his voice, laughing with gusto at their jokes, and showing all his service industry warmth for only them. If he's the yardstick of gaining respect in the music business, we failed.

BUT, we made him a good deal of money that night, didn't we?!

                    * * *

Oh yeah, in the back alley, after we loaded our gear out, Annie pulled me to her and kissed me.

Alright. Holy Joan Jett! I can say right now, I've never felt THAT way before. You know, THAT way! Well, maybe I have. Maybe, I am! I'm certainly not against it. Never was!

Alright, check it out—with the crazy life I've been living on the road, on stages, and in neon-lit clubs, my love-life has been an afterthought.

I know I'm surrounded by dudes all the time. I get the drunk guys that think they have game, slobbering around trying to talk; but I always have my crew around to protect me. But, that soft kiss from this chick with heroin eyes came out of nowhere, and I'm going with the flow. Yep, just going with it!

It's funny. Back in Tama, rumors would be flying. I'd get the evil eye everywhere. I'd have a scarlet letter branded on my ass. I would be exiled AND burned at the stake. But, this. This just makes life that much more interesting.

CHAPTER FIFTY-THREE

"Why now? Why at all? What did I do? Where do I go? How do I get there? ...and still make you proud?" Jesus took a swig of a newly purchased fifth of Jack Daniels. He adjusted the rearview mirror and looked to see if his foundation and rouge were "proper." He applied black lipstick and smacked his lips. He was dressed in a size-one black dress with a matching boa draped around his neck. He wore his fishnet stockings on his skinny legs with his brown steel-toe work boots laced on his feet as they worked the Buick's pedals.

He took the car to his hometown of Earlham, cruised through the trailer park where he grew up. He looked at the exhaust of the heated trailers coalescing above in the cold cloudy dawn. He remembered how they used to do that back then. He would watch them plume and disappear into the gray, like the smoke that used to come out of his dad's mouth and nostrils whenever a party was going on.

Next, he took the gravel roads and headed east.

He parked his car north of I-80 deep into the Keuhn Conservation Area, a vast 770 acre sliver of nature away from the heartbreak of civilization.

The expanse had wild prairie and little upkeep except for the main paths that were cut away for hiking trails and primitive camping.

There was a timber frame of a roundhouse in the prairie that he climbed onto. He was struggling with footing on the thick tree poles but managed to reach the top of the smoke chimney to enjoy the silence and gray sky.

He used to ride bikes here with his friend to escape the trailer park when there was a party. Parties always turned to binges. The binges turned to fights.

These lasted for days and ran in succession throughout the trailer park, like a viral plague that turned the adults into monsters.

This conservation area was a silent, hidden paradise to get lost in.

"Why now? Why at all? What did I do? Where do I go? How do I get there? ...and still make you proud?" He jumped down from the structure to the hiking trails down to the upland forest bluffs. He always liked the ominous look of the treeline as he approached it. He imagined himself walking into the maw of a sentient forest giant that was pulling him in.

The prairie floor turned into pebbles, crunching beneath his steel-toed boots. He looked down to see the water damage of the leather and the bright fluorescent flower design painted on the toes by his first daughter. He noticed it was flaking off.

He walked down the trail of the forest bluff that would prove treacherous if he lost his footing. His ankle joints were a little too slack and on a dangerous swivel. He took a look at the sky-lit opening at the bottom of the blackened incline. He slowed down so the weight wouldn't take him by surprise and crumple his ankles.

He reached the opening and looked around the hidden meadow that stretched around him. The prairie grass was waving in the cold autumn breeze as if taunting his impaired vision.

Beyond the meadow was another treeline that protected the Raccoon River bank. He imagined huge bears walking within the trimmed riparian buffer looking for something to eat.

"Come on motherfuckers! I'm here! I know you're migrating this way, but I never see you fat fuckers! Yeah, I took down one of your boys with a microphone stand! What you got now? All I got is this whiskey bottle——" he yelled towards the river.

No bears answered back.

He expected to see mountain lions to pounce on him from the tall prairie grass. He planted his feet as he saw a golden hide move within the lines.

The sudden threshing of the grass and the form of a five-point buck galloped away from him, deeper into the meadow.

"Crom! Beast! If only I had my dagger." His voice was starting to crack from the yelling.

He turned to the east and hiked along the footing of the treeline. There was an old *Wickiup* hidden off the trail. He wondered if the old dome hut in the ground was still standing. He remarked that if he had killed that deer earlier, he could've skinned it and tied the hide to the Wickiup's frame.

His palms moistened at the possibility of IT being there. He clutched harder onto his liquid courage.

"Here it is. Here it was. Here's what I did. Here's where I go. Here's how I got here. I will make you proud," he grumbled as he turned into the less-beaten path and saw the clearing where the Wickiup was still there.

After all of these years, he thought. The last remnants of old civilization was still standing. The weathered branches folded and clasped together like gaunt fingers of an old tree deity buried underground, clutching onto its former glory.

"Oh shit!" He saw it standing there. Black and fuzzy as usual, yet tangible like it was close enough to reach.

The Black Mark, he called it. It had the figure of a man. Ever since his dad ground his fist into that side of his face when he was a boy, the black mark made its presence in random times. But he could always find it sitting in the old Wickiup, or in this case, standing, waiting for him.

"She has cancer now motherfucker! She has cancer! You happy now? Did I interrupt you? Did you just go and do a fuckin' errand and I caught you gettin' ready to sit down and meditate on my misery, motherfucker? Or are you wanting to go, right now?" Jesus set down the bottle of Jack, tucked the skirting of his dress into his boxer briefs, clenched his fist, and got into his fighting stance.

The black mark sat down inside the Wickiup, than stood right back up again and laughed. It sat down quickly, got back up and laughed again.

CHAPTER FIFTY-FOUR

"You ever see *Night of the Living Dead*, Rick?" Ronnie asked, as he was turning the car into a gravel road on a hill.

"A long time ago. I barely remember it. Why do you ask?" Rick was in the passenger seat of a maroon Monte Carlo SS, taking a swig of his Busch Light.

"This damn cemetery will give you the fucking creeps. You'll love it. Yeah, the beginning of that movie where Barbara and her brother go up to visit their mama's grave. They meet 'Zombie Number One,' and then all hell breaks loose. You gotta remember that don't ya?" Ronnie sped up on the gravel road, spinning the tires while turning on a curve that was flanked by unkempt brush. They passed a sign that read: *Level B Road. Enter at your own risk.*

"Whoa! Watch it man! Umm. Yeah. That's one of the most iconic opening scenes of all time. Now that you say something, this DOES look like that road! Holy shit——" He looked out of his window as the autumn brush swallowed his view of the fields below, the rugged road shook the car as they ascended higher into thicker overgrowth.

Ronnie turned the headlights on. "Fuckin' shits! I tell ya... They haven't fixed this road in years. You figure they would fix this driveway out of respect for the dead. The dead get lonely, too——ya know. Don' nobody wanna come up here."

They reached an impasse, and a manicured lawn stretched out with old gravestones and markers of withered mineral stuck out like gray and silver pox sores on a mangy earthen hide.

"This place IS creepy! I can't believe they buried him out here. What's the significance of this place?"

"It's an old frontier cemetery. Goes way back. Indian and settler times. Even before the railroad down the hill come and pass through here. Even before this town, LaMoille, came to be. His old farm parents were traditional, and particular where they buried their own," Ronnie turned his headlamps off, turned around, and parked the car facing the way they came in.

"I can see that! Man, that gravestone says: 1898! I'm gonna get some great shots here while we still got a little light left. Where's Georgy's grave at brother? I got a full bottle of whiskey just for him——" Rick got his backpack with the bottle, his camera, and notebook inside; they both got out of the car. Ronnie got a shovel out of the trunk. Rick followed Ronnie as he led him to a small bank where there was a freshly laid grave that stood out among the old gravestones.

"There he is. Good ol' Georgy Manson. Here lies the coolest Motherfucker I have ever known," Ronnie put his hand on Rick's shoulder and brought him closer to inspect the etching of the fresh grave marker which read: *Georgy Manson. Here lies the coolest Motherfucker you will ever know! Born May 26, 1977 - Born Again October 26, 2001.*

Rick laughed heartily at the epitaph, and got his camera out to take a photo.

"Only that Motherfucker would think to put that on his own grave, man! I loved him with all of my heart. I just wish I was there with him that day, ya know. He was fuckin' hurting, man, and that bitch drove him to kill himself before anyone could swoop in and help him." Rick, after shooting different angles of the grave, wiped a tear, and was taken with emotion. "Man, I was outta town, being selfish——I coulda came right back to M-town to hang out with him, but I didn't, man..."

Ronnie put his arm around Rick's shoulder in a tight man-hug. "Don't do that to yourself, brotha! You had your own shit going on. He had shit to do, too! He thought of us before he had to go. Somehow, he knew he didn't have much time. Can't no one change time on the account of grief. Just be thankful he left us with a whole lotta good times——and a plan."

"Yeah, but I keep remembering our last exchange. How I wanted to take him out on tour to be our roadie and mascot. How these bitches could just fuck with your mind, take your dreams, and take your kids away. Oh fuck, I feel bad for his parents, too. That was their only son. Does that bitch have their daughter?"

"Yep. They skipped town and don' nobody know where they gon' to. Of course rumor has it that they're in protective custody down in Dallas. You know how that goes——" Ronnie looked down at the shovel and asked if he wanted to do the honors. Rick grabbed it, spun it in his hand, and asked where. "Besides, both you and I know that if the cops hadn't shot that rubber bullet while he had the shotgun to his face, there's a good chance he'd still be here today. Fuck them pigs. Here, try that fresh patch right there by your feet there..."

Rick put the shovel into the mound of soft soil behind the newly etched grave marker and started to dig. Ronnie unscrewed the cap of the whiskey they brought, poured some out onto the the earthen mound at the fore of the stone. "A work of genius if I ever knew it to be. This one's for you brotha."

     * * *

"Oh man, how much do you think we got?" Rick wiped the sweat off his brow with his "wifebeater" and took a swig of whiskey.

"I'd say a good twenty pounds. There's more, but I gotta receive word on the actual number in the books out West. But, hell yeah! This'll be a good winter if we don't get too greedy. Low profile is key. Georgy worked hard on this, and we gotta show some respect." Ronnie put the tightly-sealed plastic bags of product they had dug up in a garbage bag and into an olive-green military-issue duffel bag in his trunk.

"Sweet. Well, he had a way of taking care of family. I just wish that dumb bitch saw the bigger picture, ya know! So, you wanna hit some of this shit before we get outta here? You got a glass dick to melt this shit in? I gotta take a shower, and then we could party a little, right?" Rick put the shovel into the trunk.

"Don't call it shit, man. I got the ingredients, and it's gonna take time for me to put this plan into motion. Georgy didn't call this product 'White Man's Way' for nuthin'." Ronnie shut the trunk door and fished for a cigarette in his pocket.

"Oh shit. Is that what he called it?" Rick laughed.

"Mmm, hmm..." Ronnie lit his cigarette. "White Man's Way."

The Bastard Chronicle 17: Adult Odyssey

So, Annie got a job at the Adult Odyssey. I take her to work almost everyday now. This is the "Glory Hole" place that Squash was telling us about. It is a small brick-red building that used to be a roadhouse biker bar when the road was the main highway back when I was a little kid. I remember riding in the car with Grandma and Grandpa, and I imagined what happened in this dingy and wild-looking place. I asked Grandpa about it a few times and he said, "It's no good. It's where all the bad people go," and "It's no place for little Indian girls!" Something like that. The childhood intrigue and curiosity is paying off now. Whatever that means...

This place is on the EXACT same road, just east, past the "House by the Cemetery," Rick's old house, where our first practice took place. It's weird how this "Old HWY 30" just keeps coming back into my life.

I came with Annie on her first week. I brought my acoustic guitar and handheld recorder to get some song inspiration and noticed the distinctive smell of disinfectant and that port-a-potty smell upon entering. Gross...

And yes, when Squash told us guys lined up to the Red Light Arcade in back, it was not an exaggeration. There were people I knew from work, old classmates, and even local politicians in that line. All waiting patiently. (The mayor?! WTF? He got done in the Arcade, smoothed his comb-over and said to us, "Well, time to sober up now!" he laughed, walked out the door, and cried in his van outside...just kidding on that last part! Ha!)

It's unreal to see in such a small town that a sordid thing like this exists. I don't know who was in the glory hole room, or who was legitimately there to view a porno movie. I wasn't comfortable enough to ask. I'm a woman. I should have been afraid; but after a few beers and tunes with Annie, who gets sexier and sexier as the night goes on, I got more into the vibe.

It's like once you get past the initial shock, and see the videos, and pink sex toys warming up the room with the port-a-potty odor, it's a haven.

Some of the local strippers came in to hang out. They're fun. Were they there doing tricks? I don't know.

We got to know this one blond who says she knew the guy who worked here that blew his face off with a shotgun in the LaMoille alley. He reportedly had his daughter with him, and he was at a stand-off with the cops for hours.

I remember reading about that story in the paper. I know Rick had mentioned that one night when he was sloppy drunk.

She continued telling the story and saying how that guy was the greatest, blah, blah, blah— then she was in tears, and said the cops murdered him. Apparently, that is the word going around that the cops may have jumped the gun. (Err...bad choice of words?)

One thing led to another. She pulled me and Annie to the back storeroom, and she thanked us for being there to listen to her. She was tired of dealing with men who rip her off and treat her like an object. (Well, she should maybe choose another line of work, I thought...)

She took out a glass pipe that looked like one of the sex toys dangling on the shelves of the salesfloor. She starts taking these weird white rocks out of a bag and immediately Annie starts to get excited and says to me that this will "bring us to another level——" I asked her what she meant by that? She kissed me, and the stripper took the lighter to the glass dick and melted one of those rocks inside it.

I had never seen that done, I was like, I don't know what's going on here but it smells pretty crazy. The smoke looked cool, so we all took turns doing it.

It wasn't that bad. We just continued drinking and hanging out. She said that stuff was called, "White Man's Way," which I thought was hilarious, and we were having fun with that and started getting friendly with each other.

Like, REALLY friendly. That crazy stripper knows how to have a good time. Man, the things she can do with that pierced tongue of hers. I don't know if I'm going to hell for being in that back room with those two girls; but it was like three in the morning, and no one was around. The guys in the

Red Light Arcade had all gone home, it was just us girls in an old roadhouse on "Old HWY 30."

Oh man, did I mention the things she could do with her pierced tongue?

CHAPTER FIFTY-SIX

"I thought we weren't bringing any beer to our sessions anymore, but I guess you two have already made up your minds——" Barry said as he was seated in his swivel office chair in front of his producer's desk. Azul and Rick looked sheepishly at the 12-pack between their chairs, looked at each other, shrugged, and took a drink of their Natural Ice cans. "Are you sure you wanna do this? Maybe parting ways in the middle of our recording and mixing sessions isn't the best way. I mean, you gotta remember all the hard work I put in as well."

Barry then proceeded to mix down the three tracks that they had been working on for months.

Azul cleared her throat, and spoke in an arbitrary tone, "It sounds good, Barry. But yes, we have made up our minds and want to move forward. Besides, it looks like you have your hands full with Suite

Berry, Infant Dust, and that new band you signed——uhh, what were they called?"

"Chrome Semic Fiesta——" Barry answered.

"Ah——" Azul put the beer can to her mouth in trying to conceal her wry smile.

Rick spoke up, "We feel that we, well, let's just be real, I have done all the work for getting this band recognized and booked all over the state. We got to open for some signed bands now, without your help. We just want to go it alone and, as Azul just said, take the load off of your mind and you won't have to worry about us anymore. No contracts. No fees. We want out. You'll get credit for this mix we're doing now, and be done with it. We're recording a new CD at our buddy Cody's studio across town. We're taking Kitty with us, too."

Barry hit *Render* on his DAW to create their final WAV files to burn onto their CD-Rs to take home.

"Oof. Well, that is another issue. She left me with some not-so-choice words of endearment for me and the Bastards. Her message was along the lines of: 'Fuck you. Fuck the Bastards. You took all the credit for my work on the website. Good luck with your new webmaster. I'm taking all of my shit, and kicking you off my server.'" Barry clasped his hands together and made a gesture that suggested a cutting-of-ties.

"Well, we had nothing to do with the site to begin wi——I'll e-mail her. That's fine. I'm not worried 'bout that. Is that thing done mixing, yet? Can we get our CD-Rs and go?" Rick's patience wearing thin.

Barry swiveled around to look at his monitor to see the progress bar, that seemed to be trudging along with the cooling fans and hard drive sounding like gravel in his Compaq computer tower under his desk. "Uhh——Rendering is at ten percent," He swiveled back to face them. "Hey, trust me, I'm as frustrated as you are. If we have reached this cul-de-sac by any negative feelings, I do apologize. It's like I've said before; I only had our best interests at heart. I was more focused on the bigger picture. It takes a while to get there. Hey, where is Jesus, by the way? It'd be nice to smoke up with my buddy for one last time!" said Barry, changing the subject.

"Umm, he's been going through a rough time. Seems he's been struggling with the drink. Or, his wife is giving him a hard time. The kid, who knows. We just know he's been having a rough time. His wife called the house one night looking for him. Said he hasn't been coming home. We hope he's alright…" Azul's voice trailed off as she started to get uncomfortable in her chair, took another swig, and cleared her throat. "How far are you on the Infant Dust CD? How does it sound?"

"It's finished! It's in the process of being pressed. We'll plan to release it soon. I'd be honored if you guys would play the CD Release Show! Would that be a possibility? I'm thinking of a big, unprecedented bash at The Reverb in Cedar Falls!" Barry brightened up into his usual inimitable way while clasping his hands in excitement.

"Sure. Just let us know when, in advance. How's the progress on the mix?" Rick was pacing in the empty space across the room where he tracked his drums months before.

Barry swiveled around again. "Uhh——We are at twenty percent, my man!"

* * *

"Wow, it feels good to finally get the fuck outta there! Fuck Barry! Fuck his family! We got what we came for. Take this CD-R and burn a few hundred copies on your mom's computer. You can do that can't you?" Rick said while in the passenger seat of Azul's car as they were on the way to Jesus's house to give him his CD-R, and to tell him the news of their severed ties with Barry.

"Geez, fuck his family? That's harsh isn't it? Man, I don't like it when you say shit like that! Only a tyrant deals in absolutes, ya know!" Azul said in stern defense.

"Well, he had our shit locked up in there, and that fucker was just playing us for a bunch of fools, man! C'mon, you've seen it haven't you?" Rick barked back while he drummed 16th notes on his lap.

They argued on the way to Jesus's house, which they haven't been to since their last practice session earlier that year. It was 9:00, right before he had to go to work for his graveyard shift retail job.

The lights were on. They walked up to his door and knocked lightly so as not to disturb the nest.

"Hey guys, good to see you. I'm glad y'all came. We need to talk——" Jesus answered the door, a serious tone in his voice, immediately channeling the mood in dread as he led them to the basement where their old practice space used to be.

"Is everything alright, dude? We heard Amy was looking for you when she called the Compound," Rick said.

"Hmm, yeah, about that. I got fucking crazy again. I ain't been home, because I've been dealing with some fucked-up shit in my head. I don't wanna upset the kid. Fortunately, I still got my job——" Jesus turned the light on in the cold basement that no longer had musical equipment inside. "I found out my mom has lung cancer. We're trying to set her up with medical treatment. Chemo. All that stuff."

Rick and Azul were shocked and immediately sympathetic.

Jesus continued, "Me and Amy are moving out of here and moving to Jefferson, a small town two hours away from M-town. It's less expensive to live there, and I'm transferring to a better paying position at another store. Things will be easier for my family. So, now, when I'm driving to band practice, I need to make damn sure that my time is gonna be worth it. If we say we're gonna get something done, we need to do it. Ya know what I'm saying?"

Rick and Azul understood and solemnly agreed. They just listened as Jesus talked about his mom, about the family dynamic in dealing with her diagnosis, and why he was moving out of Des Moines.

"It's gonna be a tough time for all of us. I'll be working on my drinking again, definitely not smoking anymore; but I'm telling you, man, it's hard. Everything is amplified when you got a kid involved, ya know what I'm saying? We gotta make this band work. I'm glad we are cutting ties with Barry. We've been doing good on our own. I can throw that contract in the trash now. If we're on the same page, the three of us have been the band this whole time. With all due respect to Squash and whoever percussionist we hire. It's always been the three of us. So let's fucking do it, man!"

"We'll do it. For your mom." Rick nodded in determination.

"For ALL our moms," Jesus added.

The Bastard Chronicle 18: Great Plains Audio

Local Lix Rock 103 is promoting a big thing where local bands get to record a live set with a studio audience. The set then airs on the show later in the month! It is a joint promotional deal for the radio station and Great Plains Audio, a new recording studio on the west side of Des Moines.

One of Barry's boys, who is a web designer and singer of the band Chrome Semic Fiesta is on our side now, doing our new website.

We went live with this big announcement right after we got the green light to go in and record!

* * *

Rick and Rosita rolled up with some people in the Burnt Burrito. We got a few carloads of Little

Bastards to be the studio audience. Annie rode with me. Jesus and Squash met us there.

We arrived as the cloudy day was turning to night. It was cold, but we looked forward to be on fire inside the professional studio. We've never been in such a nice, clean facility. It was just east of the foreign car dealerships. Big prime real estate!

We met the engineer. I can't remember his name. He introduced us to the studio owner. (Can't remember his name either…Great networking, girl! Not…)

The engineer had a lengthy list of bands he recorded from Omaha, where he was originally from. They wanted to capitalize on the scene here. The owner just pays the bills.

Rick has been bringing around some shady people lately, mainly, this one skinny, older white dude with the craziest brown 80's mullet I've ever seen.

Ronnie. That's his name. It's like he still has "Hysteria" and "Shout at the Devil" still bumping in his cassette deck in his Monte Carlo SS. He's nice to me, but obviously tweaked out all the time and tries to get in on EVERY conversation. Even when it's supposed to be a strict band meeting, he's always poking around to add his two cents worth, and then some. ("Fuckin' shits! I tell ya…" is his catchphrase, I swear.)

What's also weird is that his wife, who is the total opposite, just hangs around and doesn't speak. Ominous. Cold. She just kinda hides behind her unusually thick glasses and plays the part of Ronnie's wife. Yeah…

We had a great time though! It was definitely hard for the band to get the energy going in the big drum room while everyone else was in the control room with the engineer.

Rage Against The Machine recorded their first album like this! It's the most professional studio we've ever been in! I'm glad we got this opportunity to see how shows like the "BBC Live" or "Iowa Public Radio" broadcasts do it.

I didn't get to pick the recording engineer's brain like I wanted to because of all the extra people around. Plus, we had to tear down and haul our gear out at a reasonable time.

Perhaps, we will return, and I could play with all the great toys in that nice studio!

* * *

Speaking of toys, Annie had a fifth of vodka and was getting blitzed. On the way home, she was crying, holding onto me, and kissing me. I tried to be comforting, but I was so tired from working all day, doing the show, and loading gear. I just wanted to go home in silence and sleep. She kept going on about how people thought she was ugly, a drugged-out whore. My god, what about my needs? I have female hormones, too! They need rest to regulate. It was overwhelming.

But, the whole entourage came back to the Compound and guess what? Another party! Great, I had to work in the morning.

She stayed with me in my room. We turned off the lights and let the darkness create a sort of chrysalis for us to entwine in as we lied in bed together, away from the noise. Just outside my bedroom door, Rick was running around naked and chasing everyone around the apartment with bottles of whipped cream and spraying cans of Busch Light all over everyone.

* * *

As we lied there on my mattress, she said, "I've never been with a woman before."

I said, "Me neither."

I don't think that makes us official. Maybe, it does.

But, her heterochromia makes me weak.

Her expensive perfume and cheap vodka smells good on her skin.

Together, we're two different flavors of sweetness on one plate.

The odd duality of companionship.

When life gives you something you weren't looking for, do you take it?

The Thieves' Conundrum Compendium 8: Fort Madison

Back in my hometown! We played this place called Vinnie's on the main street area next to the fuckin' Mississippi! It was a triumphant return to the place where I was conditioned to fail. To spend the rest of my life at the prison.

Fort Madison is a prison town. It's only claim to fame now. 'Bout half of my friends are in there already. Mid-twenties. Slam. Doors shut. Life wasted...

The fucking Mississippi River runs through here, but growing up, it always felt like the world forgot about us. Not that night! I had alot to prove. With my band in tow, we kicked ass, got free drinks and food all night, and conquered!

It was a Friday night show! We didn't get back home until Tuesday morning. We were trying to get Jesus and Squash to stay with us, but they were being pussy-whipped fuckboys! So, it was me, Rosita, and Azul;

(Who just got laid-off from her casino job) and we stayed with my old homeboy: Tray.

I showed the girls around the old neighborhood. Visited tons of friends. They met Mom! It was so good to be home. We didn't stay long, though. I guess my rationale was that if I stayed there too long I wouldn't be able to leave.

I showed them my uncle's place on the river. He has boats, and we wanted to go boating! He wasn't home for some reason. His place looks like something from the "Friday the 13th" movies.

I started chasing the girls around with a machete that was hanging in his garage. Haha! I think I might've scared 'em for real! I was just playing. They almost ruined the whole trip by being freaked out for real. I apologized though! I told 'em to chill and I laid out a bump for a peace offering.

They accepted! Ha! They never say "No" to THAT do they? White Man's Way! We just got more beer after that, cruised around some more, and went back to Tray's. I think that was Sunday...

We got back to his house, where he lives a few blocks away from the famous railroad train bridge above the Mississippi River! We call this place: The Thin Line of Purgatory! It's the space where we walked on the wooden railroad ties that ran along the bridge's steel girded frame on the bottom while the trains ran right above our heads on the tracks. This is where Tray and I would go to get away from life. We'd take a boombox, bring some beer, and hang out where certain death was above us(the railroad track) and below us(the deep Mississippi). As above, so below. We use to take the high school girls here, fingerbang 'em and shit. Fuck, it was good times, man... Long gone dayz.

⋆ ⋆ ⋆

Before we left, Tray gave me his dad's old cowboy hat! I'm flattered that he gave me something of his dad's! Nobody else is wearing cowboy hats in the music scene nowadays, so I am gonna sport that shit.

Man, we were smoking alot of ice, man. I was kinda worried about having Azul party with us. I don't wanna corrupt her like that. Fuck it!

She's gotta hang with the big boys, right? Girls gotta show they can hang, especially, a badass guitar player like her. She's one of a kind. Shit, man. She was all in though and could hang with the rest of us.

Rosita knows all about getting high. She tried to run away from it in her hometown. But, she's safe with me! With me, it's different. I'm in a fucking band, and now I'm hustling that shit!

We're the fucking Bastards & Thieves! There ain't fucking no one like us, but people wanna be us. Their silver lining; we crush that shit up and fucking smoke it!

* * *

FLAME...FOIL...FLAME...FOIL...FLAME...FOIL...FOIL...FLAME... FOIL...FLAME...FOIL...

FLAME...FOIL...FLAME...FOIL...FLAME...FOIL...FOIL...FLAME... FOIL...FLAME...FOIL...

FLAME...FOIL...FLAME...FOIL...FLAME...FOIL...FOIL...FLAME... FOIL...FLAME...FOIL...

FLAME...FOIL...FLAME...FOIL...FLAME...FOIL...FOIL...FLAME... FOIL...FLAME...FOIL...

FLAME...FOIL...FLAME...FOIL...FLAME...FOIL...FOIL...FLAME... FOIL...FLAME...FOIL...

FLAME...FOIL...FLAME...FOIL...FLAME...FOIL...FOIL...FLAME... FOIL...FLAME...FOIL...

FLAME...FOIL...FLAME...FOIL...FLAME...FOIL...FOIL...FLAME... FOIL...FLAME...FOIL...

FLAME...FOIL...FLAME...FOIL...FLAME...FOIL... FOIL...FLAME...FOIL...

Inhale...eXhale.

The Bastard Chronicle 19: What Day is This?

I need a new pedal board! I've been putting that off for months. Seems like every time I get a little ahead, I get a lot behind. Sometimes, ya know, I feel stuck; but then I'm moving so fast that I can't seem to find a tree stump someplace to gather my thoughts to what I wanna do next.

The pigs have repo-ed my car. Out of the fucking blue! They showed up on a hot day to fucking take my car out of the lot parked at the compound. I shouldn't have answered the door, but did. It was all white people. Asking my name and shit. What are you doing asking my name and what were they doing at my house? My Band Headquarters! Fucking mookomans! White devils are always trying to take something from Natives, right!? But, there they all were. About 5 of them! A older woman, and older man, two young guys, and a girl. I think they were a family… fucking family business, but whatever!

How could Auntie Sandra work at a job like that all of those years? Repo…expensive cars. GRR!

I had to call up Grandma to borrow money. Why did I agree to getting such an expensive car? The payments are too much! I hated doing that. Calling up Grandma to borrow money. I was afraid I would just break down and cry if I heard her voice. I didn't though. Rick, Rosita, Anne and I were cleaning the house, taking care of bills, silk-screening shirts, and doing band shit online. I was pumped to take care of business and that's what everyone was doing. Everyone is doing. Ya know. Taking care of business, my business, needs cash flow.

Do I ask the tribe for money? My uncles and cousins are getting all kinds of money from the tribe! They're on the tribal council now! They're the reason I'm out of the job! Mass Layoff! WTF?! Buying Harley Davidsons, expensive cars… EXPENSIVE CARS! GRR!

I'm not like my cousins back in Tama! I'm not like another dead cousin or lazy per-cap baby cousin sitting in jail!

Fucking tribe never does anything for women anyways! They punish women and treat us dirty when we have our periods. Banish us. Exile us and leave us in the wasteland with nothing…for having fucking periods!

It was right for me to cut my hair off. I'm glad I did. Look what I got now! Now my hair is growing back and when I can braid it up, we'll be signed, THEN I will finally ARRIVE!

I hate doing that. Borrowing money. Fucking mookomans! Fucking white devils, decide to take MY car that I got as a graduation gift for all my hard work! It makes me do MY work! MY fucking band! I had to do it, I had to! I'm leaving in *a little bit to get that money. I might stay around to feed the horse. I don't know yet. I love Magenta! I hope Grandma doesn't ask me to stay for supper. I don't know, man. I won't be able to eat it without throwing up anyways. Time is wasting. I need to get my car. Can't sell my guitar, my amp, my pedals. I need a pedal board too! FUCK! I need those. Those are my livelihood. Or, will be! They will be OUR livelihood! We're the best band in the fucking Midwest! I mean, really! We're gonna be signed in a year! I need those to make our CD! To play live! I just hate having to do this and ask my fam for some money. But, it needs to be done. I really don't want to tell Mom, but I might have to. Fuck, I don't really want them to see me like this. Helpless. But yeah, I guess what I'm really trying to say right now is, I don't want them to see me like this…*

The Thieves' Conundrum Compendium 9: Fort Dodge, VFW Hall

Azul just fucking spits right in this one chick's face in the audience as we are playing! We debuted a brand new song on stage called: "The Golden Calf." Haha! It was classic! The chick didn't mind it though. Lesbo! Haha!

I guess it was better than when Azul leapt off the stage, out into the pit, and almost gouged a dude's eye out with the head of her guitar! That was a few shows back, now that was fucking gnarly! I'm glad we didn't get sued for THAT one. His eye looked like a popped cherry and was purple all around the flesh area! She gets violent when she gets going. I guess it pays to be a hot enigma like her! Haha!

Ah fuck, we just played the basement of this VFW Hall, and it was great. We played with a bunch of metal bands and us. We brought some of our crowd, my good buddy Felix, and his ol' lady.

* * *

It's good to be back in Fort Dodge! The last time I was here was when the "Empty Caste" recorded our demo out at Junior's Motel. The legendary recording studio that is just south of here. Great place! That was a helluva time. Fuck, we just drank, partied, and managed to record a five-song demo there! Everyone was so tweaked out that none of us slept that whole time. I wouldn't mind going back there!

* * *

We've been recording at Cody's studio in Des Moines for months now, and the CD sounds like dogshit! The Sweet Barry CD sounds better than the stuff we're recording now! We just stopped trying. We just end up partying whenever we go there to record. Cody's one of those dudes that can tweak for days, and stay down in that basement studio like a vampire. Ya figure with all the time he spends down there he'd make it sound good. But, we'll just make out with what we have. Azul has got the artwork down, we got so many shows to play, and shirts to sell. We need more product!

* * *

Line...

Line...

Line...

Line...

Line...

Line...

Line...

Line...

Line...

Line...

Line...

Line...

Line...

"Ain't nobody gonna build nothing till God's on your side"

The Bastard Chronicle 20: Ft. Madison & Keokuk

We went to Rick's old stomping grounds again. The
prison town. The Mississippi Mudville. Whatever
ya wanna call it. We get great shows there! We
played two nights back-to-back in Ft. Madison and
Keokuk, the border town a few miles from there in
the southeastern tip of Iowa. Illinois and Missouri
both border there. Strange culture. I can see how
it must've been a beautiful and bustling economy in
the Industrial Revolution days.

Seems there's, umm, a lot of drug use there. I
know M-town's pretty bad. Maybe, it's everywhere,
and I just don't see it. Of course, maybe the
surroundings of the river valley kinda amplifies the
symptoms beneath the dregs.

We played our set on the first night and the
crowd was rowdy. We loved it.

Though, once again, we had to play fricking "WOMD" twice, again! Why don't our other songs get encores?

After that, the bar owner told the bartenders to "Get them anything they want!" Before, we've gotten free drink tickets and all of that. This was our first "Band-gets-the-keys-to-the-bar" moment! Fuck me, we got trashed! It seemed like the party didn't stop. We just hauled our gear to the next one.

We found the venue, ate a little dinner in this weird, satin-lit Chinese place in the downtown area, loaded in, did a soundcheck, and continued the party.

Again, we won over the bar owner's blessing for the keys to the bar! Fuck, man it was ridiculous. I made sure to cake on some more makeup so as people couldn't see my obvious discoloration. We had to do lines to keep up with the madness. It was insane. (I hope I don't have to go to rehab for this shit…Aye!)

One creepy and significant moment comes to mind. There was this white supremacist dude that came to the Friday show AND the Saturday show. He came up to me after we had played the first one and was really friendly. He complimented how I looked like a "curly-haired, warrior princess" onstage, "dancing like my ancestors" to our music. When we got to the percussion parts, he said he was in "heaven."

Mm-kay…

He sported a big red swastika shirt, suspenders, white laced boots, tattoos; his whole outfit was unsettling. I was ready to scream for the guys to come and save me if this Nazi guy decided to kidnap me or start some shit. But, he didn't.

He asked me if I would be interested in going to a powwow he was organizing around there. I was confused. The only other powwow I could think of being close to here was the Rock Island Powwow, which my grandparents took me to when I was real young. Anyways, this dude scribbled on some paper the name of the powwow, a phone number, and his name: Tracy.

Flash forward to the next night. I was surprised to see him there again! Afterward, he got to talking about how he admired me; he envied me.

I asked, "How is that?"

He said I had an identity. A culture and heritage to call my own in this country full of bastards and thieves.

I was like, "Wow. I never thought of it like that. Thanks, man."

I shook his hand and that was that. I still got the paper in my bag. I don't know if that was legit. Maybe. But I'm not gonna find out anytime soon. But what he said really stuck with me...

The Thieves' Conundrum Compendium
10: Duluth, MN

We finally made it out of state! Next we are gonna hit Omaha, Lincoln, hopefully Chicago! We're branching out and getting heard outside shithole Iowa! Feels good. We put in alot of work. Hundreds of E-mails. Hundreds of phone calls. We reached out to tons of bands. We finally got a show with this metal band from Duluth, doing an all-ages at this park. The building was like a rental hall with a pretty sweet stage.

The town was fucking gorgeous, right by the great Lake Superior! It reminded me of Fort Madison, except WAY more vast!

Squash booked us a hotel room on top of the bluffs. The Buena Vista hotel. That shitty hotel lived up to its name. We could see the whole scene. It was pretty gnarly!

When everyone was passing out for the night, Azul and I went downtown to look for a White Castle, since we don't have those in Iowa. She was obsessed!

There wasn't a White Castle, but we did find this small casino in the middle of town and played a little. It was like something you'd see on a western movie. We were so drunk and obnoxious that we got kicked out! Apparently, all they kicked us out for was saying, "Fuck" too many times!

* * *

Squash and I are starting to not get along. The guy can be a fucking cheese-dick. So fucking judgmental! He shouldn't be throwing fucking stones in a glass house, that prick! He cheated on his old girlfriend and smokes weed all the time. He's in no position to judge what I do. I do double his work load as far as this band is concerned!

He and I were so close, man. All the good times we had, and he's acting like this?! I just don't know what to say at this point. I straight up wanted to kick him out of the band, but the others won't let me. They say he is too big of an asset to lose with his "tech genius" and light system. Fine! Whatever! If he stays out of my way, I'll stay out of his. Fuck.

* * *

The show was a bit of a disappointment. We traveled almost 10 hours to play to about 20 people, that's including the bands. But hey, we got them on the mailing list. We'll add them, and use those contacts for later. We didn't make any money. We just handed out our CD. A rough mix of the "Cody Demo" that we fucking hate with a passion.

Everyone liked our stupid "Weapons of Mass Destruction" country song. We fucking hate that, too! We had to play that twice...again!

Times like these, I wish I didn't have to haul my drum kit around. Just to be a frontman. Drink fucking beer, get high, and be a rockstar. Yeah, I wouldn't have to haul all that shit, I'd just sell merch at the end of the show. Sounds nice! I'll present that to the other two. If I could get the right drummer, teach him all the parts, I could do the hand percussion shit, play a bass part. Whatever! I can do anything!

The Bastard Chronicle 21: Cedar Falls, The Reverb

We first played this venue when we entered a Tuesday night "Book Your Own Band" thing. We brought a few of our Little Bastards and got our foot in the door. The soundman liked us. The staff was cool as hell, and the crowds were good after the buzz about our band got around.

It is a great venue (I saw Dog Fashion Disco and Strapping Young Lad here! Yes!!!) that is in the center of University of Northern Iowa's campus town, The Hill, in Cedar Falls.

Like Gabe's in Iowa City, it has a treacherous two-story staircase for bands to haul gear up to. I almost fell back from carrying my half-stack speaker cab up that beast! Luckily, Jesus followed me and caught me before I fell back! Jesus saves indeed. (More on that half-stack later…)

Flash Forward to this night's show. We were releasing a remixed version of our "Cody Demo." Infant Dust was releasing their newly recorded CD. But the show was billed as a Suite Berry Records CD Release Party featuring Infant Dust, the webmaster's band Chrome Semic Fiesta, and in SMALL, PINK, CURSIVE letters: Bastards & Thieves "CD release" in quotations! Just like that.

Ya know, maybe just because we have a GIRL in our band, OUR designated font on this particular flyer HAS to be small, pink, and demeaning...or something like that!

Even back then, as an artist, I have been peculiar about Barry's art choices for flyers when we were working together; but I think this was the ultimate last word as the flyer had an elaborate and professional layout featuring Infant Dust's new CD artwork. They are clearly his golden child, and we are the unloved bastards of the past...

We played first. The venue was getting packed, and we were gonna give them a show that none of Barry's bands could follow.

Truth be told, it was good to see all those dudes. Especially Travis, as we hung out at the bar.

But before we played, Rick had to have a few bumps. I joined in. Even Jesus partook, saying he needed a "pick-me-up" after working and driving all day.

The thought didn't enter my mind that Rick already had been drinking hours before. When we started the first song, he was already WAY too fast on the tempo and was running out of breath, not hitting the notes right on the second song! I had to step in on vocals to fill in the empty spaces, and I was already getting winded. It was all a jumbled mess, and I bit the side of my mouth. Real bad!

I was bleeding from the mouth and started to thrash about the stage to take advantage of the set time to look like a raging demoness. The kids started stagediving, so why not?

While raging, I decided to tackle my half-stack, and it fell. I was dumbfounded and had to pick it back up as I was playing, only to find out it wasn't able to stand right anymore. One of the casters underneath had broken off as I tackled it!

I felt so stupid and just stood there letting the feedback of my guitar ring out-of-tune.

The soundman rushed up to help me and had to take off my amp head and place it on the stage floor and prop the half-stack sideways and reset the mic.

As that was happening, Squash was giving Rick dirty looks throughout the set. I swore he might have taken a swing at him with his bass. They were not locking in as a rhythm section. That, I could hear!

Jesus had put his makeup on wrong, right before our set, and got some shit caked in his eye! He tried to concentrate on his parts. That poor diva, I should've been the makeup girl and applied it on for him…

We got through the gig somehow, and it was the sloppiest we have EVER played. Great crowd though. We haven't practiced that much either. Squash hasn't been coming to practice, and I do worry…

There was bad morale after we had unloaded from the stage. There was no green room for us, so we had to sit among the crowd on the side wall with our gear and feel sorry for ourselves in our blood, sweat, and proverbial tears.

Squash said he had to leave early and loaded out to his car right away with his Long John Silver's girl helping him.

I was hoping tonight we could clear the air and solve the tension between him and Rick. But Rick was moving a hundred-miles-an-hour and working the merch booth with Rosita, hollering around and downing beers.

Jesus and I were bummed out. We loaded out to the staircase of death as I got help with my broken half-stack this time by an old friend's help in Travis. What a sweetie.

Afterward, he got something really big and shiny out of his van.

We found out what that big shiny thing was when he and Barry came onstage before Infant Dust was set to play and unveiled a huge plaque that had the CD, artwork, and press-kit inside. Just like a gold-selling band might get from a million-dollar record company!

We couldn't believe it! Why bother with a band of their stature? Along with all of the merchandise and CDs they had printed up, why even go through the trouble of having that blingy thing made!?

For a second, I thought that maybe we had made the wrong decision to part ways with Barry and his "Sweet" Berry Records team. It was definitely the last thing we wanted to see as Barry took the mic to thank everyone, except us; and he made photo ops of the plaque with everyone, complete with champagne, as Infant Dust ripped into their set.

You won, Barry...

I don't remember going home. But we made it. Considering Cedar Falls is about 60 miles away from M-town. 160 miles for Jesus. I feel bad for him.

The Thieves' Conundrum Compendium:
House of Bricks

Hi there! It's been awhile since we've last met! Gosh. We've just been so busy with the band. But I've got to tell about some really funny shit that went down!

* * *

This segment is brought to you by our old sponsors at Suite Berry Records...

* * *

Barry was putting on an all-weekend "festival" at the House of Bricks. He was swinging his cock around with his teenage boy eunuch bands. He even invited some heavy hitters from the scene to be suckered into his "Sweet Berry Records Presents!" weekend.

Both Friday and Saturday night were booked, and both of his bands played the prime spots on both of those nights, the All ages and 21+ shows.

The sucker bands who were far more talented then his bands on their worst days were promised a fair share of the door and free T-shirts for each band member. Each shirt had the Suite Berry Records logo on the front and a "Support Local Music!" slogan on the back.

As if the bands all asked for that shit...

The Friday night show, which I attended, goes off. Bam. Everyone's had a good time. The bands are waiting to get paid for the night. That's how it goes. Everyone's hanging out after the bar closes, counts are made. Each band gets their fair share...but wait!

"No one is getting paid," says JC, the owner of the H.O.B. Barry had collected ALL of the money, which was an undisclosed amount, and took off out the back door!

WTF?!

His boys were left with the T-Shirts and everything!

One of the guys in the other bands got drunk and started to berate Infant Dust as they were packing up their gear. It turns out that the Infant Dust boys had nothing to do with it. They were just there to play a show, sell some merch, and crash at a hotel to do it again the next night.

Nothing happened. But the online message boards, there was some sure-fire shit-slinging there! Everyone who was on there were tearing apart Suite Berry and the two bands! People who weren't even at the show were commenting. It was brutal!

"Fuck Sweet Barry! Who is this guy? Where did he come from?"

"Fuck Infant Dust! Bunch of no-talent rich boys!"

"Chrome Semic Fiesta = Chrome Semic Fatboys!"

That was some of the shit that was said...Just brutal, man!

The next night was canceled. J.C. said it was canceled by the "organizer." The bands who weren't Barry's bands wouldn't have showed up anyway after that news spread like wildfire!

But, Infant Dust and Chrome Semic Fiesta's reputation is fucked in Des Moines! Musically, they suck, but it's not fair to them at all. Fuck Barry for taking advantage of those kids! Fucking thief!

On the Des Moines Music Online Message Board, the vocalist for Chrome Semic Fatboys, I mean, Fiesta, a.k.a the Suite Berry webmaster(who happens to be OUR webmaster now!), was trying to set the record straight and said that the bands who played signed an agreement to "waive their performance fees for purchase of Suite Berry Records T-shirts for each member of the bands."

"Promotion for all" was his defense. Moot point. Apparently, you can't build a movement when NO ONE wants to be in it!

The other bands claimed there was no such "agreement" signed.

After awhile, the webmaster, after being called every name in the book, resigned his platform and said, "Alright everyone, fuck me! Fuck me! Every one of the bands can get their money for playing. I'm sorry, man! Fuck me! It may take a few days, but we will pay everyone!"

Barry didn't once get on there and say his piece. Not even on his own website! He had his boys take the blame, and the stones thrown. Nobody's heard from him since. Both of his bands, whose reputations are ruined in Des Moines, and perhaps all of Iowa, haven't made any contact. Barry's website has been taken down.

That is the end of Suite Berry Records.

The Bastards & Thieves survived with our name intact. Our stock is rising! (Applause)

Thank you, thank you.

   * * *

Am I gonna get tired of being right all the time? I don't think so. I can do anything.

   * * *

This next segment will be brought to you by our NEW sponsors:

Georgy Manson's "White Man's Way" The Future is a New Silver Lining!

Georgy Manson's "White Man's Way" is the Manifest Destiny of Your Mind!

Georgy Manson's "White Man's Way" Will Make You Want to Fuck!

Georgy Manson's "White Man's Way" Bringing Families Together and Making Dreams Come True!

I like that one^^^

PT IV

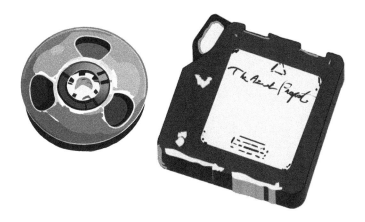

CHAPTER SIXTY-FIVE

Q: I want to backtrack on what you said earlier about growing up on the Meskwaki Settlement. You were raised there, but you were not an officially enrolled tribal member. How does that work?

Well, like I said before, it's a patrilineal culture. The father's bloodline is expected to thrive, flourish, and is preferred over the mother's side. Ask any enrolled dude, I guess the logic is that the father's side, their blood quantum will be kept "pure," as opposed to the mother's who will bring in outsider genes into the gene pool.

It's a suppressive, archaic way of thinking. Because, hey, outsider blood got in anyways.

When I was growing up, white girls were getting knocked up and getting free money from enrolled dudes all the time, because their children were automatically enrolled under Meskwaki tribal law and those kids got their mommy and daddy a monthly check. Easy money!

Growing up without that benefit made kids like us work that much harder to make our mark in the world.

Some don't even try. Drugs, drinking, all-around negativity crushes all.

Q: That's unfortunate. I would imagine there is abuse of power there as well.

Yeah, when the band was a year and a half old, my family was going through a major shakeup. My grandma had passed away, and she was our last remaining link. Or our remnant of the past. She and my grandpa were the ones that raised me when I was little.

Back then, my grandpa was the tribal chairman and had the vision to bring in the casino as a source of exponential growth for the tribe.

He got a lot of opposition from the old guard that used to say, "That's not the Indian way!" or, "You're gonna corrupt our youth!"

I remember my uncles having to be his bodyguards to protect him during tribal council meetings from irate dudes threatening him. It was a crazy time!

But those same people that opposed it back then are reaping the benefits today.

But anyway, I went off on a tangent. There was a major familial shakeup during the time of the band——

My uncles, and cousins were on the tribal council. Their friends, too. There was even a slick white preacher guy on the sidelines calling the shots. So, yeah, it was real life nepotism, oligarchy, there was some shady shit happening! (Laughs)

Those guys would be rolling up on Harley Davidsons to tribal council meetings. All of a sudden, my cousins would be buying guitars, expensive toys, new cars, new houses.

It turns out they were just taking all of that money from the tribe.

With my grandma dying, from cancer, by the way, it allowed the mice to play, as it were. Her house, our old house, was torn down against her last wishes; and basically, Christmas didn't exist anymore in our family! (Laughs)

Q: That sounds awful. How did that affect the band?

So, the band was getting CRAZY busy; we were moving so fast. We're getting noticed. Momentum was building. No other band could touch us live! We were wanting to get a CD made and get signed. That was our goal.

I guess, there's a time where you're so, in pursuit of your dream, so much stuff happens that falls through the cracks. You forget about where you've been and where you came from.

And in my case, I found a whole 'nother side of me that I never knew existed.

CHAPTER SIXTY-SIX

"Hey, Az...how would you like to open for fucking Slayer?!" Rick's voice crackling the other end of the phone line as Azul was at her mom's place doing remixes on the home computer.

"What are you talking about?"

"Check it out! We got a chance to play this really big, fucking gargantuan festival in Davenport that this guy named Bob is putting on! October tenth. Save the date——"

"That's my birthday——"

"No shit!?" Rick laughed. "We got a little less than five months. This is gonna be a helluva birthday present! Anyways, this Bob guy, turns out, he is putting everything on the line. He owns this club called Banana Joe's, right on the edge of the fucking Mississippi River, and he's gonna use the parking lot for the big stage and have two stages in the club. He laid it out to me, and it's a legit deal. Fucking, Slayer! Can you imagine this shit, and what it could mean for us?" shouted Rick in his animated style. Azul pulled the phone away from her ears, still processing the news.

"Shit, I can't believe it, dude. Uhh, wait, so what's the catch? What do we have to do?" Azul asked while scrolling the mouse on a WAV form she was editing on her software.

"You don't sound excited. What, does my breath stink or some shit——"

"Stop."

"Alright, alright. It's a legit deal. We need to sell the most tickets. I mean, sell thousands of dollars worth of these tickets he'll be giving us soon. I have to give him the word today! How long you gonna be at your mom's house? We gotta get on this shit immediately. We can start selling to everyone in M-town and Des Moines today."

"How many tickets and at what price?" Azul clicked *Render* on her software, biting her lip at the number he was about to say.

"For starters, fifty tickets at twenty-five bucks apiece. Now, the thing is, these are advance tickets sold through the bands. He's promising us that our share of the profits is five bucks out of every ticket sold and the opportunity to get the best slot possible."

"How did this come about? Are we the only band he's offering this?"

"I got the connect from another band, so we are not the only ones. This is a festival, so a ton of locals are gonna be on it. Some national touring bands, too. The thing is we have to sell the most out of all of them to get the opening spot, right before Slayer! Imagine that shit——"

"Damn, it's starting to hit me. But, man, we gotta get on our grind then. Have you called Jesus yet? He's gonna freak! He learned to play guitar learning Slayer songs. Did you call Squash, yet?"

"Uh yeah, you wanna call Squash? I'll call Jesus after this. I hope he's got his new phone line hooked up at his farmer's house in Jefferson. Yeah, he IS gonna fucking freak! So we in?"

"Fuck yeah, I'm in." Azul looked at the rendering time and got up from her chair to get a snack.

"You don't sound real excited."

"I am! I am, I've uh——been remixing these tracks of our demo. This is like the third remix we did. I can't keep polishing this turd. We really should get into a real studio and pump out a real demo. A REAL CD! Do you think we can do it before the Slayer show?"

"Ah fuck, I'm all in. But how we gonna pay for that when we gotta worry about selling tickets?"

"Umm, I'm sure we can think of something. God, it's hitting me more and more, now. Fucking, Slayer!"

"Fucking, Slayer."

CHAPTER SIXTY-SEVEN

The Bastards and Thieves continued gigging throughout the summer. The announcement for the Slayer show was made on their website, which Azul now had the sole responsibility for after the fallout of the Chrome Semic Fiesta frontman and webmaster.

The band pooled their resources and sold tickets at a steady rate.

The promoter of the event doubled up the capacity and opened a new club next to Banana Joe's to accommodate the projected record attendance. The festival was taking shape as the weeks went by. Twenty local and national bands were added. The festival in October was now billed as: Pigstock '03.

* * *

Azul was living on unemployment for the preceding months as a result of the intertribal scandal that involved her cousin's family who were members on the tribal council. There was a mass layoff at the casino where she and many of her extended family worked.

The closure came at an inopportune time as the band's fortunes were ramping up.

Azul booked studio time at Junior's Motel, near Fort Dodge. The locally famous studio where multiple acts, including the Empty Caste have recorded. She asked her mom, who was still employed at the casino, for a loan of 600 dollars for the weekend rate.

The band then had to choose which songs to record.

　　　　* * *

After a practice session, the band went across the street to the Chippewa Lanes Bar, where they held a meeting.

"So, we've never had good-sounding versions of '*Total Sexual Thing*' or '*House by the Cemetery*.' Those are still great songs. Why don't we do those?" Jesus said after he ordered a beer.

"True, but we've never recorded '*9/11*,' ever. We haven't touched that one since after our third show. We could work on that. It's got potential——" Azul added.

"Yeah, but you remember how many bands came out with songs called '9/11' after that? It was crazy! Maybe if we change the name of the song, add new lyrics, or something," Rick responded while tapping a beat on the table.

"Maybe, or we could write a new one. But we have to record '*Weapons of Mass Destruction*.' That's the fuckin' radio beast, whether we like it or not; and it'll be huge." Azul took a swig of her beer

"Man, why spend our time recording a song we hate? Shouldn't we just do all the heavy songs for this CD if we're gonna be selling this at the Slayer show? How many songs can we do in a weekend?" Squash asked. He was seated at the end of the table.

"Junior's Motel told me that a canister of tape, which cost one-hundred-fifty bucks, by the way, holds a little less than thirty minutes. So, whatever we got, we need that much. If we're not doing '*9/11*,' then we should do what represents us now, as opposed to doing the old ones that are the percussionist songs. We don't have Ben or Mick as percussionists anymore," Azul answered.

"Yeah, but when will we get a chance to get those old ones on a good recording ever again? You said we were gonna get it mixed at Catamount? That's gonna be super-expensive! Can we even pull that one off? That's like over a grand isn't it?" Jesus asked.

"I talked to the head producer, Tom. He doesn't discuss price, he said, 'Arrange that with the studio manager.' I mean——man, look—— Stone Sour just recorded and mixed a hit record that's all over the radio now. If we say we've been to the same studio they went to, that'll make us look like instant players."

"So, when are we going there? Have you even booked a date at Catamount yet?" Squash asked.

"If we can decide tonight what we want to record, I'll hit them up tomorrow and that'll be that," Azul pulled at her bottle with raised eyebrows.

"I think we can do that. I got a little side hustle going on. We need that product, and we need it, now. Man, we need a sponsor or something. I say let's do those heavy riffs we've been working on, turn those into a couple of songs, do '*Weapons*,' and decide on a couple other ones for next week. We can make thirty minutes—— easy! I'll make some shit happen on my end this weekend," Rick getting more animated as he stood up to order another round. By the end of their meeting they agreed to record five songs and write one in the studio.

* * *

"What clan are you?" asked the Chippewa Lanes Owner standing behind the bar.

Azul made eye-contact and smiled, "Beaver Clan. At least that's what I was told. Meskwaki's don't really consider me a member, but my grandparents still included me." She leaned forward on the bar counter then looked over his shoulder as if looking toward the past.

"That's good. Learn your identity as much as you can from your elders."

Azul frowned and nodded, "I know…"

"Yeah, you better be careful. Some Indian ladies from the tribe been coming to the bar here, asking about you. I got a bad vibe. Bad medicine, kind of vibe." He refilled her beer glass. "This one older lady got real drunk with her friends one night. She started talking about her dead son, saying that it was your fault. She kept going on and on. Talking 'bout putting bad medicine on you."

"Bad medicine? Really?" Azul asked for more information and he did his best to describe who she was. She pieced his descriptions together as Lou's mother.

"My uncle used to be a Medicine Man up north. I've seen some things and heard stories. That kind of stuff exists. So, watch out for any messengers. Deer or owl——"

"Right. *Witikos*. I'll keep an eye out——" Azul sighed, thanked him, turned around on her barstool, and stared to the east. "Fucking, vultures!"

CHAPTER SIXTY-EIGHT

The band met at Junior's Motel at sundown. The studio was located south of Fort Dodge, near a small town called Otho. Cornfields were in panoramic view as they drove to find the building on an unbeaten path off the main highway.

In the Burnt Burrito was Rick, Rosita, and Azul. Jesus and Squash drove themselves in their respective vehicles. They timed their rendezvous perfectly as they pulled into the farmhouse property where the studio was built upon.

Azul got out of the van first to stretch while the two lovers stayed inside. Squash got out of his car with his gear packed in the backseat and met her on the driveway.

"Why the fuck is she with you guys?" Squash laughed and shook his head. "What, is she gonna play on the album or something?" he asked pertaining to Rosita's needless presence.

Azul glanced at the van, shrugged, and shook her head in acknowledgment. "Ya know, I forgot she was there until you just said something." They both chuckled. "——and before you ask, we left the *other one* at home." Azul, pertaining to Annie, who wanted to tag-along to the session like Rosita.

In the 70's, the studio was converted from a chicken coop. The architecture was built to professional specs by the owner over the years.

A finished and weatherproofed wood carving of the name, "Junior's Motel," flanked by musical notes on each side, greeted the visitors of the rustic and faded red-painted building.

On the other side, to the west, was an unfinished stone tower standing 20 feet, looming above the studio's roof that was built to overlook the expanse of the vast cornfields surrounding the area. This fortified anomaly set the tone for what the band craved in their first true professional album-recording experience.

"Crom! That castle tower begs for a photo op. If only I had brought my swords and chainmail!" Jesus spoke in his best medieval voice as he rushed to take a closer look.

Azul walked to the left of the wooden sign to find a set of sliding glass doors with venetian blinds inside covering an amber glow. "This must be where he told me to load in our stuff."

She tapped a beat and slid the door open. A tall, lanky middle-aged man with a worn baseball cap, wearing a flannel greeted her. Another man, dressed the same way was lounging on the couch in what looked to be the drum room. She scanned the high ceiling and sound-baffled room.

"Whoa! Hey, uh——I'm Azul. We spoke on the phone. I booked the weekend. We're Bastards & Thieves."

"Hi Azul. Nice to finally meet ya in person. I'm Kurt. This is Joe, my buddy. We were just gonna head out for a bite to eat in town. We waited for you to get here so you can get situated. We got some nice couches for you to crash on here in the drum room. We got some inflatable mattresses you can put anywhere," Kurt walked over and hand greeted everyone as they entered into the warmly-lit room.

"Yes! I like that! Is that an organ?!" Jesus spotted a vintage organ-like instrument on aluminum legs with a pedal beneath.

Kurt corrected him and told him it was a pump organ that belonged to *"The Clown from The Nine"* that was left there.

"No shit! I love this thing!" He pumped the pedal and played a B-flat minor chord progression on the instrument as Kurt gave the group a quick tour of the studio.

"So, I set my drums right beside where Jesus is playing that thing?"

"Yes. That's got the best drum sound in this whole place. Don't ask me why. It just does. The control room is in the old part of the studio. That's where we'll record everything else."

"I guess we'll be doing some vocals in that vocal booth there! Kinda nervous now that I see this——is that the old drum room? Ooh! Is that gonna be where the rest of us are gonna be?" Azul ran to the door that led to a vestibule that housed another door to a spacious room that had an old grand piano, enough space for a whole band, and another sliding glass door iso-booth offset from the main area.

"Fucking wow, man! Holy shit! Let's write a piano song and record it guys! Look at this——" Azul's voice cracking, unable to hold her excitement as the others followed.

"Ah shit, you guys are gonna be in here while I'm stuck tracking in the first room. How is that gonna work?" Rick asked. Kurt said that they have a video camera set up to face the drummer. He wouldn't have a monitor to see the band, but they would be able to see him.

"It's a good thing we practiced a lot before coming here——" remarked Squash. Rick furrowed his brow, he didn't know if Squash meant to be sincere or sarcastic.

"Well, we demoed everything before we came here. If we've all been listening to the songs, I think we should do okay. And Rick, I could loan you my teddy bear if you're too afraid to be in that drum room all by yourself," Azul teased. Rosita laughed and cuddled up to him.

"This is amazing! We should totally sleep in here tonight, babe——while the others, ya know, sleep in the other room. It's so isolated in here I think we should..." Rosita spoke in her raspy voice and got quieter into Rick's ear.

"I'm calling dibs on the big brown couch!" Azul excused herself; Squash played some quick arpeggios on the piano.

Kurt led them all back to the drum room where Jesus was still playing the organ.

"This place is nicer than I remember when the Empty Caste was here about four years ago...damn, time flies." Rick observed as he put his worn black gloves on for loading gear.

Jesus woke from his trance. "Yeah, totally! Of course all we did was party, too. We just didn't know any better!" He laughed, and told the others to listen to the riff he had been working on as they were taking the studio tour.

"Sweet! Sounds like the Bastards and Thieves are writing a song in the studio——aww shit!" Azul cracked her knuckles and rubbed her hands together in artistic glee.

* * *

The next day was cloudy and cool. To the band, it was perfect weather to stay locked inside a cozy studio to work on recording their music. They were the most prepared they had ever been.

They started the session at 9:00. The basic tracks for the songs were recorded by five in the afternoon.

They were lounging on the drum room couches having celebratory beers. Rosita was at the farmhouse on the other side of the property for a shower.

Squash had already left with his gear right after he recorded his parts. The brusque departure disappointed Azul and Jesus. As for Rick, it was a relief from the tension between them.

"Have you guys even tried to iron out your differences?" Jesus asked Rick.

"We talked a little bit after last practice. Nothing ever came of it. He just says, 'Yeah——everything's cool. Just, a lot is going on——' blah, blah, blah. 'Reagan came back to me, we're working things out.' So, I don't know. He has sort of a passive-aggressive thing going on with me. But I'm not blowing my lid for your guys' sake. We got some great shit done today. It's come a long way."

"Yeah dude, the recording part went by so quick! The miking and setting everything up was the longest part, but then after that, we all kicked ass. Kurt really knows what he's doing. He said we made his job way easier than usual; so all of those shows we played really paid off."

"I think your song, Azul, and '*Weapons*' are gonna be the singles. The guide vocal you did was really good. I didn't know those words until I heard your track. Did you just write them?"

Azul, with a cloth in her hand, *giving Mocha a bath*, "I've had those for awhile. It's just been a long time in getting the confidence to actually sit down and work on them. I'm still trying to harness my voice. For years I hated the way my voice sounded. After hearing it on playback while doing my demos, my voice would just stop; and I'd start stuttering. I've been fighting stuttering all my life. Though it hasn't shown up these past few years, it's always been one of those things I look over my shoulder for."

Both Rick and Jesus were surprised and both said they never noticed.

"Yeah, maybe I'm over it now, or I'm just at a point in my life where I'm more comfortable with myself. Growing up, it felt like some fuckin' invisible hand was always around my throat, preventing me from using my voice when all I wanted to do was scream and be heard. I mean, as a result, I've always felt I got ripped off in my childhood."

Jesus stretched his hands and nodded in agreement. "Yeah, I think we all feel we've been ripped off in our childhood. But, that's why we all found music. I mean, look——it brought us all together and here we are——" He jolted in pain as he relieved the tension in his hands to a resting position in his lap.

"Damn dude, I know a masseuse chick who could give you some treatment for those hands. You gotta quit your job. We need your guitar playing hands," Rick popped open another can.

Jesus assured that as long as *we're workin'* all the miles traveled and nagging pain would be worth it in the end. "Guys, we got a new CD now. Fuck, that feels good!" Jesus yelled out as he reached for a beer. "This is my last few——" he added, laughing.

"Well, you deserve it! You're a good man. A great father. Maybe the booze is talking——but I love you, and you're the best of all of us. You're a fucking great dad! Fuck! I wish my dad was like you," Rick emphasized by standing up from the couch.

Azul agreed as she raised her beer high. "Fuck yeah, you're way better than my dad! My dad wasn't EVER there for me."

"Mine was the biggest wife and child-beating asshole ever. He smashed his fist into the side of my face when I was little! Imagine how that fucks up a child's mind, seeing that shit and always scared it'll happen again. That fucker is rotting in some prison somewhere. Hopefully, in hell——" Jesus raised his can.

"Mine ended up being the town drunkard and fucking drank himself to death in a fucking cemetery. Ain't no way in hell I'm gonna end up like that! I'm gonna fucking play music with you two. We're gonna take over the fucking world!" Rick lifted his beer can high. "Alright, bastards, we have an obligation to ourselves and to each other that we're not gonna end up like our fuckin' dads! They're dead! And we're gonna be the fucking band of bastards that the kids like us are gonna look up to for years to come! Ya guys good? C'mon let's chug and beer me you fucking bastards!"

The three cheered and bashed their cans together after Rick's grand statement. It was a beer bash that the three core members indulged in for the rest of the night.

The Bastard Chronicle 22: Studio life-Back to Reality

Ah, what a beautiful experience it was to be away at the studio with my boys!

Rosita just happened to be there. She wasn't too annoying. But, the band, we were on another plane of existence. Her presence just brought it down a notch or two. She kept asking me on Sunday if she was glowing. Being really giddy too. Wonder what that's about?

The vibe was awesome. We had the radio on low as we were sleeping. "Hearts of Space" on Iowa Public Radio was on. I remember laying down on the couch both nights, and I was feeling the creative flow in the air. I would get up and look outside, and there wasn't a cloud in the night sky that you could see all the stars.

We got everything finished and then some! We got a hidden track on the CD thanks to Jesus' love affair with the pump organ. It sounds awesome! I can't wait for people to hear the final version!

After Jesus laid down a Jew's Harp part (It was SOOO funny; we couldn't stop laughing!) on "Weapons of Mass Destruction," Kurt was nice enough to let me have a go at the full-size mixing console to mix it down onto a CD. That was a moment...I get goosebumps thinking about it now! Co-Producer: Azul Morgan! Fuck!

We left the studio with our rough mixes, the master tape, (encased in a big plastic 2" tape canister with, "The Azul Project," written on the label by Kurt!) and a van-full of gear to take back to the Compound in M-town!

* * *

When we got back in town at midnight, the lights weren't on. We opened the door to the stairs on the back porch and immediately felt a blast of heat. I knew something was wrong as I was the first one at the door. I rushed up the stairs. The door wasn't even locked, and I opened it! God, it was so hot. Like an oven. Dark as fuck. I reached to the left where the light switch was and turned on the hallway and the bathroom light.

Rick and Rosita came in shortly after and went to their room, turned their light on, and everything was where they left it.

My room was okay, too. We turned on all the lights. It was so hot.

Rick checked the thermostat and said it was on full blast, so he immediately turned it off.

At that point, Rosita is freaking out and repeating, "Where's Annie?"

I had a sinking feeling in my gut as I'm sure we all did.

I rushed into the kitchen and to the attic door. I opened it slowly, gulped, and swung it open——Dude…

It was pitch black and I saw her white body laid out on the stairs! I fucking screamed! It was the most ghastliest thing I have EVER seen!

I almost lost it until she jumped and started moving like a fucking zombie. She moaned something, and I flew back into the kitchen!

On the other side of the door, where the living room is, Rosita was behind the door, and she pushed it shut in the nick of time as I got out of its swinging path. It closed. She felt it push back. She screamed!

It was Annie in her underwear! Pale as fuck. She literally looked like a White Zombie! She came stumbling out towards my direction and says, "You're home!"

What da fuck?! Her eyes were pure red. She smiled and said she was okay. She had just passed out. With her hip bones and ribs showing, that was by far the most gaunt and unhealthy I've ever seen her.

Rosita turned her around, looked her over, and hugged her. I just shook my head and walked to my room. I let those two have their moment.

Later, I talked to Annie, and she denied she was in any trouble. She just got bored and got too wasted. But I did notice some pretty nasty marks around her neck, like she tried to strangle herself, or passed out with something tied around her throat.

She does like to be choked…during sex. So, I don't know…

* * *

What was she thinking as she was fucked up AND by herself during the whole weekend?

Man, I can't stop thinking in my head: Annie, what are we gonna do with you? Is that fucked up?

Because, I feel guilty for not taking her with us.
'Cause now that image of her pale body contorted on
the stairs is burned into my mind. I see it every
time we go up to the attic to practice now. It
could've been so much worse.

The Thieves' Conundrum Compendium: WTF

Fuckin' aye I got sloshed with Will! We even had some fun with his pain pills! He came back from job training with the railroad. He'll be on the road all week when he starts. Good for him! He's got his shit together more than I do.

I couldn't do that railroad shit. I have hard enough time taking shit from the bosses at MY day job. I'm my own hustler. I was born to be independent.

I was the one supporting my mom and baby sister back home, making ends meet and getting my hustle on, selling dope, odd jobs, putting in the band work and all that! Skies are the limit with the many plates I been spinning!

        * * *

Well, hey! Reagan called me. I haven't heard from her since she got back together with Squash, what's new?

SQUASH IS IN FUCKING JAIL!!!

WTF WTF WTF WTF!

He'll be serving time for a year. It's something drug related. Something he kept from us the WHOLE TIME! That dumb asshole probably just got 'possession with intent to deliver,' or something like that. They'll jail you for anything in this goddamn state of Iowa. So, where does that leave us?

WITHOUT A FUCKING BASS PLAYER, AGAIN!!!

He sold a shit-ton of tickets! I'll give him that! He knew alot of people. But, hey, he won't get to play for any of those people now! What are we gonna do? Find another bass player? When will we have time? He owns the lighting rig, and he's the only one who knows how to work it!

WHAT A DICKHEAD!!!

* * *

Well, fuck! Guess what happened?! Rosita just tried jumping out of the Burnt Burrito! As I was driving!

Yes! Just took off her seatbelt, pulled the latch on the passenger door, and tried leaping out to the gravel shoulder! Next to a goddamn creek bridge! I was livid! I'm lucky I slowed down in time, and no one followed me!

She and Annie had been drinking vodka all afternoon while I was at work. She went to pick me up, which was 15 miles away from the compound, I saw she was hammered, so I told her I was driving back. She started freaking out, and she tried jumping out.

That crazy bitch!!! What's the fucking world doing to me?!

* * *

Okay, so I went out with Will at the Chippewa, and I saw Mandy there last night. Rosita saw us!

So, yeah. Big deal!!! Nothing fucking happened! We were just talking. Nothing. No rubbing up. No hand-holding. We talked about her son, fuck that, OUR son. I STILL DO consider him my son as long as I live, no matter how me and Mandy's lives divert. That's just the type of guy I am. I wanna give him the type of support he needs because the kinds of guys Mandy sees are pieces of shit! All of 'em! But, she gave me her new number and we're meeting up at the park with my little stepson so he can see me again. I want to be there as much as I can.

Nobody told me that Rosita had walked into the bowling alley and saw us talking. Saw us talking! Nothing more! What was she doing leaving work early that night?!

So, she kept all that bottled inside, took me to work the next day, got a coupla bottles, and unleashed terror when she picked me up!

It's a good thing Annie is here to calm her down. They're both staying at Rosita's aunt's place...fuck, they could stay there as far as I'm concerned! Fucking pathetic.

Azul just got her unemployment check. She'll be home. She probably thinks she's gonna come to a nice, quiet house. Fuck that. I'm gonna call some people. I'm getting fucked up.

CHAPTER SEVENTY-ONE

The Tallcorn Tower was an old skyscraper hotel that was built in the early 20th century. It was the premier landmark of the time that could be seen for miles around the city. The building was once a shining beacon of civilization with its descending vertical neon lights that sang: *Tallcorn Tower*. Now past its bustling downtown heyday, it was a tenement to the destitute and poverty-stricken.

Azul and Rick parked in the back lot. At the foot of the building was the 7 Rayos liquor store, which was closed for the night.

Rick sprang out of the car and told her to follow him. Azul grabbed her backpack filled with beer and a full bottle of whiskey. They both had beer cans in hand as they took to the alley way where no one was around.

He put his beer down, stepped back, and took a running jump to pull down a fire escape stair ladder that was hanging down from the second floor. A loud screech of rusted iron pierced the humid night.

A raccoon scurried out from under a dumpster nearby. A woman's laugh was heard in the distance.

"C'mon. I've done this before. Climb on up."

He helped her up as the rusty ladder weighed down from their steps. They climbed to the second floor fire escape catwalk. Holding onto the guard rails of the structure, Azul couldn't help but look at her hands and smell them. She was repulsed from the rust stains caking her skin. She gagged. Rick asked what was wrong.

"Nothing..."

They continued climbing the fire escape higher as the wind became cooler. They slowed their ascent on the sixth floor catwalk where it went around to the main street side of the tower and stopped to admire the view.

"That's fucking sweet, dude!" Rick exclaimed.

"This is great! Imagine how this was back in the day when movie stars and famous people were ruling this block. Fucking Jean Seberg days, man! Look. There's the old railroad station where the old *Stone's Restaurant* sign is." Azul admired the vintage neon sign that the red letters appeared to be bursting out from the darkness. She mused, "It's like a priceless heirloom of M-town's past, man. Generations old, yet still standing as a reminder of dreams that came true."

Rick scoffed. "It is cool. But it's just a stupid sign. You're getting all heritage-y on me again. Look at what it's surrounded by now. The world's falling apart. We're at war. The way I see it all of this downtown area is gonna be gone in like fifteen years."

"So doomy, man! When did you get all pessimistic pissy-pants on me? Rosita's fucking with your jedi-force, man." Azul laughed as she took a pull on her sweating beer can.

"Eh, fuck. Maybe you're right. That's why we're just gonna enjoy the night. We just recorded an album, and WE'RE OPENING FOR FUCKING SLAYER!" Rick shouted as loud as he could with arms outstretched into the night sky as Azul wooed out as loud as him.

Rick turned and walked to a fire-exit door propped open with a coffee can full of cigarette butts and ashes. Rick nudged it aside with his foot too hard, causing it to tip over. Its pungent contents fell to the sidewalk below. The ashes blew hard in their direction.

"Goddamn it!" Rick shouted.

"Watch that shit! I'm gonna die from tetanus, eating ashes, and you don't know what kind of diseases are on those cigarettes..."

Rick coughed and shrugged it off.

The rank of alcohol and smoke engulfed them as they entered the hallway. The faded maroon carpet was a collage of countless spills, cigarette burns, and bodily fluids. Azul wrinkled her nose while trying to wipe ashes off her clothes and hair. She continued to follow Rick down the hallway. There was music booming.

They stopped at apartment-six. Rick knocked a rapid succession of beats on the old solid white door.

"Apartment six. Floor six? Hmmm...We'll see how this plays out," Azul said and the door immediately opened.

It was Spike. Shirtless. Displaying his pink, burned, and scarred torso for Rick and Azul to see.

"S'up Rick...S'up Az."

Rick in his animated fashion, "Hey! We're Social Services. We came to check on you. Why don't you and Charlie like us anymore? We haven't seen you at shows lately. We were worried that you fucking skipped town and shit!"

"Aww shit, we don't have no ride, man. Sorry dude, I——"

"I don't wanna hear it!" Rick laughed. "When we make it big, I'll invite Charlie backstage and not invite you. We'll make Az put a restraining order on you for stalking her, and you'll be banned for life from our band."

"Naw man! I'm sorry guys..." Spike rubbed his face and scratched his freshly shaved skull.

"Let us in! I'm just playing. S'up? You guys got beer?"

"Yeah man. Come on in. *Mi casa es su casa,* my friends. For real, man——"

"Oh shit, he's trying to talk Spanish now that Azul's here. Making up for your excuse for not coming out to the shows!" Rick joked.

"Naw...it's all good, man. Just listening to some Maiden, man."

Azul walked in after them and instantly heard Iron Maiden's *"Number of the Beast"*. She chuckled. "Ah, the ongoing irony of the number six. That's the third one..."

The apartment's cream-colored walls were mostly bare. Naked light bulbs on dusty old chandeliers were clinging from the ceilings in each room. Beer bottles were everywhere. Full ashtrays, potato chips, beef jerky bags, drug paraphernalia, and bottles of prescription drugs provided a labyrinth for their Pomeranian to explore. Its auburn coat, full and bright, emphasized that the dog was the healthiest one in the apartment.

Rick and Spike went into the kitchen to put the beer Azul had in her backpack into the fridge.

"Oh my gawd! Sup, Az!" Charlie came out of the bedroom with arms outstretched to hug Azul. She was wearing the same black Jack Skellington hoodie she wore the night they met with a white tanktop underneath. She had the same faded jeans with holes showing her pale bony frame. Just like Spike, she had a freshly shaved skull which was rubbing against Azul's cheek as they hugged.

"I love you so much Az! I wanted to make it to your last show, but we had no ride and Spikey was freaking out again. I love you so much Az, I do——" she said as she hugged tighter and sobbed. As Azul rubbed Charlie's back, she could feel her ribs through her hoodie.

"It's okay sweetie. Don't cry. Whatcha been doing lately?"

"Oh sorry if I'm hugging you too tight Az. I just love you. Oh my god——" between sniffs she continued, "Ronnie freaked out. Spikey freaked out. Something about us owing Ronnie money. I try not to pay too much attention to that shit, 'cuz I've been working on my art again. Here, come see!"

She pulled Azul into the bedroom where clothes and dog toys were scattered on the floor. The queen-sized bed was unmade with random things littered on top of it.

She had several 11x14 inch sketches of art laying on a makeshift area that was comprised of two fold-out desks and plastic totes.

Upon first sight, Azul saw that her works ranged from doodles, to abstract images done in pencil and watercolors in various stages of completion.

"These are really good, Charlie I didn't realize——"

"I know right? It's all been coming together again. I'm able to work in all kinds of media, but I really want to be able to interpret my dreams that I used to have when I was younger. Ooh! I've been talking to my brother again! We sat down and started talking about Mom, and our stepdad and his bullshit. I told ya my stepdad was the reason I couldn't do art, right? Yeah, that fucker hated all artistic expression, which is why my brother left way before I did——" Both of them took a drink of beer. Charlie wiped her tears and continued talking. "Spikey, I know he can be kind of a trip sometimes; but believe me when I say, he's been helping me to find myself. We're gonna move out of here soon, and we're gonna head to California because we have a connect out there that we met a few weeks ago. That's gonna be great because I'm getting sick of this place. And my brother said, he loved me! Do you believe that shit? It's been like years since he's said that!"

"How long ago was the last time he said that?" Azul asked.

"Shit, I'd say I was probably like eleven when he left home. He was like eighteen. I didn't see him or see his band play or anything until I saw him like a couple weeks ago. Oh my god, it's so crazy!"

"How's he doing?"

"He's been doing great. I mean we got fucked up and partied for a few days. It was rad. He has a swimming pool in his backyard! He has a platinum record out now. That's my bro, but he still is my best friend after all these years, ya know——"

"Really? Is he gonna help you out with your art? Your financial situation?" Azul looked closer at her artwork on the table and flipped through images of a baby in different colors splashed out on solid colored backgrounds.

Charlie continued talking like she didn't hear the question. "His house is so nice. I'll take you there sometime, and we can party. He's out on tour now; but when he gets back, we're gonna get together again. I might have to start looking for a job soon to keep the phone line on until then, ya know!"

Azul uncovered a watercolor painting of a black colored baby with white angel wings. Dark red strokes were dashed outward from the image. She looked up to Charlie to talk about the image.

"Hey! Who wants to get high?" Rick called out to the two in the bedroom. In the living room, Rick and Spike were both sitting on the couple's tattered green couch cutting chunks of meth on a tin serving platter placed on the coffee table. Eight lines. Two for each person.

The young women turned to the doorway to join Rick and Spike. The opening harmonies of Iron Maiden's "*Hallowed Be Thy Name*" played on the stereo speakers.

CHAPTER SEVENTY-TWO

The four had taken Azul's Diamante to a cliff of a deep rock quarry that was located in the bluffs near the Iowa River. Azul had parked her car near the edge. Charlie was taking pictures with a disposable camera of both Rick and Spike posing atop the cliff as a sliver of sunlight shone in the east.

"Get a shot of Spike breathing fire, dude!" Rick told Charlie and he backed away from Spike.

Spike, holding a bottle of Everclear, took a swig and held the 190 proof alcohol in his mouth, spit at his Bic lighter in the other hand, and a bright flash of flame spewed out of Spike's mouth into the cold air above. He let out a death metal growl. He ignited another flame as everybody cheered.

"I fucking love you Spike! You fire-breathing motherfucker! I don't care what people say about you, but you're right to fucking show your dad up! You're better than that man. You're fuckin' better than that, man. Fuck him if he doesn't see that! You better believe what I say, dude——" Rick with beer in his left hand, put his right arm around the shirtless Spike.

"Who's saying what about me? What, motherfucker!?" Spike pushing his face up to Rick's.

"That you...are a fucking hustler, man. A true fucking hustler. Like me, motherfucker! You and me brother——" Rick squeezed Spike's gaunt shoulder blades as they both cracked a smile at each other.

"That's a good shot! Kiss each other now! Wooo!" Azul yelled as she was sitting on a plateaued boulder next to her car.

The two drunken young men locked lips as Charlie frantically snapped and wound the plastic camera, both women cheering and laughing. "That's it fuckers! The cover of the album!" Azul yelled.

"Fuck that! The shot's no good anyway, we're just fucking backlit by the sun, so all you're gonna see is some black figures in the foreground of the sun coming up——" Rick then explained about lighting, exposures, and his dream of becoming a professional photographer after music.

"I coulda figured THAT out, dude. All the disposable cameras you own. The pictures as wallpaper at your guys' place——The Compound. You could totally kill that shit! Make your own studio——" Charlie encouraged while winding the finished roll of film inside the camera.

"That would be nice. Fuck, if we had capital to do it, man, I'd be all in. We'd have our own Bastards & Thieves in-house production company!" Rick and the two women continued rambling about ideas.

Spike with his teeth grinding on a disassembled pen as a homemade pipe was preparing to melt another white rock on a sheet of tin foil atop the trunk of Azul's car.

He lit the foil apparatus first, inhaled the smoke, passed the pipe to Charlie, he lit the foil for her, and so on.

"Yeah, if you're talking about more capital, dude; we got the hookup. We got a little network going with Ronnie and some dude out in Cali. Came over here to M-town. He's a cool dude. I'm pretty sure you've met him before. Name's Felix. He has a whole crew with him in Des Moines and shit——" Spike said while lighting a cigarette.

"I know that dude! He came to a couple of our shows already! We got fucking high as fuck in Fort Dodge! The gig where Azul spit in that chick's face!" Rick laughed outloud in rapid-fire staccato and he told the rest of the story of that night with Azul. "Ronnie's my boy! He's over at our place all the time. I'll talk to him about that shit. Maybe we can set something up about securing our spot on the Slayer show. Maybe get a new backdrop, get some new lights, a whole new setup. Fuck, we can go there right now, man. I'm sure we can talk business and still party. Let's go hit 'im up after this!" Rick's idea was resonating with the rest of the party. Spike walked closer to the edge of the cliff while the others were getting ready to go.

"Ya know, man. I wonder if anyone's committed suicide up here? It's beautiful up here. Just think, I could fucking end it all right now, if I wanted to. As much as I like burning myself, dude...I could just fucking throw myself over this fucking cliff right now. Shock and awe campaign, man. The last thing I'd see is that beautiful sunrise over there, and be done with this shit. My dad wouldn't have anything to bitch about wit' me no more——Think about that shit..." Spike looked wide-eyed at the sunrise as the sudden confusion grasped the others cold.

"Spike——" Rick yelled. "What the fuck are you talking about brother? Don't do it!!!"

Spike began rushing toward the cliff. The women yelled, and Charlie sprang to rush after him.

Spike sprinted to the edge then stopped and rolled just short of the precipice. His legs arched over. He turned on his belly as his arms scraped the surface. His fingers clawed and caught a hold of solid rock. He pulled himself to safety and rolled onto his back in a fit of insane laughter. The young women were in hysterics. Rick lost his balance. His knees gave out as he rolled on his back, in the same state of insane laughter as Spike.

* * *

Inside Ronnie's duplex, he led Rick, Azul, Spike, and Charlie to his bedroom, where his wife, dressed in an old faded-white bathrobe, was sitting on the side of the bed. She was cutting lines of meth on a sheet of glass which was on a tin dinner tray. A single dusty bulb in an old ceiling fan lit the room. Azul remarked to Spike and Charlie that the room looked like their bedroom. Charlie just let out a snort. The wife let out a wide sniff.

There were children's clothes, toys, dirty diapers strewn about the room.

Ronnie was rambling on in rapid-fire pace. The conversation morphed into Ronnie and Rick talking about how great the Monte Carlo SS was. After she made two lines for each of the group, Ronnie's wife unscrewed a half-full bottle of Jack Daniels for them, not saying anything the whole time as they took turns snorting their lines.

"Oww! Fuckin' aye! Fuckin' shits! I tell ya——" Ronnie shouted in his nasal tenor that alarmed Rick and Azul. They watched him with wide-eyes as he complained about "*The Burn.*"

Spike held Charlie in his arms, and they both stared at the floor and listened to their hearts beat through their chests.

The wife was still stoic as she scooted herself off the bed to light a cigarette at her vanity.

A little boy started to cry outside the bedroom door. Azul was startled. She wiped her nose, rubbed her eyes, and tried to make the necessary adjustments to make herself look proper. She looked around the room to see if she was the only one visibly ashamed, and wondered how long he'd been standing there, watching them get high.

"Hey buddy! How ya doing? I'm Uncle Rick!" Rick said in a high voice to the toddler-age boy, who was rubbing his eyes, clad in only a diaper and a cowboy hat laced to the brim around his neck.

Ronnie picked him up to soothe his crying. "You hungry, buddy?" He took him to the living room and switched on the TV. An older boy then appeared in faded red pajamas, peeked in at his mom on the bed, made a quick glance at the others, and went to the living room to sit in front of the TV. A little girl, who was of median age to the two boys, ran down the hall to join them.

Azul felt uneasy as she glanced at the wife, who took a drag from her cigarette, exhaled, and yelled in a piercing tone, "Tom, you better feed your brother and sister before you go to school! Make sure they finish every goddamn bite of their cereal and don't waste the fucking milk! Only use half a cup for your sister 'cause she's lactose intolerant, remember——"

Azul, startled at the sudden roar of the wife, escaped to the living room.

The two oldest children were seated on the floor, transfixed to the cartoon on the TV. Ronnie was seated on the easy chair with the toddler boy on his lap. He still spoke in his rapid-fire tongue to the boy while engaged in small talk to Azul as she sat on the brown love seat peppered in cigarette burns and spill stains.

Azul felt a headache coming from the dehydration and constant grinding of her teeth. She tried focusing her vision, as the whiskey shot was making her see double.

"Fuckin' shits is soaking through to my damn clothes! Tom! Change your little brother. He made a goddamn mess on my lap!" Ronnie yelled. Tom got up from his place on the floor to get a diaper in the back room.

The smell of the toddler's dirty diaper got to Azul. She began to feel lightheaded and in-vertigo. She could taste the bottle of warm whiskey again and bent over.

She threw up all over the floor in front of her.

Azul wiped her mouth then wiped her eyes with the sleeve of her hoodie. She bellowed in anguish. "Oh my god! I'm so sorry!" She wiped her eyes again. A glass of water was brought to the right side of her face with Ronnie's skeletal hands.

"It's alright girl…" Azul heard Ronnie as if there was an echo effect on his voice. "Someone is partying somewhere! All the time——" He threw his head back in laughter. His brown mullet morphed into a shaking live muskrat on his laughing skull. Azul desperately took the glass and drank the water as she watched the blurry vision of Ronnie laughing in slow motion with a wild rodent on his crown and the sound awash in the echo effect. She moved her eyeballs to the left of Ronnie where the girl had bumped into her knee and stood where she was sitting.

"You throw up like Mommy," the girl said in a tiny voice. Azul looked at her, and the sentence took a while to manifest in her mind as she saw Ronnie's wife stomp from the hallway like a woman possessed.

"Don't you dare tell anyone what Mommy does goddamnit!" The wife, with her fleshy arms, grabbed the girl and yanked her back to the hallway, where the girl crumpled and slid on the wood floor. The girl screeched, and the whole room was in commotion. Azul shut her eyes tightly, shook her head, and tried to comprehend what was going on. She could hear the screeching little girl being taken back by the stomping steps of a giant. A reverberating smack of hand on weak flesh, followed by the cry of what sounded like a small and wounded animal being carried away into the M-town slaughterhouse.

"Fuckin' shits! I tell ya..." Ronnie's voice reverberated in Azul's head. She opened her eyes and was startled by little Tom rushing in front of her and stopping at Ronnie to give him the diaper.

Rick suddenly came into the room, took a wide vaudevillian look at the scene, and yelled at the top of his lungs. "Oh shit!"

Cavernous reverberations of laughter ensued.

Spike and Charlie joined in.

Azul looked around in confusion, and eventually reared back in laughter with the rest of them, rejoicing in their delirium.

     * * *

"What day is it?" Azul seated in the driver's side backseat, asked Rick, who was in the front passenger seat. A young Latino man was driving. He was a sharp dresser and wore strong cologne.

"It's Friday," the man answered in a slight rasp on behalf of Rick. Earlier in the afternoon, he came to the Compound to pick them up in his sleek, black Mercedes Benz. He introduced himself to Azul as Felix.

Azul and Rick's neighbor, Scott the Metalhead, was riding in the backseat with Azul. Scott, a Compound regular, told them about a punk and metal show happening in Omaha, which was three hours west of M-town at a venue called the Sokol Underground. They all thought it would be a good idea to sell some Slayer tickets while there.

Scott the Metalhead was born and raised in M-town. As his name suggested, he was a die-hard metal fan who never missed a live show. He had a laid-back hessian stoner vibe about him, and was a constant show-going presence in the scene.

"Yeah, it's Friday. Y'all been partying hard this week?" he asked Azul, who smiled first and nodded, then rolled her eyes and shook her head. "Heh——It's alright, man. I don't judge. We all got work to do. We're in fuckin' M-town, man! There's absolutely nothin' to do but get high——" Scott laughed. He claimed he never did meth like a lot of his friends did, but proudly admitted, *I smoke a lotta weed, man.*

"It's just that, well, I've been on unemployment for a couple of months now. Days tend to kinda mesh together, and I don't know what the fuck——" Azul said to Scott, and mentally tried to piece her last few days together.

"Let's set up another rail, man. You sure you're not in Scott?" Rick unrolled a sheet of tin-foil with rocks, and apparatuses inside. Scott said to go ahead. Azul at first refused, took a drink of her beer, than said yes after a few seconds. "Well, hey! That wasn't hard. We'll hook ya up. This shit is the shit. *White Man's Way*, ya ready? Felix has got it, man."

"Yeah, man. We're here to have a good time, man! We're all good. I got stacks and shit. In that exact order!" Felix laughed. He talked about his big house in Des Moines, and how he got to Iowa from his old East L.A. stomping grounds. "Me and Rick were talking about backing you guys up. The Bastards and——What was it?"

"Thieves," Azul and Rick uttered.

"Ah shit, that's cool!" Felix nodded in approval while rubbing his neatly trimmed chin hair. "In Spanish that would be *Bastardos y Ladrones*. I like that! Yeah, man. I got all kinds of money. All you have to do is ask. You guys and girl are my homies. We can make a lotta good shit happen."

Rick looked at Azul and gave her a signal and an approval nod toward Felix. Then they talked to him about how well the ticket sales were going, what they accomplished so far, and what they planned to do. Scott was going with the flow while putting in his two cents to the conversation.

"That all sounds good, man. I like you guys. As hustlers, ya know? You don't see too many around here in Iowa. I like the drums you guys do. The show you put on is insane. Hey Azul, you Latina, right?"

Azul was surprised at the sudden shift in direction of the conversation. "Uhh, yeah. Well, kinda. My dad, who I've never met before, is part Mexican and part North Dakota tribe. I got my hair from the Mexican side. That much is certain. Word has it, he was a big time cowboy back then. He named me. My mom was just as crazy as him back in the day. Not so much now. I just know a little bit of the language though."

"I thought you could speak it, like, fluently——" Rick genuinely surprised, as he fashioned the foil and got his hit ready to flame up with the lighter underneath.

"I wish I did. Ya know——and perhaps someday I'll meet my dad. Or, *mi padre*. Right Felix?" Azul laughed and poked at Felix' shoulder.

"I'll teach you some Spanish if you want. Hey man, my dad is in prison back in La Mesa, Tijuana. Man, it sucks. Worked all his life and got busted as a fluke. I still get letters from him once in awhile. It's a tough life. But we gotta look after our own out here, ya know?"

"What is he in for? Or is that something you talk about?" Azul was apprehensive about her question.

"Ah, you know...stupid shit. Business with the wrong people. He made quite a bit of money. He took care of us and shit. He even had a nice place in prison. He lived in El Pueblito. It was like a little town inside the prison. Crazy, man! But that all changed about a year ago. The Feds took over and tore that shit down. *Mi padre* has to live with all of general pop now."

"Geezus, dude! I can't believe they had like, a little town in the prison. Well, I'm glad he's okay and still looking out, bro——" Rick melted the rock on the foil and sucked in the metallic smoke with his hollowed-out pen.

"Hey dude, I got a glass pipe for that shit. We can use that for later——" Felix reached into his glove compartment to pull out a small bulbous glass pipe with black burn marks on the underside.

Scott didn't partake in their ceremonial smoking, but he had his own pipe with weed bought from Felix. He stuck to his own vice.

The four made the long drive to the Sokol Underground, which was in the lower area of the same building as the Sokol Auditorium in Omaha. The show had some local Nebraska and Missouri River Valley bands that they were unfamiliar with.

They did not sell any tickets. They were much more concerned with making trips out to the car to hit the pipe and to drink beer.

At one point during the night, Felix showed them what he had in the trunk of his Mercedes: six rolled-up wads of cash and assorted plastic baggies of drugs stuffed in an olive-green military-issue duffel bag.

Azul noticed that Rick had the biggest smile she had ever seen him put on as they took turns looking inside the bag. They went back into the Sokol for the headlining band. She commented on his smile.

"What's with the biggest shit-eating grin I've ever seen you do? What's on YOUR mind?"

He sniffed loudly, gave her a tight hug, a kiss on the cheek, and said to her, "It's all gonna work out!"

CHAPTER SEVENTY-THREE

The party of four in the Mercedes were on the road all night. They didn't get back to the Compound until five in the morning. Scott the Metalhead, said his good night to the group as he walked home a block away. The remaining three went inside. They hung out in the kitchen. There was a message on the voicemail that Rick had been expecting from Bob, the promoter of the Slayer show.

"Hey Rick, this is Bob out in Davenport. You need to get down here to give me that ticket sale cash. You said you had two-thousand and two-hundred dollars in cash. That's sweet! I got the tour managers screaming for retainers and guarantees. I need some serious cash to appease these guys. You're my number one band! If you could deliver that later on, I'll be at the venue all night tonight. Give me a call and let me know when you're gonna be able to get down here, and we could make the exchange, man. Look forward to hearing from you soon. Buh-bye!"

Rick put the phone down on the kitchen table. Azul and Felix were standing by the sink. "Well, that was Bob the Promoter. We gotta deliver the ticket money to him today. We have to! We have to! You guys down to do it now? We hafta go now!"

Azul raised her voice and stated that no one was going anywhere in their current condition. She asked him what he said.

"We gotta deliver the cash at the venue in Davenport. He said he'll be there all night tonight——"

"Yo, why can't we just Western Union him the money and be done with it?" Azul stretched her neck.

"Hey, why can't we just Western Union him the money? 'Cause we're in no position to bargain. That would look bad on us if we make HIM go out of HIS way to head over to Western Union pick-up when we can just hand him the cash, see us in person——"

"Alright, alright! Okay, then. Let's get some rest. We have time. Then later on this afternoon we can all make the three-hour plus drive together. We can take my car, Felix' car, anything but the Burrito. It'll be fun, right?" Azul stretched her arms out. She yawned and immediate pain shot through her jaw. She then had cramping pain in her entire mandible area and tongue. "Errhh, owwwww…"

"What's wrong? Jaw lock up?" Rick laughed. Felix was stoic, and looking out the kitchen window at the dark blue of dusk shrouding the neighborhood.

Azul didn't say anything. She went to the bathroom to wash herself and get ready for bed. She took two sleeping pills and slurped water out of her hand. She washed her face and neck, letting the coolness soothe her senses. She brushed her teeth and gargled mouthwash. There was a metallic taste in her mouth that didn't go away. She then wanted nothing more than to change into her pajamas, slam down on the bed, and fall into a deep sleep.

* * *

Azul was jolted awake by muscle spasms in her legs. Her abdominal muscles tightened up, and she immediately rolled onto her right hip where the pain subsided. She didn't hear anybody outside her door. She heard the tapping sound of a light rain outside. She looked around her room to see it was as dark as when she fell asleep. Confusion swept through her as she took a sip of her water bottle on her nightstand. Her alarm clock happened to be unplugged. She looked at it and let out an annoyed growl because the clock's electrical cord prongs had never fit snugly in her wall outlet. She always mumbled to herself after discovering the inconvenient state of her alarm clock, "I'm not working anyways. I have no place to be that requires me to be woken up at such an abominable hour. Hmm. *Abominable Hour*. That's a cool title for a song——"

Suddenly, she gasped. She remembered that they had to deliver 2,200 dollars to Bob the Promoter in Davenport. She sat up and let the blood correct itself in her body. She could still taste nothing but metal. She got up and had a cramp in her left leg. The sensation of her legs never having gotten any rest made her more anxious as she hobbled to unlock her bedroom door.

She went to Rick's door, and it was wide open. None of the lights were on. No one else was home.

She noticed a mailing envelope that was haphazardly duct-taped to her door. Rick scribbled the number of Bob the Promoter, *Meet at 9:00! Banana Joe's!* underlined.

When she read that, a sick feeling of fire shot in her belly, a feeling of hatred compounded by the alcohol damage she had in the lining of her throat and intestines.

"How could he?!" she thought, as her stomach growled. She knew she was hungry, but the thought of food made her want to vomit.

Sighing, she took down the envelope and felt the bulge inside. She unclasped it to find all the money was inside, along with some of their band stickers, and a copy of their CD-R demo. She snorted at the ridiculousness of the shameless promotional inclusion in that precious package.

She checked the time on the kitchen wall clock that was hanging by the phone. It was 5 o'clock. "AM or PM?" she asked herself.

A feeling of panic swept her. She grabbed the phone and wanted to call home and talk to Mom or Zach, but she knew she couldn't do that. Going through the numbers in her head, she felt disgusted that all the numbers of the contacts she knew were related to the band. Everything relating to the band was related to getting high. She flipped through the address book they had kept next to the phone and finally thought of a friend she hadn't hung out with in a long time: Lisa.

"She's probably doing nothing." She dialed and let out a sigh of relief as Lisa picked up after the third ring.

"Hey Lisa, this is Azul! It's been awhile. Watcha doing?"

"Hey, just got off work. Thinking of what to do tonight. What are you doing?"

Azul explained that she had to deliver the money to the promoter in Davenport and needed some company. She said she would buy her a 6-pack of whatever she wanted to drink for the ride.

"Ah shit, I like that! Let's roll. Just honk, I'll be waiting."

She felt better as she hung up the phone. The drive to Davenport was a long three-hour drive east on the interstate, the exact opposite way of Omaha.

Feeling filthy, she took a shower. Hoping it would get rid of the tingling feeling all over her body. The water and soothing lather of her fragranced soap calmed her down. The stench of the cigarettes and booze from the night before was washing away. But she knew the chemical foil flavor in her mouth, nose, and throat was something that would take days to get rid of.

* * *

The dark rain clouds made everything bleak at 6PM. She started the car and thought back to her simpler life on the small acreage back at the family home in Tama. She could just drive straight there if she wanted to, since it was off to the east, 15 minutes away from M-town.

She missed Magenta. The smell and feel of his white velvet hide pressing against her cheek. His glistening eyelids matching hers as they appreciated each others' company. Watching him eat was always a pleasure as he liked to dig his snout into the pile of fresh oats inside his feeding pan.

She wanted to head to her mom's house, pick them up and go there, but an empty feeling arose as she thought of her grandma not being there anymore to comfort her. She wiped away the tear that came from this grim realization and put the car in drive.

She had a responsibility to her bandmates——and her dream.

She picked up Lisa at her grandparents' house where she still stayed, with her daughter, who had grown to be a toddler. She watched her daughter hug Lisa on the front porch before leaving.

"Wow, the last time I saw her, she was just a small baby," Azul said to Lisa as she got in the car.

Lisa giggled and said it hasn't felt that long since that time. "I need to get away for a few hours. She can be a fussy little critter. Besides, my grandparents don't mind being alone with her. They do a better job of raising her than I do. Matter of fact, they said they like it better than raising me AND my mom! Ain't that some shit?"

"I know exactly what you're talking about. My mom was that same way. We were living at my grandma's house when I was that age, too——" Azul fought back the lump in her throat after she said, *Grandma*. She touched Lisa's arm and thanked her for giving her company.

"*De nada.* I needed this, too," Lisa said and buckled her seatbelt.

Azul drove to fill the gas tank at the Jiffy convenience store in downtown, near where they used to work together. She got Lisa the 6-pack she promised. Azul opted out of food as she was still nauseous but bought a water.

"You heard another robbery happened at this damn place? I'm telling you this Jiffy needs to just close down, or move outta this neighborhood!"

"Oh really? That's not cool…" Azul was at the gas pump filling her car and looked to the Tallcorn Tower, which looked dark and ominous as it towered above the Jiffy. The cascading neon lights flickered as the only letters illuminated where A-L-L-O-R-O-W-E in Tallcorn Tower. "All or owe? What does that mean?"

"What? What do you see?" Lisa looked at Azul's hypnotized gaze as she pointed toward the tower. Lisa looked at it and was confused.

"The lights are blown out on some of the letters…"

Lisa, looked again. "Oh damn. That building is so full of tweakers. Don't even get me started girl! Stay the fuck away from that place!" She got in the car. Azul was squeezing the pump handle to a white knuckle grip. She loosened it as her bursal sacs in her joints cracked, sounding like popcorn to her. She put the pump back, screwed the gas cap on, and wondered what *All or Owe* meant.

　　　* * *

The storm clouds threw Marshalltown under a dark shroud as they left it behind. They turned east on the familiar road of HWY 30, towards Tama, a road that both of them had grown up traveling on. The familiar sites seemed to wave goodbye as they passed.

"Hey, my family's old property is just south of here. I'm finding myself missing it a lot more after my grandma passed this year." Azul pointed toward the Meskwaki Settlement which was off of HWY 30, within the hills and tree lines of the Iowa River Valley.

"Ah man. I'm sorry. I saw the obit, and I thought of you. How'd she die?"

"Cancer. It was a long time coming. She was a fighter. She managed to stay around a lot longer than what the doctors originally told her how much time she had. But, you know, it hurts that I didn't go to see her more often. I always think of when I was younger, that woman, along with my grandpa, gave me a home and comfort that no one else could've given me in that time. I was lucky to have both of them. None of my other cousins had the privilege. I always thought they were rotten because of it. They ended up being no-good, good-for-nothing, ya know, that gave me a reason to try to not be like that. We had a guitar around the house. Grandma played piano during church. I got the music juice from them."

"That's amazing, girl. I can totally understand the grandparent thing."

"It's not enough though. Her last few years, I wasn't around to return the favor. Be there for her. I was off doing this shit. STILL off doing this shit. All these extra things I have to do and put up with to build a music career. In Iowa, of all places! Fuck, man…" Azul felt her eyes sting from dehydration. She took a drink of water.

"But you're doing it! I'm damn proud of you. At least you're not likely to stay in M-town, or Tama. Anywhere, but here! But, I got a feeling that your grandma would be proud of you and supportive. She didn't raise no runt. That's for damn sure." Lisa looked out to the Iowa River as they crossed the bridge near the Settlement. "My brother just got busted for selling meth. He got sentenced a couple of months ago. He's facing twelve years for that shit, man! I'm so pissed because my baby is not gonna see her uncle growing up. Who knows how he'll come out and if my grandparents will be alive when he gets out."

"I'm sorry. I didn't know he was involved in that…" Azul was surprised at this news and immediately all the things she had witnessed in the past months replayed in her head. Lisa spoke in-detail about his involvement, how the family found out, and his eventual arrest.

"My brother, for all intents and purposes, is a good guy. But, he got way too confident in his slinging skills. He had a few runners working for him. The cops got one, and they ratted him out. They even put it in the newspaper that he was a drug *overlord!* That issue sold a few copies! And you've met my brother. There's nothing *overlord* about that kid——"

As Lisa was talking, Azul's mind drifted as she was thinking about her involvement in the band.

Azul, before, felt alienated from everything else deemed normal for so long, that in her fragile and sick state, she could feel herself clamoring for normalcy. She did not want to have to worry about driving hundreds of miles to pay a promoter she had never met. She was tired of dealing with acquaintances, fans, industry people, fake friends, and drug dealers. She was being surrounded by people she never thought she'd ever be involved with. She had grown to hate the hard partying that was around every corner of her strange sub-culture. The financial hardships were on her mind constantly. She always questioned if she was making the right decision after her college graduation, which for a Native American and Hispanic youth, was a social milestone.

She was losing control of her life. The music was fading from being the one thing that mattered.

They entered onto Interstate 80, which was the long stretch of highway which seemed to stretch longer as it got darker and the rain was at a constant pour. She felt her body tensing with the highway noise.

To calm down, she imagined riding on Magenta's back on a lazy summer afternoon. She could smell the horse sweat and feel the muscles working beneath her. She remembered holding onto the reins, feeling confident that she had him under her control, and all was well.

Then, she remembered a time when a huge bull snake slithered by in their path. Magenta shuttered in fear, jolted back, rearing his mighty frame, almost bucking off Azul. She felt herself clutching onto the reins for dear life at the thought of it.

Back in reality, she was white-knuckling the steering wheel and clenching her teeth. Her whole body stiffened into her seat.

She realized that she had tightened up, then had a muscle spasm. She lost her cool and started to panic as Lisa was in the passenger seat still talking and drinking her beer.

"Umm, sorry Lisa I, umm, hafta pull over somewhere..." Azul murmured.

"What's wrong, yo?"

"I fucking have to pull over somewhere, fuck, fuck, FUCK!" Azul screamed the last word as her heart was pumping blood faster than her body could keep up with.

She jerked the steering wheel with her hands as her legs came up to cradle the bottom radius. Her muscle cramps took over.

"Holy shit! Azul, what's wrong!? A deer?" Lisa put her left hand on Azul's shoulder, and put her right hand on the steering wheel over Azul's hands to correct her driving.

"Fucking deer!? No, no fucking deer, you fucking——stupid, okay! I'm freaking the fuck out now. I need to pull over. I need to pull over." Azul looked in between the swiping of the screeching windshield wiper blade, she saw an interstate exit sign. Perched on top, a white owl with its full wingspan stretched as large as the width of the sign itself, swooped toward the car and away from the headlight's path in a brief second.

"Fuck! Seriously?!" She jerked the wheel again, causing the cars following her to brake fast. The car hydroplaned for a second, and she caught the interstate exit after a near-miss. Lisa spilled her beer on her lap.

"I'm pulling over here. Over here. Over here right now—— fuck me. FUCK ME!" Azul screamed again as she stopped at the exit's stop sign.

She looked towards the passenger-side window and found there was an old truck stop that was completely black with only a single light on the edge of the parking lot. She decided it was safe to park there.

"What's wrong with you? God! I spilled beer all over. You almost got us in a damn accident. Are you okay?" Lisa yelled, totally oblivious to Azul's condition.

Azul turned recklessly into the lot and stopped the car under the only working parking lot light. She opened the driver's center console, where she had five small shot bottles of vodka, grabbed them in desperation, twisted one open, and rushed out of the car. She was taking deep breaths then emptied the shot bottle in her mouth.

Lisa got out of the car and rushed towards Azul. "What's wrong? What happened?"

Azul licked the bottle of spare droplets, dropped it, unscrewed another. "Stop asking me stupid questions! Just, stop asking me stupid——Fuck——" She took a swig of her second shot bottle. "Okay! Okay! Okay——" Her voice began quivering uncontrollably as she focused on her breathing.

"What? Did something happen to you?" Lisa was taken aback by Azul's sweltering hostility.

"Fuck! Nobody did anything to me! Is that what you think? Oh Jesus Christ, fuck——" She took another shot, gritted her teeth as hard as she could while feeling the sudden rush of vodka set afire her insides.

"I'm sorry! Okay. Just breathe, now. Breathe. Tell me what's going on," She tried to embrace Azul who started pacing erratically in front of her.

She pulled away to take another drink from the small bottle.

"Shit. Fuck! I'm sorry Lisa. I'm sorry. Umm——shit, man!" Azul's eyes teared up as her voice cracked and was reduced to a constant tremble. She finally realized that Lisa didn't know what was going on inside her.

"Well, could you keep this between you and me?" She reached into her hoodie pocket for a loose cigarette that she happened to have and saw her hands were trembling as much as her voice was.

She pulled out her lighter to try to light the cigarette in her mouth. She got the flame to light the tip of the cigarette. The tobacco smoke filled her mouth. She retched.

"Azul. Babe. You're sick aren't you?" Lisa said, watching her.

Azul threw the cigarette down and crushed it with her cramped left foot after her retching stopped. She then put weight on her toes to try and alleviate the cramp.

"Umm, don't tell anyone back home. Shit, I don't have my notepad to write any of this down for my report, huh? Uhh——shit, man——" Azul took a deep breath, and cracked her knuckles; hurting her. Lisa inched closer to listen.

"I haven't eaten anything. I've been fucking drinking and partying for I don't know how the fuck long——Umm, ever since we got back from the studio. Rick, me and a bunch of people have been, ya know, just fucking partying and shit——" Azul swallowed, her mouth getting drier. "Yes, I've been doing meth, too. Smoking. Snorting—— lot's of it." Azul looked at Lisa to see her reaction. Lisa's eyebrows rose indefinitely and was paying special attention at that moment. She didn't interject, letting Azul talk.

Azul went through the whole time she started drinking with Rick up until the Omaha trip. She had trouble remembering details, but she managed to count that it had been an 11-day binge.

"I've never felt this bad coming down. I don't know what to do. I just...I just want to fucking die right now, Lisa..." She began to cry. Lisa finally came over to put Azul in her arms to comfort her.

The rain was still coming down on the both of them under the one light at the edge of the parking lot. The interstate a few yards away still roaring with the sound of cars.

One minute into their embrace, as Lisa was calming her down, a white van pulled into the lot and parked alongside them.

The lights startled Azul as she shrank into Lisa, who embraced Azul's malnourished, trembling body in her arms. Lisa smelled the cold sweat and alcohol in Azul's hair.

They both read a logo on the side of the van: Meskwaki Friends Church.

A bear-like Native man with long white hair in a white dress shirt wearing a beaded necklace stepped out. A woman with permed hair, dressed in a white blouse was in the passenger seat, looking out at the strange women standing in the rain.

"Hello? You ladies doing okay?" asked the Preacher.

CHAPTER SEVENTY-FOUR

Azul was checked into Covenant Rehabilitation Center in Cedar Falls. It was known as the best place where every addict in Central Iowa went to detox.

She laid on her bed, trying to remember how she got to Covenant. She sighed and looked around her room dressed in scrubs two-sizes too-big for her frail frame.

She barely remembered being wheelchaired in. She recalled meeting eyes with a few of the patients in their rooms down the long hallway of the detox wing. Their different states of maladies were on display like a traveling freak show as she got closer to her room.

She asked the nurse what she was giving her when she got to her bed. It was Diazepam. She then looked at the IV stuck in her right arm and watched the yellow solution being dripped in. She assumed she was hooked to a *"Banana Bag."* As long as it was going to pump a cure into her that allowed her to sleep, she was hopeful.

She thought of the stories she heard of her cousins, friends, and her own mother being former patients in the same facility. She swore she would never be a part of that club, but now she couldn't say she was any different from any of them. She cried and felt remorse for ever looking down on their character for detoxing there.

She wondered if anyone would come to visit her. Then, thought it better that no one see her in that condition. Then, she longed for someone to come again. Her confusion was throwing her mind through a loop as her stomach growled.

She remembered the itchiness on her face. Her skin felt like it was covered in a thick layer of wax. She scratched and felt worse at the sight of skin flakes coming off of her. She turned to her side opposite of the IV and closed her eyes only to see nerves dancing in the darkness. She further hoped the medicine taken earlier, along with her IV, would put her to sleep.

She thought back how she and Lisa had told the Preacher and his wife that she was very sick and needed help. The Preacher obliged and said that they would help as much as they could. His wife didn't seem to mind and told them to climb in.

Lisa asked what they should do about Azul's car, but Azul didn't care at that point. She felt like she would die right there if they didn't rush her to the ER. The closest hospital was in Grinnell, a small college town nearby. It was only 20 minutes away from where they were parked. They all agreed to take her there as Lisa got the keys from the ignition, locked the door, and they both got in the back of the white van.

"Okay you ladies, please excuse the mess——" The Preacher spoke in a soothing baritone voice. "We were at a big potluck in Iowa City, and we have a bunch of boxes and food. I forgot my cellphone at the place! I'm not used to carrying those things around. They cost a lot of money, so the wife said we'd better turn back. Good thing we did because we were following you. Saw you almost run off the road! We turned around to see if we could help. Good thing we did——the Lord works in mysterious ways——there's that and we can all be thankful I listen to my wife——" he chuckled, smiled at his wife, and glanced at the rearview mirror at the two women. "Yeah, there's plenty of meatloaf, soup, potato salad, frybread in the coolers if you wanna help yourself——"

Azul retched again. She spit out some of her vodka and water at the preacher's description of food at that moment.

"Oh shit! Uhh——sorry, sir——" whimpered Lisa.

After a slight pause, "Well okay, no worries! I'll shut up about that food and getcha to the hospital. Let's go!"

The rush to the hospital was a cacophony of highway noise, a pounding in her head, a ringing in her ear, and sporadic voices as she clenched onto Lisa, who held her during the ride.

All the while, she was forcing down the vodka shots she had in the pocket of her hoodie to desperately make the shaking go away.

She couldn't remember anything else about the ride, or the ER visit in Grinnell. She remembered certain blips under a blinding light, of the Preacher talking about knowing her grandma and grandpa, getting blood drawn from the nurse, screaming at someone to fuck off, a hand touching her and someone telling her to lay back down, and a white man in a white coat telling her she was going to Cedar Falls.

It was as if a long, crucial piece of time was wiped out of her memory.

A nurse then came to check her IV and asked how she was doing. She didn't know. The nurse turned on the TV for her.

"You should be feeling more relaxed now. We got you on some good stuff that will help you sleep, okay Azul? I really love your name honey!"

"Thanks." She passed out moments later.

* * *

"Hey babe!" Lisa walked in the room with a large lavender purse and a small gift shop teddy bear. She walked over and gave a still bedridden Azul a hug.

"You have a kickass room! You've been watching a lot of TV? How ya doing?"

"I can't feel my ass because I've been sitting here the whole time. Been watching the History Channel a lot. Fuck the news. It's nothing but Bush, war, Bush, and angry old white fuckers all the time. But hey, thanks for the teddy bear. I love it," she smiled and held it to her cheek, then reached out to hug Lisa again. She then noticed the familiar envelope of money sticking out of her uncharacteristically large purse.

"Oh shit! The money. I was worrying about that! What happened? How'd you get it?"

"Do you remember telling me to get your car and to take the money to the promoter guy like a hundred times?"

Azul thought for a few seconds. "No, I don't. Be honest. Was I that bad?"

"Oh man…" Lisa paused, took a sigh. "You were crazy. It hurt me to see you like that. For real——you were freaking me out AND you drew blood——" Lisa showed a small but deep cut on her forearm where Azul had dug her thumbnail into.

"I don't remember that either," Azul looked at Lisa's forearm thoroughly and noticed a bruise on her upper arm. She gasped, "I'm sorry. You know I'm not like that. It wasn't me. There's no good reason for any of this shit, really——" She showed Lisa her arm with the IV stuck in.

"Well, you look and sound better. Have you been eating?"

"I managed to stomach a little food this morning. Soft part of a waffle, applesauce, some oatmeal. I figure I'll work up to solid food soon. I hope."

"Good. Oh yeah, the money. Well——it's crazy that I have so much money with me. Heh! I've never had this much money on me in my life. That's why I borrowed one of my grandma's old gaudy bags. It looks like a chopped-off elephant's ear. Look!"

They both laughed. Lisa gave her the envelope. Azul took out the wad of cash and started to count it but stopped because her hands were still shaking too much. She sighed and asked Lisa to do it.

"Twenty-two hundred dollars," Lisa said.

"Good. It's all there——" Azul plopped down in relief, and pushed the button of her bed to a more upright seating position.

"The Preacher's name was Victor. His wife was Vickie. Get it? Ain't that some shit? We owe a lot to them."

"Yeah. I do remember him saying he knew my grandparents. That's a trip..." Azul trailed off in thought.

"Well, after the ER in Grinnell, they took me back to the car just off the interstate to that abandoned truck stop in a town called Malcolm."

Azul snorted. "Oh my god——way out there? We were practically in the middle of nowhere."

"Right. I kept thanking them for doing all of this. I was still pretty buzzed and got emotional. They said it was fine. They were doing their 'Christian duty.' But, we got to the car, and I got the money. They followed me back to my grandma's——so it was all good."

"Wow. All in one night, and I was getting checked in here——" Azul thought for a bit. "I've been in detox now for like almost two days altogether. I think——"

"This is the third day."

"Jesus..."

"Your mom and little brother came to the ER when you got checked in. I called them after a lot of loud deliberation with you——I'm telling ya! You were freaking out and saying you didn't want to see them. You kept saying you had everything under control——"

"I don't remember any of that," Azul got a lump in her throat, "I miss them so much."

"They'll be here. I told your mom I was coming up here today. She said she'd be here after work with your brother. She passed on a message to me for you not to worry, and she has a surprise for you."

"Oh man. I don't know if my body can handle any more surprises. Hmm. Well, she's been through this whole detox rodeo thing before. I took her to this very place a handful of times. I know she was probably pretty pissed. I hope I didn't say anything too bad."

"She was the one who committed you here. You should be thankful, Azul."

"Yeah right. It all seems to get worse as I find out more about the truth of what I did."

"Umm... You did say some pretty bad things to her. I'm warning you. You tried to get your brother to agree with you. He was hurt, too. They've never seen you like that before." Lisa looked at Azul as she turned her head and stared out the window at the humid gray sky.

"I didn't mean to say those things..." Azul said as she asked herself if she really did mean them.

CHAPTER SEVENTY-FIVE

"So, hey Rick I'm glad I got a hold of you. This is Bob in Davenport. I hope the band's doing good. This call is in regards to the ticket payment you said you were gonna send over a couple of nights ago. Just wanted to touch base and see what was up. Haven't heard from you. I'm depending on you guys for those pre-sale tickets. This is the biggest show of the year for us and for you, too, man. What the fuck? I'd appreciate if you'd give me a call back. Hope things are good. The Slayer thing is a big deal. You guys are guaranteed the opening set time right before them, that is, if you get those tickets sold. You said you had twenty-two hundred. That'll secure that spot Rick. No bullshit. No other band has delivered anything close to that yet. Again, give me a call back. Today! Thanks."

"Fuck, man! What the fuck is going on here?!" Rick slammed the phone down on the kitchen table and pushed it away, knocking over a dozen beer containers.

"What's wrong baby?" asked Rosita walking in half-awake from the bedroom.

"That fucking bitch didn't deliver the fucking money like I asked!" Rick put his head in his hands and let out a frustrated grunt.

"Oh shit——the money?" gasped Rosita, gathering consciousness.

"Yeah, the fucking money for the tickets! Slayer show! Biggest show of our lives! The money we ALL worked hard for! Remember?!" Rick snapped.

"Gawd… I remember. Have you heard from her?"

"I had all the fucking directions written down and everything she needed. The money was in the brown envelope, all nice and fucking neat. I put Bob the promoter's phone number on there, and I drew a map on the sheet of paper! God! Is that too much to fucking ask? What are you looking for?"

"My smokes, baby, that's all——" Rosita was looking around the trashy kitchen.

"I gotta do everything around here now? Is that it? We put a lot of fucking work toward selling those tickets. Where is she? Is she at her fucking mom's house? Fucking useless kid! I'll be fucking pissed if she took off with that money! What'd she do? Skip the country? Took it back to her ancestors down south? What da fuck?"

"My cigarettes aren't in this room. Where did we go last night? Oh wait——they're in the van aren't they!"

"How should I know? Go see! I have twenty-two hundred dollars missing, and you're looking for a pack of cigarettes?"

"Okay! Stop it. My head is starting to pound right now. I'm going to the van. I'm gonna go across the street to get a water first. Do you want anything?"

Rick was pacing the room. "No, I don't need anything——I gotta figure out what to do. I gotta find Azul. Fuck——"

Rosita slipped into her flannel shirt and corduroy slippers that were a present from the House of Compassion charity clothing bank.

"I'm going. You still got that good Felix shit, right? Get a bump ready when I get back, baby?"

Rick looked at her slippers, thought for a few seconds, and said, "Sure. Hurry back we got stuff to do."

Rosita walked down the staircase to go outside. Rick went to the table to fetch the phone that he manhandled into the beer bottle and can pile and got his address book. He flipped to find Felix's name.

"I hope you were serious about that band sponsorship deal, Señor Felix…" He dialed the scrawled number and thought outloud that Rosita had her moments of genius sometimes.

CHAPTER SEVENTY-SIX

DOSHA MY DAUGHTER! HOW YA DOING? I'M FINE. THE SUN IS
SHINING HERE. I HOPE IT IS OVER THERE IN IDAHO! LAST TIME I
SAW YOU YOU WERE A WEE LITTLE ONE. YOU HAD REAL PRETTY
HAIR. I BET YOUR A BIG GIRL NOW. I'D LIKE TO BRING YOU UP
HERE AND TURN YOU INTO A REAL COWGIRL. AHO! WE CAN RIDE
HORSES ACROSS OUR LAND. WE GOT A FEW HUNDRED ACRES
OF LAND HERE ON THE REZ. YOU HAVE A BIG FAMILY UP HERE.
GOT DOGZ TOO. NO CATZ. KEEP GETTING SNATCHED UP BY THE
COYOTEZ. AT LEAST OURS ANYWAYZ.

I HEAR YOU PLAY GUITAR! THAT'S GOOD! PRAISE GOD. I'D LIKE
TO BRING YOU UP HERE TO COME SING FOR ME AND THE FAM.
WE GOT A PRETTY BIG CASINO UP HERE ON THE REZ. THERE'S A
BIG STAGE HERE WITH LIGHTS AND EVERYTHING. YOU CAN PLAY
ON THAT STAGE! WE CAN ALL GET TOGETHER AND HAVE A BIG
FEAST. IT'S IMPORTANT THAT WE NATIVES GET TOGETHER AND
GIVE PRAISE TO OUR CREATOR. HE IS GOOD.

YOU HAVE TWO SISTERZ AND A LITTLE BROTHER! MAY (20), FRAN (19), AND TEDDY (16). I ENCLOSED A PICTURE OF THEM ALL. I THINK THIS IS FROM 2 YEARS AGO. THEY ARE GOOD KIDZ. YOUR ARE THE OLDEST. IS THAT COOL? YOUR LITTLE BROTHER TEDDY IS IN JUVEY NOW. HE STABBED A TEACHER IN THE NECK WITH A PENCIL. SHE LIVED THO. HE GETS IN TROUBLE ALL THE TIME. YOU NEED TO SHOW THEM THE WAY. HOW TO ACT. YOUR THE OLDEST AND I HEAR YOUR DOING WELL! FRAN GETS IN TROUBLE ALOT TOO. I HEAR SHE'S PREGNANT NOW. I'M GONNA BE A GRANDPA! THAT'S PRETTY COOL ENIT?

I HOPE TO HEAR FROM YOU SOON. I GOT SOME MONEY FOR YOU. THERE GONNA BE DRILLING FOR OIL ON OUR LAND SOON. I'M STAYING AT THIS ADDRESS NOW. 6 WEEKS SOBER TOO! GOD IS GOOD! I ENCLOSED A PICTURE OF ME WITH YOUR AUNTIE. I CUT OUT THE BEER CAN IN PIC. I'VE BEEN LIVING IN SEATTLE FOR A LONG TIME. I MISS THE SEA AIR. BUT IT'S GOOD I COME BACK TO THE REZ. WE GOTTA GET BACK TO OUR ROOTS SOMETIME IN THIS LIFE. AHO! WE CAN ALL COME TOGETHER ON OUR RANCH AND BE A FAMILY AGAIN.

LOVE YOUR DAD, BUCK

P.S. "DOSHA" MEANS HI OR WELCOME IN NDN. HIDATSA. AHO!

* * *

"Well... He definitely sounds like a bit of a hick," Azul chuckled as she perused the letter and its contents; the aforementioned two pictures in polaroid form, a handbill for the casino on the reservation, and a funeral program for her dead paternal grandmother.

"Up that way, they're definitely cowboys. It was a big rodeo culture back in the day. Those boys would travel all over and compete. His drinking sure has caught up with him though if that picture is recent. Man..." Mom studied the pictures with Azul.

"After all these years. Hmm. I don't have his hair after all..." she paused. "So, he sent this to where I work? How many hands did it pass through?"

"He's been calling around to all the different departments of our casino, asking for Azul with HIS last name and not ours. Nobody knew anyone with that name. I guess he couldn't figure out that your last name was Morgan. OUR family name. Maybe he didn't remember, or he really is that dumb——"

Azul snorted. "Yeah, well someone talked to him and said I worked there. He never got to you though. Did he?"

"Well, I've said in the past that if he ever found me I'd show him to you. You're my daughter, and you deserve to know who your father is, regardless of all the bad things that happened. But, no. He never reached me."

"I'll just assume that everyone at work knows all my family business now, AND I got sent to detox," she sighed, glanced at the letter. "I'm a big fucking mess, and my estranged father thinks my shit is together? What am I gonna do?"

"Well, there's always gonna be vultures around that talk shit. Don't worry about them and worry about your own. Your health is your first priority. I'd tell you like your grandma not to talk to Buck. But it's your life; and if he wants to be in it, then it's up to him to make up for all that lost time. You don't owe him nothing. Talking that BS about you showing the way to your lost brother and sisters, those are his kids! It sounds like he's feeling sorry for himself the whole time and on the *Forgiveness* step in his recovery program."

"What's a recovery program?"

"A.A. You're gonna hear a lot more about that stuff now."

"Nuh-uh——"

"Yes you are, you watch——"

"Nuh-uh——"

Mom snorted and scratched her daughter's head. She ran her fingers through her hair. "I'm glad you're alright though. When's your dinner?"

"Well, your timing was right. I hear the lady down the hall with the trays coming in any minute."

"I sent your brother across the street to get Wendy's. He should be back here soon. Gee, I heard that guy that owned that restaurant died recently——"

"That was last year, Mom."

   * * *

Her steak tips dinner arrived on a robust tray piled with potatoes, vegetable medley, and fruit cocktail. A desert of carrot cake was included; she ate the whole meal with gusto. It was the first decent meal she had in weeks.

Her mom and brother stayed with her for the rest of the evening and planned to stay in a hotel nearby after visiting hours. It was a much-needed gentle time with her family as she cried a half-dozen times. She apologized for being selfish, not being there for them, and what she said in the ER.

The doctor came in to tell her that they would let her go *at noon tomorrow*, but she had a long way to go for a full recovery. Before leaving the room he recommended A.A and N.A. meetings for 90 days and to come back to see him for a follow-up.

"Ninety days. That sounds really impossible right now; sobriety, especially in M-town." Azul wiped her face with her dinner napkin. She noticed the tingling in her face wasn't there anymore.

"What about your band? Your music? Is that something you're willing to let go? It's what got you here——" Mom asked.

"I'm not going to quit, Mom. It's a part of who I am. At least, I thought it was."

"Are those other guys gonna support you when you're down and out? I don't see them here."

"I haven't talked to anyone yet. That reminds me, I better tell them. Well, maybe not. I'll just send the money to the damn promoter after we leave here. I really don't wanna talk to Rick right now. Rosita and him are most likely back together and STILL partying. We were hanging out with some really shady people lately. I have to get out of that house. That's the first thing."

Azul and her mother sat quietly and watched TV. Zach fell fast asleep on the easy chair in the corner after his dinner.

"Hmm… must've been a long day for him. He looks so peaceful, all passed out in the chair," Azul admired her sleeping brother.

"Well, ya know M-town. You hear things. The kids have been talking. Your band, your whole scene is pretty notorious for parties, drugs and all that. I guess it's been worrisome for him being your little brother, hearing all the talk that goes around in his crowd. A lot of them getting in trouble too. Skipping school. Getting on the police blotter in the newspaper. Hmm… Seems like kids were all innocent a few months ago," Mom said and looked at Zach.

"Yeah, I think about that. Hope no rumors are going around that I'm being a big slutbag——"

"Better not."

"Well, there's this one cute blond girl at the porno shop that does this wicked thing with her——" Azul started.

"Shh! Shut up! Don't even go there!" Mom quickly hushed her. They both laughed, startling Zach awake. He looked at them, the TV, then tossed to his other side to go back to a light snore.

"I've been getting crank calls at my office. Weird stuff has been happening since the shutdown at work," Mom's voice got serious, she took a breath and continued, "I had five calls with just silence on the other end. My supervisor said to just let them call, log it, and listen. Around the third call, I could hear breathing. Like a woman's. The fourth call I could hear music in the background. Kids playing. Still nothing. I got a pretty good idea who it might be——"

"Lou's mother." Azul not surprised by the news.

"Yeah! So, the fifth time I picked up I said I was gonna have the call traced and get the cops involved for harassment. Then an old Indian lady's voice said, 'Your little half-breed got what she deserved after what she did to Lou.' That pissed me off! Right away, I said, 'Bitch! She's still alive! You failed,' before she hung up——"

"Eee, really? How did she know I was in the hospital——wait, small towns. Word gets around quickly. Well, call the cops anyway because there's no excuse for that shit, and you and I don't believe in that witchcraft stuff."

Mom thought for a moment. "Ya know your Uncle Theo might help you. He's a Medicine Man, I think."

Azul looked at her sleeping brother again then out the window at the night sky.

"I remember you telling me that, and ya know, I can't stop thinking that shit happens for a reason. Maybe, I got Buck's letter because it might be good for me to go up there, ya know, since I'm taking this time off for myself now. Plus, he said he had money for me. That might prove useful to get my shit outta the Compound and get a place of my own."

"If that's what you feel is the right thing to do. We can back you up. You have family here to get you up there, money-wise."

"The more I think about it; the more determined I feel. I can take a weekend, finally meet Buck and the family. Meet my brother and sisters...and yes, maybe Uncle Theo can help me in the 'curse' department." Azul couldn't help but smile at the mention of *Curse*.

"It'd be good for you. Maybe we can come up there with you."

"I'd like you to. But I should probably do this alone. I know you worry, but I'll be alright. Besides, you and Buck might shack up and get back together, right?"

Mom winced and made a vomit sound, and they laughed.

They sat in silence for a while. The night nurse came into the room to tell them that visiting hours were over and that Kim and Zach would have to leave.

"We're gonna check in to the hotel just down the street. Get more rest. I'm glad you got to eat. Think about what you wanna do some more. If you want to meet your father, get some of that money he owes you; then we'll get the wheels in motion. Okay?" Mom hugged her daughter and kissed her on the forehead.

"Okay. Hey! Wake up little monster. You're going to the hotel with Mom," Azul called out to Zach, who woke up immediately, came over to hug her and said, "Good night. Love you." Azul was surprised to hear how deep his voice had gotten.

They left the room. She turned off the light by her bed, eased back and thought about Buck's letter. She said to herself, "Idaho? Oh my god…"

CHAPTER SEVENTY-SEVEN

"What's up Rick Rocker! You get any sleep, man? That shit was pretty crazy last night, right?" Felix and Rick slammed their mitts together and embraced. Both men elated, like the oldest of friends, to see one another.

"Oh shit, man! No doubt. I figured we got this shit down, man. That stuff you got is the best I've had. I mean, it's like the purest. Once I get in a zone, I turn into a fucking megalomaniacal beast, like my grind is on beast-mode and shit!" Rick was still grasping Felix's hand while shaking it with pure gratitude during every emphatic syllable.

"Right, man! It should make you play better. That's what I like to see when it comes to that shit, man. Fuck beast-mode. You got GOD-mode bro! Let's go inside. I'll cut you a little line, man. For old times sake!" Felix indulged in his East LA accent, let out a boisterous laugh, and pulled Rick in with their everlasting grip.

"Aight man, oh shit. Wait! I gotta get Rosita. She's waiting in the van," Rick turned away towards the parked van on the street. "Rosita! Rosita! Baby, come 'ere!"

Rosita heeded the call and came out from the driver's side, almost tripping on her pink sandals when she started to walk. She wore a gray tube-top with small white and pink girl trunks. Her red-rimmed sunglasses covered half of her face as she adjusted them to admire the Spanish-style stucco house that Felix lived in.

"Holy shit! Dude! I love your pad, man! Felix! I didn't realize! You are the shit! I'm moving in! Is this like your house out in LA?" Rosita's raspy voice cracked with excitement as she came to the doorway.

"Oh man, this is just my crash pad. My house is all over the place. Me and Rick are gonna be taking turns renting suites out at the casino, the Marriott, everywhere! 'Cause we're all gonna be able to afford to live like that after today my friends!" He held out his hand to lead her inside, sporting a wide grin as he and Rick started talking about a new shipment of product that came that day.

      * * *

"Just don't talk about God like that, man! I love you, but I swear if you're gonna keep talking about this shit like it puts you in 'God-Mode,' I don't know if I can hang with you anymore bro..." Rick was cleaning Felix' island tabletops in the large kitchen that was adjoined with a full dining room and the main living room with the 52-inch television with surround-sound playing Latino music videos, "I mean, it's like you're not afraid of lightning bolts striking you dead whenever you say that."

Felix was sitting on his leather sofa sectional with an attractive young woman with curly black hair cuddled next to him, bobbing her head to the music video that was playing. "What are you talking 'bout homie? What, you have a problem with me using the word God? *Aye dios, mio!* I'm not meaning anything by it, bro! God-mode. God-mode. Whatcha saying, dog?"

"Dude! Watch that shit, Felix! I don't wanna die today! I gotta open up for Slayer before that happens," Rick started putting dirty dishes into the sink while using his arms to emphasize his words. "I swear you don't believe that shit you're spraying! I know you don't believe it, that's why you do it!" He shook a wet dish at Felix while Rosita started dancing barefoot in front of the television. Felix's curly-haired companion got up from the couch to join Rosita, "You don't think a lightning bolt is gonna strike you down, just like that? It's gonna happen if you keep doing that. Just you watch! I don't wanna plan a funeral today——"

"Shit, funeral? Really? Naw man, I'm here to stay! I'm making more money than my grandparents ever did! Soon, you will too, and your band is gonna make it big! I'm telling you because I love you, man. You ain't got nothing to worry about, man. Shit——being struck down——I'm the one that's gonna be doing the striking down, homie! I got the goods, the bitches, AND the heat! In that exact order," Felix slapped his hands together for even more emphasis. "You don't think I got heat? Shit——I grew up Catholic, so I ain't gotta worry about anyone striking me down! My grandpa said that, 'Hard work will always win you a seat in the kingdom,' you know what that means? It means I'm good——GOOD! I work hard and things take care of themselves, bro. God is looking out for me. No need to fear, bro—— no need to fear!"

The curly-haired vixen and Rosita were dancing closer together, their breasts touched, then their slim serpentine bodies began to entwine.

"Just don't use the G word when describing the stuff man. It leaves a little bad taste in my mouth is all," Rick cocked his head to the two sultry women as a music video full of scantily clad women was playing a slow Latin beat. "It's well; that's pretty cool about what your grandpa said. My grandpa used to say, 'Ain't nobody gonna build nothing till God's on your side'——" He sniffed loudly, hawked a loogie in his mouth, and swallowed the numb chemical mound back into his throat, "I miss him a lot you know——"

"I miss my *abuelo*, too. He was the best a little guy like me could ever ask for. Hey, they grew up in some crazy times. What do WE got? 9/11? The Internet? War in the Middle East? What do guys like us hafta worry about 'cept make as much money as possible as this world is getting angrier and angrier. You realize that?" The two started to get distracted by the two drug-induced vixens in front of the ones on T.V. "But, you know, with this shipment, we're gonna take care of business and have some fun doing it, ya heard bro?" He licked his lips at the sight of the two women as they removed both of their shirts and started fondling each others' breasts while both of their tongues explored the other mouth.

"So, this sponsorship deal, you were talking about, does that still stand, brother?" Rick bobbed his head to the music while watching the two women get fully unclothed. "If that's the case, maybe *God-Mode* can stay in your vocabulary. We'll, uhh, supply the lightning bolts, man."

Felix got into the music and nodded his head. "Yeah, sure thing, man. Anything you want Rick Rocker; anything you want, my man——"

CHAPTER SEVENTY-EIGHT

Azul crossed the North Dakota border through the small city of Fargo. The Red River ran through it, and she drove by the Sports Arena. She was impressed, but wary, that this would be the last bit of civilization she would encounter before the great unknown that stretched ahead.

Her route ran straight on I-94 northbound from Iowa through Minnesota, then turned west to North Dakota. Her destination was at the heart of the state on the Fort Berthold Reservation. The home of the Three Affiliated Tribes: The Mandan, Hidatsa, and Arikara.

She knew very little of the history of the tribe and her family. She was afraid that if she thought about it for too long she would get anxious and have another panic attack in the car. She knew that being alone on the trip she was taking a huge risk by not having Lisa by her side and angels in a white church van to save her this time.

So, as a soothing travel companion, she made a mix CD of country songs that she grew up with. She didn't want to buy country CDs, so she hung out at her mom's house to get on the family computer to download songs from Napster. This gave her a chance to be with her family before the long journey to meet her *new* family.

Buck's letter had a phone number scrawled where he could be reached. She called after her stay in the hospital to find out, to her surprise, it was her Aunt Karen's number. It turned out that she was expecting her call. Azul had never met her, but they talked for an hour. During the call, Karen passed the phone around to her daughters, nieces, nephews and to her husband, Buck's brother, Uncle Theo.

Buck lived on his own in a house on their land. This immediately intrigued Azul as she pictured a vast ranch. She guessed he probably resided in a bunkhouse.

The only land ownership Azul had ever known was her grandparents' acreage in Iowa. It was just enough room for a house, a large garden, and a corral for horses with a small barn for hay.

She learned that the family in North Dakota had a few hundred acres of land, and they had multiple horses over the years. Azul learned that her penchant for horses was not merely circumstance. It was in her blood.

She stopped for gas at a station off the interstate, got some food, and called Aunt Karen to let her know that she was in Fargo. It was 8:00 PM when she called.

Aunt Karen answered and said they had booked a room for her under Uncle Theo's name at the Four Bears Casino and Hotel, located next to the great Lake Sakakawea.

Karen said she was lucky because the Mandaree Powwow was going on, and it was one of the most popular ones in the nation. Both natives and non-natives from the United States and Canada attended the yearly event. Uncle Theo was on the tribal council, so he had the clout to book one of the blocked rooms in the hotel.

Karen confirmed that it was an eight-hour drive from Fargo. Azul sighed, "Great. Am I gonna need a gun? All I have is my trusty bat and some mace."

Karen responded, "Just coffee——" she warned that the drive was long, but the landscape was *pretty much flat and barren*. "I haven't heard of anything bad happening on these roads recently."

Azul half-jokingly replied, "Yeah, they might be all dead or disappeared——"

"Oh, don't talk like that! I'm praying for you. You'll be fine. I can't wait to finally meet my long-lost niece! Aho! *Aye*——" Karen assured her in her motherly northern Rez accent. She said to some children's voices in the background that Cousin Azul was in North Dakota and to go pray for her in the living room. This sent a warm feeling in Azul's heart as she smiled, made an about face, and said her byes to Karen and the children.

She looked at the harsh neon lights of the last gas station surrounding her and looked beyond to the great frontier that stretched ahead. The late-summer sun was resting on the dusty horizon of the great plains.

She had the *Farewell* theme from "Dances With Wolves" playing in her head. She snorted at the ridiculousness of that theme being recalled in her memory as she thought that the scene where John Dunbar takes off on his maiden journey to the great plains, atop Cisco The Horse, paralleled with her own journey.

She got in the car, turned the ignition, skipped to track-20 on her mix CD, and drove west to the sounds of that very theme from John Barry's soundtrack on repeat.

The Bastard Chronicle 23: Smoke Signals

So, with all of my time, strength, and resources, after my fall from grace, I finally met my long-lost family. At least some of them...

I didn't know what to expect. Driving up there was pretty dope. I didn't realize such pretty country was so far up north. Being from the Midwest, it feels that everything is centered right there, and at the same time, conveniently forgotten.

Even with all the band travel and the gigs played all over our state and the surrounding ones, we really are in a small area.

I was still feeling fragile, but I was slowly regaining my health. I'm on B-1 Vitamins now and a mood stabilizer; and since I'm on unemployment now, hopefully, Buck's money he said he has for me will help me get out of my living situation.

After this major setback, the band's future is in doubt after the Slayer show. I don't know if I can hang with Rick's bullshit anymore. But after my visit, I am hopeful.

I got to the Rez early before dawn and couldn't see anything except some fires from a few oil rigs in the distance.

I got to my aunt and uncle's place the next day. The drive was on some really treacherous terrain with roads that could really pass for highways to hell.

The house is on a ranch surrounded by some huge hills. I didn't see any animals though. That was a curious concern as Mom made it sound like these were big-shot cattle farmers and cowboys. It really was like another world.

I thought of Magenta. He would like this place. So free. So vast. He would probably run away, and I'd never be able to find him...

I met my aunt and uncle, and they had two little girls and a boy to call their own. My cousins. Then some more cousins came over to meet me. Then some other aunts and uncles. I was overwhelmed! I still can't remember everyone's name! Next time, I'll definitely write names in a notepad or something to remember.

I told Uncle Theo about Lou's mother and the bad medicine thing.

He smudged me, said some prayers, and gave me a pouch of tobacco to keep with me at all times. He said I had good strong medicine; and as a Beaver Clan, I would be alright.

I never told him I was Beaver Clan! Eee! How did he know!?

* * *

It was a warm reception overall. I dug it! But there was an uneasy feeling because there was an obvious absence from the festive nature of "Princess Azul's Homecoming Jubilee": Buck.

After dinner at the homestead, Aunt Karen pulled me to the back porch where they had a couple of dogs running around, some remnants of old ranch life with chicken wire fence, horse pens, and an old broken-down pickup. (We have those back on the "Sett"!) She pointed to an ugly, rusted-out trailer with flimsy plywood covering some of the windows with a blue tarp flapping in the breeze.

"That's where Buck, your dad, stays. He should be sleeping it off now. He's been drinking again. I'll send my oldest over there to make sure he's okay, then he'll come get you. But, don't worry. My son will just be right outside."

I asked why he needed to do all that. She lit up a cigarette and shook her head.

"He's a weird one, your dad, nowadays. Misses his mama. He does weird projects around the house to stay busy——" She took a drag then continued, "He lost his toe. His left eye is gone. Doc told him he needs to quit drinking and eat right before he loses everything."

I didn't know what to say as I looked over at the ramshackle trailer home, a dwelling I totally did not expect for an old hotshot "cowboy" to be living in. A light turned on in one of the windows. I asked how long he's been like this.

"Oh, he has his good weeks. But, since you said you were coming up here, he tricked one of your oldest cousins to run him into town to get him to the casino and the liquor store. He's been drinking ever since. Uncle calmed him down though. I say to him; I'll sick the dogs on him if he creeps around late at night! Gee. I worry for my kids when he's like that."

Wait…an OLDER cousin? I asked her, trying to keep mental tabs on how many cousins I actually have.

She smiled, said "Yuh. You have a lot of family you haven't met yet. Your sisters are in Seattle now. Your brother is locked up." She looked over at the trailer then shook her head again.

I felt uneasy after that. The light in the trailer window went out, and I noticed how dark it had gotten. She said I would see him in the morning.

She offered for me to stay the night in the homestead, but I politely told her I would stay at the hotel (which is really the ONLY one on the Rez!) Uncle already gave me a comped room, complete with a check for my expenses and then some.

She understood and said something about going to the Powwow tomorrow. I just wanted to check into a nice hotel room and feel a hot shower wash years of confusion away for the night.

The hotel and casino was about 20 miles away in Newtown, which was located on the Rez's main tribal office infrastructure next to the great Lake Sakakawea.

On the drive there, I could see sporadic lights from meager Rez houses burrowed in the dark hills. The Powwow lights in Mandaree could be seen from miles away from a flat vista.

I couldn't see the lake much. It was mostly pitch black; but as I arrived, I could see the great lake sparkle by casino light.

CHAPTER EIGHTY

"Was that you?" Leo, Aunt Karen's oldest son, who stood 6' 4" with long hair, boomed in his thick Rez accent.

"Wuh?" A nasally voice came from deep within the trailer.

"Was that you a coupla nights ago? Peeking through the windows? Stay the fuck away from my sisters! You come sneakin' around again like a creep, I'll put some buckshot into your pervert ass!" His deep baritone filling the trailer as he held the door open.

Azul winced at the smell of old upholstery, beer cans, and cigarettes. She noticed black patches of mold on the ceiling and was about to say something when Leo whispered in her ear, "Don't be afraid of how he looks with his eye socket open like that. He forgets to wear his patch sometimes. He used to scare the girls when he would walk around after the docs took his eye. Poor guy. He can be a sweet one, but he got a tough break."

She just nodded her head and looked around at the cobwebbed, unwashed, shag-carpeted trailer with cans and bottles, porno magazines, and a strange life-size doll of a busty brunette woman with olive skin dressed in a satin gown sitting on a love seat in the corner.

"Oh my god——" as she was about to ask what the doll was, a 5-and-a-half foot Quasimoto-like figure dressed in a Seattle Seahawks jersey came out from the hallway, combing his thin graying brown hair and put his small comb in the pocket of his wrinkled khaki shorts. A haphazard blue patch was taped over his left eye.

"Aho! Greetings. Dosha, Daughter. Leo, good to see ya! Aho! Heh-heh, you're pretty. I see you got your mom's skin. Good. She's always had good skin——" He walked over on his tiptoes to not make the thin floor boom so much under his weight. Azul instantly remembered she used to do this when she lived in a second floor apartment with her mom and stepdad when Zachary was a baby, so the neighbors wouldn't complain from the heavy footsteps above.

She swallowed, looked at Leo again and said, "Hello——"

"Woo——It's hot in here, enit? I'll go turn on the air-conditioner. It's noisy, but it does the job. Holay, lemme go here real quick——" Buck sidestepped and turned around awkwardly, hitting his knee on the edge of the coffee table, some glossy porno magazines slid off. "Ouch!" He stammered an apology and hobbled to the air-conditioner propped in the furthest window that had Christmas ribbons tied on the vent that immediately danced to the cantankerous beat of the sluggish unit.

Azul inhaled deeply and took another look at the trailer from her vantage point, "Looks like you got some cleaning up to do." She winced at the old microwave dinner trays stacked next to the full kitchen sink. Flies were everywhere.

"Yuh," he chuckled, coughed and apologized for the mess, "Hey, maybe you can help me, you know. That'd be something we could do. You can teach me how to do it, eh?"

She grimaced at the thought and remembered she used to be a slob until Zach was born. She slowly became domestically-oriented as she cared for her baby brother into her teens.

"Uh, no that's okay. What's with the uh, lady over there?" She coughed and pointed at the expressionless facade of womanhood on the dingy love seat.

"Oh, yeah! Leo knows her. This is Josetta. My fiancé! Praise God, enit? She's gonna be your new stepmother!"

Azul was in shock. She looked over at Leo who nudged her shoulder and said to Buck, "She looks kinda cold. Maybe she should have changed into something more appropriate for meeting your daughter, enit?" He patted her back, and gave her a signal that it was all a harmless charade to play along to.

"Yuh, good idea! Come on *Mami*, let's go change you into something more appropriate for our company today, aho!" Buck hobbled over to the love seat, made a grunting noise like he was in pain, bent over to pick up the doll, and asked Leo for help; to which Leo sighed and grudgingly agreed, cursing himself for having said something in the first place.

"Alright, I'll take her to the back and put something on her while you stay here with Azul——" Leo picked up the doll, Buck immediately responded.

"No, no, no. I'll go back with you! Besides, heh-y-y-you won't even know what her b-b-best outfit is."

Azul let out a snicker, raised her eyebrows and watched as Leo hoisted the doll with ease on his shoulder, it was pliable enough that it draped over his frame like an unconscious teenager.

Buck was deflected from helping. He then began following him like Igor to his Frankenstein, back to whence he came. "Where's your cane?" asked Leo as they went to the back room.

Azul was left alone to study the open living area of the trailer.

There were some vintage rodeo posters from the 70's hung on the living room wall. Several framed pictures of his youthful days in competition stood on the two bookshelves in the room.

His brothers were also represented. She recognized Uncle Theo in one of them.

There was a picture of a man with long hair dressed in buffalo skin regalia that appeared to be from the early 1900's.

The biggest picture in the collection was, what appeared to be, Buck's mother. She recognized her from the picture on the funeral program he included in the letter. Upon closer observation of that photo, she had a close resemblance to her.

She gasped. Her grandma was a younger woman, posing next to a white pony that looked like her Magenta. The uncanny resemblance hypnotized her. She felt a force within her awaken that was stirred by all of the events that aligned themselves for her to see that image. She felt in that moment her youth was foretold in that dusty and grainy photograph she never knew existed.

The two came back a few minutes later with Josetta in tow, dressed in a leopard-skin leotard, and a black negligée. "There we go! Here's a proper introduction; this is Josetta, my——"

"Fiancé. Yeah, I know. Umm, is this my grandma in this picture with the pony?" Azul, changing the subject while grabbing the picture to look at it closely.

"Oh! Uh, yuh. That was back in the sixties. We had a big ranch then. Right where this trailer is now. We had a lot of horses. Oh man, you shoulda seen it. Your grandma was quite a lady. She had her favorite horses. That one was one she didn't have long, but she liked that one. Yuh——" Buck explained as Leo plopped the doll down onto the love seat again. Buck stepped in and crossed its legs as if it was sitting casually.

"Wow. How did she die?" Azul asked Buck, turning her head to look at him closely for the first time. She didn't see any facial features that were like hers. She looked into his jaundiced right eye. His skin was flaccid and pale.

"Holay…umm, cancer. She uh, sh-sh-sh-she uh, held on for awhile tho. I was in Seattle most the time tho," he stuttered and flinched at being face-to-face with Azul for the first time. He groaned a bit under his breath, then asked, "Hold up your hands. Hold 'em up wide so I can compare."

She drew back with hesitation, but looked at her hands and noticed she was shaking. It was not from the *coming down*, but from meeting her father for the very first time. She held up her right hand while still holding onto her grandmother's picture in the other. Buck held out his hand to hers and stood studying it for a few seconds.

"Your hands are smaller, but that's 'cause you're a girl. But you have the same lines. The same muscles. Shape. Aho! I see it now!" He inched closer and joined his palm to hers. He clasped his fingers through her fingers for a second and let go. "You thirsty? I got some Kool-Aid if you want some——"

"I'm okay," She stood rigid, curiosity came over her. "That's odd. What you did. What's the significance in the hands?" She opened her palm to see what he saw special inside.

"Oh! If you were a boy you could've been a bullrider. In our family, we got strong hands," He hobbled, with cane now in-tow, over to the refrigerator for Kool-Aid.

Azul furrowed her brow and wanted to ask if that was the reason why he never came to see her ever, but relented, "Oh, well, I guess that's something I wouldn't have known had I not come today, right?" She looked around for any more mementos to ask about.

Buck retrieved his Kool-Aid pitcher, which happened to be the Berry-Blue flavor, and looked for a glass in the dirty dish rack, "Yuh. Me, your uncles, nephews, cousins, all bullride. Even Leo there, until he got bucked that one time, enit, Leo?" Buck found a cup and signaled to Leo, who wasn't paying much attention but looking at the multitudes of porno magazines and their cover vixens' seductive poses.

"Uh, yeah. Got bucked off. When I was twelve. At a branding. Messed my back up——" He sat down on the tattered couch and nodded his head at the mention of the unfortunate accident.

"Damn, dude. Sorry." She walked over to put her hand on his shoulder. She looked over at Buck as he drank his blue Kool-Aid. He took one big drink out of the cup and tipped the pitcher to top it off again, just like she did since she was a little girl.

"Yuh. Gotta be tough to be in the rodeo. A lot of the kids gave him shit——*EEE*, excuse me, I mean *heck*——but he got up again, enit!" He pointed his head to one of the big vintage rodeo posters placed in the middle of the main living room wall, "That one over there is from nineteen-seventy six. I won the championship rodeo. Got first place. Took the title to Mandaree! Aho! That was a good night. Here, I'll show you some more pictures——" He moved with purpose to the bookshelf below the poster to one of two large photo portfolios stacked together. "This is me when I took the title in the last eight seconds. Oh, man. Longest eight seconds of my life. But, my proudest. The sweat was in my eyes, the bull was like Satan wrestling with me! I can still hear his huffing and puffing! Man, I swear, I saw God put his hand out to me through the clouds in the sky! He told me to hold on. And I did what he said. Kept holding on without losing my hat! Man, you shoulda seen me! I remember it like it was yesterday. I never rode better than that day. I quit school to become a champion bullrider! I won. Then I became the champion! Best day of my life..."

The Bastard Chronicle 24: Powwow Highway

I'm crying as I'm writing into this journal. The sunset is beautiful out here. The summer is coming to a close. I'm crying because all my life I've never known my dad. And now I do, and I was just let down…

LET DOWN.

That's the only way I can describe it now.

*　　　* * *

The sunset is really beautiful out here with the sky so free. This is like God's canvas out here, man.

In the daytime, the terrain is dusty brown. I imagine this land as a gigantic horse hide. I can only imagine if it turns green at all around here. Maybe it does. Not much rain here. It's almost fall time. I can come back in the spring when things turn for the better.

Maybe, it did get a little better now. I can say I've finally met my dad.

A man, if you can call him that, that lives in a dumpy trailer on his family's ranch in the middle of fucking nowhere.

A man, if you can call him that, who is a porno freak and fucks dolls. Gleefully!

A man, if you can call him that, who said THE best day of his life was at a rodeo in '76. A man with four children!

Someone, I would definitely avoid at all cost under any normal fucking circumstance.

Someone, that dissolves in a crowd and retreats into the shadows without ever sticking with the program of being there.

Someone, who completely misses the point on empathy and regard to their own flesh and blood.

No one, who I would regard being of flesh.

No one, I can rely on for guidance or a straight answer to a simple question.

No one, I can understand for the life of me.

I seethe when I'm there among others. I could easily turn cold and unflinching as he in his existential plane of ignorance he chooses to lie.

Why did I turn out so different? And why am I the same?

I have his mannerisms. His stutter. His selfishness. His love and longing for the spotlight. His fucking alcoholism. His drug addiction. His hands.

Don't LET yourself DOWN, Azul...

* * *

Why and how on earth do people like him? If they knew what I knew or know what I've felt for not knowing...would they care?

* * *

The dude lost his eye from drinking too much. Can I rip the rest of his face off?

* * *

...at least he made good on the money. I got a couple grand. That should help in getting out of tweaker central when I return home.

* * *

It's pretty out here. No. I'm not tweaking while writing. I'm being a poet! It's what I do. I'm carrying this journal around at the Mandaree Powwow right now. Writing is also in my blood, like the cowboy stuff. It's something that he doesn't have. I get that from my other side.

I'm going to my hotel room after this, and I'm heading back home in the morning; but I'm liking the vibe right now.

Mandaree is like those little towns that we play in Iowa, except, smaller—yet bigger. It's a gathering of beautiful Native People from all over the country in their regalia, dancing to old songs written before a copyright was invented. It's a whole different world here. You can see the lights from the grounds for miles at night, just as bright as those burning oil wells. You can hear the drums all throughout the day. Follow the drums and hear the bells and voices, and you will find a world within a world.

Mandaree is so small. The only sign of commerce here is a small independently-owned convenience store that one of my aunties works at. I finally met her. She's nice.

My mom and her were tight back in the day. Mom snagged and hooked up with her hot-shit, bullrider brother for a few nights on a 49 and here I am. A couple of decades later, and I'm here. My aunt still works here.

Would I want to live here? No.

Would I want to end up here? No.

But I can say I've been here.

Because I now know I came from here.

CHAPTER EIGHTY-TWO

The opening riff of Slayer's "*Chemical Warfare*" played in Azul's trusty Discman to psyche herself up for the moment they were to hit the stage for set-change.

The Bastards were scheduled to perform as the headlining band inside the nightclub that was filled to capacity.

Slayer was set to perform right after them on the festival-size main stage which was located outside in the parking lot area where it overlooked the emerald-lit Centennial Bridge on the Mississippi River. Over ten-thousand fans were in attendance.

In an agreement with the stage manager and soundman, to ensure quick set changes for each band, the Bastards were asked to let every band use their drums and amplifiers. That was a total of eight bands from all over the Midwest.

They were scheduled to play a 30 minute set, but the show had already run 10 minutes behind. They had just learned that the tour manager had emphatically ordered the promoter that "NO bands were allowed to play at least 10 minutes before Slayer." Meaning, that the Bastards could only play for 10 minutes total.

Every second was important as the band defiantly intended to play at least 20 minutes and gain as much time as they could in their soundcheck.

When the band before them got done playing their set, they helped them haul their gear off the 3-foot high stage and brought theirs on, and rushed to plug everything into their amps.

They also had to reconfigure the drum kit, construct the percussion rig, set up their strobe lights and samples, do a microphone and monitor check for everything in a span of a few minutes.

Jesus, as usual, was ready to play and check his levels to the soundman first and achieved it in under two minutes. His hair was in tendrils. His makeup was caked on. His cheeks covered in rouge. He dressed in a size-one satin evening gown with his newly healed Bastards & Thieves logo tattoo in full display on his upper-right arm.

"Stay calm guys," he said as the others were in a rush while trying to avoid tripping over anything as the soundman's assistant was getting the drum kit microphones set up.

Azul wore black eyeliner to accentuate her almond eyes and black lipstick for her pouty lips. She sported a blue du-rag with her thick raven black hair now long enough to be braided in dreadlocks flowing freely from the back half of her head. She wore her favorite Isis(The Band) girl T-shirt and black Dickie slacks.

"We're doing good. Chester, dude, your shit is already miked; and you're running direct, too. We don't have time to set up the light show and samples, just plug and play, man. Thanks!" she shouted over the music that was playing on the PA as they were setting up.

Her pedal board was plugged in and ready. Then she taped the cords to the stage as was her ritual to ensure no tripping hazards. She made her way to her amp to turn it on and took her guitar out of its case. She felt the oppressive heat of the stage lights above, a bead of sweat came from her brow as she rose to strap on her brand new, blue Paul Reed Smith Custom guitar she christened: *De Be Sa Ke*, her Aunt Sandra's Meskwaki name.

Chester, who was dressed as a Goth, in full leather, spikes, and fishnet shirt, still had the same Fender Precision bass he brought to their first writing sessions as a band back in Rick's house by the cemetery two years ago.

As soon as Azul told him the plan, he relaxed right away, plugged in his bass, did some warm-up finger exercises while the soundman told him through the wedge monitor in front of him that he had his levels *good to go*.

Cousin Wayne was in a sour mood the whole day and was complaining to everyone within earshot because he had to share his drum kit with all the bands that played that day, despite his agreement to share. He adjusted his kit to the way he played, insisted on adding his second kick drum and extra toms, adding extra work for the soundman.

Azul was seething under her breath as Cousin Wayne's two drunk brothers were on the stage as a part of his "entourage." They were getting in the way and trying to be a part of the show in which their presence was not at all required and was a security risk for the musicians and stage crew.

The Bastard Chronicle 25: Highway of Clusterf%&kery

The Bastards and Thieves have finally arrived at the moment of truth! How we got here is a testament to our hard work, perseverance, and our "Weapon of Mass Destruction!"

However, our heroes didn't arrive on the big stage unscathed. No way! There are literal pieces of us lying all over this Highway of Clusterfuckery.

So, let's open the Journal of Murphy's Law and let us see where we stand right now…

* * *

As soon as I got back from meeting my family up north, I came back to the Compound and the whole place was lit up, and there's another party going on.

Rick was up in the practice space, drunk as always, and we started talking about the money we owed Bob the Promoter. I told him I sent a money order to him after I got out of the hospital. The money transaction was taken care of, albeit a few days late.

I mentioned that I almost died...

He started going off on me! He said that he asked Felix to bail us out because nobody knew where I was. I asked what "Bail out" meant, and he said that Felix had loaned us the cash and gave us some extra to spend on CD's, shirts, and a new backdrop.

Long story short, I said he jumped the gun and put us all in danger. He said I was full of shit...

I took some of my things and crashed at Mom's place.

A few days later, Rick calls my mom's and wants to talk to me. He said he was sorry for acting like a douchebag and says he broke his arm!

Fractured it! Can't play drums for at least six-months!!!

I was FUMING but managed to swallow my anger and said, "Alright, we'll get through this," he can still sing, so I started calling around and e-mailing people for any possible drummers that might wanna play with us on the Slayer gig. I phone tag a couple of guys, but nothing came up.

Rick had spent a few horrible days coming down...

He was real vague on how he broke his arm. All he said about it was "...it was just some bullshit that happened."

Love the transparency, dude!

I've seen him punch stuff while on a bender before. I could see his knuckles were smashed. He must've punched something or someone and just busted his arm on impact. Meth isn't a good substitute for Calcium, hence, the forearm fracture.

Jesus was oblivious to what was going on in M-town and showed up for practice. We explained everything to him. Out of nowhere, he suggests calling Chester back to fill in on bass. So, we did.

He agreed! Good man! It was great talking to him again even though he left us hanging a couple of years ago. Water under the bridge. He's in another band now but promised to not flake on us during this crucial time for our band.

We were desperately seeking a drummer. Bob the Promoter has $4,400 dollars from us. The same $2,200 sent twice; and by the looks of it, we have the spot we wanted.

I heard that Marlin was out of jail. His charge for vehicular homicide was dropped. He just got a little time added for his barred-driving charge he already had. Geez!

So, I called up Marlin to see if he could play drums…

First, when I called he said, "Damn! You shouldn't be calling. My aunt's here now, wait…" It sounded like he went outside; then he asked what was up.

We talked. Everything is still good with us, and he said he couldn't do it. After his time in jail, he hasn't touched a single instrument and just spends his days getting high and eating NDN Tacos at home.

I didn't bring up his aunt or the witchcraft as much as I wanted to. There's a time and a day for that.

He suggested our old bandmate and my cousin: Wayne…

Great! As much as I didn't want to, I called my ol' Cousin Wayne and made magic happen. I knew what I was getting the rest of the band into and knew it would be painful. But my ol' Cousin Wayne said, "Yes," and we have a band!

It's a good thing he's a good drummer because we didn't have to waste time in teaching him or Chester a lot. Each guy is autonomous in their own way.

With Wayne in the band, we sold even MORE tickets. And not in a good way because HIS family is now coming to the show and they are the reason why I'm out of the job, as well as hundreds of people that work at the casino.

His dad, (Not worth mentioning his name...) is the one on the Tribal Council responsible for the shutdown! Along with some of my aunts and cousins, they were caught on-camera stealing hard drives, surveillance tapes, and who knows what else from the casino! Along with the buying of cars and motorcycles, they are now buying votes, loaning money to their relatives to vote for them; and they're even printing their own propaganda newsletter. Basically, a fascist regime!

It's all over the news! The people of the tribe finally thwarted their plans and kicked 'em out of the building. There was a lot of incriminating evidence they stole. Along with the general manager of the casino, who is an "ordained minister" at the church they all go to, my cousin's family are responsible for violations and hundreds of thousands of dollars stolen from the casino. Fucking great, right? Good old fashioned embezzlement and nepotism!

And now, our band: Bastards & Thieves is REALLY involved with big-time thieves! AND drug cartels! Real-life criminals...

Not only that, Cousin Wayne is a pathological fucking liar! Like, big time. The main reason I didn't want to play with him ever again. But, here we are. He brings in the family drama after practices, like I wanna be involved. He's lied about little things, and the lies get bigger and bigger as time goes on.

   I just shake my head and tell myself that we need to pull this off no matter what. But, these bad people are all up in our business; and now it feels like the band, the core which is me, Rick, and Jesus, have absolutely no control…

CHAPTER EIGHTY-FOUR

Rick was complaining about pain since he broke his arm. He also had a history of back pain that he kept from the band up until then. When they found a drummer in Cousin Wayne, he was relieved that he didn't need to haul his drums around anymore though he still complained about his back and a sharp throbbing pain in his wrist that was further exacerbated by his broken forearm.

When Will the Patriot moved in, he had a prescription to use muscle relaxers that he got from the VA in M-town. Rick and he would indulge in his prescriptions leisurely. But over time, Rick started to crave those pills as he would crush and snort them along with using his crystal meth. Will and Rick's long-lasting friendship was getting strained by the latter's increasing appetite for opioids which was the main reason why Will had since moved out of the Compound after Rick's arm-break.

Felix had a side operation that invested in large quantities of *Ox* pills to sell and, with Rick's patronage and eventual partnership, saw their business acquisitions soar into profitability.

But with Rick's physical woes, the eventual addiction came into prominence on the road to the big gig. Even though he hadn't done meth since the arm-breaking incident, he had traded one addiction for another.

Jesus was the first to notice on one particular practice night. Rick was in a glassy-eyed stare, and his vocals were sluggish and behind the beat of the songs.

"Are you gonna be okay to do this, man?" Jesus asked him that night. He said that he would rather not do the show than see his friend start mixing his pills along with the other temptations that were available to them.

Rick assured him that he knew what he was doing.

* * *

Rick was in his regular shirtless state with his large blond goatee braided down to his chest. He wore his trademark cowboy hat, the gift he received from Tray of Fort Madison.

He had two full pitchers of Mountain Dew with a plastic cup in his teeth from the bar. He had a cool demeanor all day that was very unlike his usual electric charisma he was known for. He was trying to make his way through the crowd of 300 who were on hand to see this new band from M-town who were good enough to play right before Slayer.

He managed to make it to the front of the 3-foot high stage. One of Cousin Wayne's brothers shouted to the people standing there to make way for *Rick the Rocker*.

The crowd was perplexed to see this cowboy-hatted guy with a cast on his forearm with two full pitchers of soda in each hand trying to hoist himself onto the small stage where there were wedge monitors and cables in his way. But he got his right foot up to the stage, pushed his weight up, his knee buckled, his other foot caught the edge of the black stage skirting, then fell forward. He spilled the two full pitchers of Mountain Dew all over the stage.

"Oohhhhh...shit!" Rick bellowed after landing on his face. He used his good arm to get himself to a crouching position. He tried scooping up the mass quantities of ice with his plastic cup which he had chewed one side of and smashed into his face. There was nothing left in the two pitchers.

"Motherfu——" Azul reacted swiftly by moving her pedal board out of the way then was startled by Cousin Wayne's snare drum that went off like a cannon in the floor monitors as she was bent over.

The soda was spilled all over Rick's area of center stage. The soundman's assistant had a couple of throw towels to sop up the mess as he cursed loudly and stormed off the stage as the drums started doing the pre-set soundcheck.

"Hey guys, I need something to drink. I need something to drink——" Rick kept asking Azul and Jesus. One of Cousin Wayne's drunk brothers told him not to worry. He had a pitcher of beer behind the amps and a glass, and he immediately poured one for him.

Jesus was being heckled by someone in Spanish. Jesus looked at them, shook his head, and proceeded to ignore them. Azul noticed this after hearing the words, "*fucking maricón*," and saw that it was Felix and two of his friends having a laugh at Jesus's expense.

She immediately tightened up and started to yell in his defense when the soundman asked for her guitar through the monitor. She stopped and played some riffs at full volume while looking at the front-of-house soundboard for his cues all while making sure Felix and his crew didn't taunt Jesus any more.

Then, her drunk cousin got right in her face and *wooed* as loud as he could in his beer and sweat-soaked mania. "You're doing it cuz! You're doing it! Wooo!"

Azul recoiled and told him to get off the stage. She tried to get the soundman's attention again to see if her guitar levels were good but heard him say through the monitor, "Ready when you are."

Rick immediately went into his crowd banter, "What's up Davenport? Y'all ready for fucking Slayer?! We're Bastards & Thieves from Marshalltown and Des Moines! Is someone gonna get me a shot and a beer up here!?"

Azul groaned and looked toward Jesus who just shrugged and turned on his effects pedal for his trademark pre-show noise intro.

She turned to her left to see Chester had dipped his head in his pitcher of water, reared back his black mane and splashed the stage and her.

She flinched and smiled, shook her head and said, "Fuck it!" then turned her guitar's volume knob on to let her amp feedback. "It's my birthday, right?" She got her pick ready, saluted the crowd, and waited for the count-in to the first song.

The crowd was packed in the club. A few of the "Little Bastards" from M-town, many of their friends, and select members of their family were among the swell of excitement as the count-in on the hi-hat brought forth the mammoth pounding of the bass drums and barrage of thrashy 8th and 16th notes that immediately got the mosh pit going, the heads banging, and the kids on the stage to dive.

* * *

Immediately as it started, it ended. The Bastards got off stage-right as they let the sweat and adrenaline steam out of their collective bodies, and they retreated to an area that was closed off with a black curtain.

A double-door was propped open to the large patio that stretched across the club's side that faced the main stage parking lot area which was filled with over ten-thousand fans rocking alongside the moonlit Mississippi River.

Slayer were enshrined with amplifiers and an elaborate stage design complete with strobes and crimson red stage lights as they played one of their staple live songs, "Disciple." It was a sight to behold for the band as they watched the crowd chanting the refrain of: "*God hates us all*." They toasted with their collective waters and beers for pulling it off.

"We did it!" Rick pulled the sweat-soaked band members in for a group hug. Their camaraderie was shared by the five of them alone. All of the practice, miles, and hustle awarded them this moment.

Throughout the day they had handed out sampler CDs of their basement demo and flyers for their scheduled set time, even selling tickets to people outside trying to get in. They sold 15 T-shirt packages that included a demo and random stickers for $15.

After they played, they sold five more and got 20 new fans on their mailing list.

The small victories would not have been possible without their perseverance and trust in each other.

The band watched their heroes perform their set by moonlight. Cousin Wayne and Chester were air-drumming while sitting next to the backstage water trough.

Azul was again relieved their part of the show was over. She had Mom and Zach with her, sporting their *Guest List* lanyards.

Rick's mental fog had lifted as he indulged in post-show cocktails with Rosita by his side.

Jesus and his wife Amy were laying out on the banana yellow lounge chairs. He had a headache the entire day, but said it got better as soon as Slayer played their classic set-closer: "Reign in Blood," which the Bastards, like the musical bastards they are, included a stolen portion of in their own set "for the hell of it," at the risk of a potential public-performance lawsuit.

But they did it for fun. They were young, true rebels, making mistakes along the way; but no one could take this moment of victory from them for the rest of their miserable lives.

The Bastard Chronicle 26...or The Blue Chronicle 1

Everyone was wiped out after the Slayer show. We all took separate vehicles and stayed in separate hotels.

The next afternoon I just followed Mom and Zach home.

I saw Squash's ex on the highway. The Long John Silver's girl. I didn't see her that whole time. It would've been great to catch up with her.

Speaking of her, we got a prison letter from Squash. THE premier bassist in our "classic lineup." He is locked up in Fort Madison. Seems he's got the extended tour of the place.

Anyways, he's doing alright. He misses playing with us. Misses the good times. He even had some touching words to say about Rick. I never knew him to be so open and sentimental in real life as he was in the letter. Well, maybe prison will do that to you. I hope to never find out or any more of my dear friends for that matter…

Chester and I had a brief talk when we were loading out our gear at 2:30 in the morning. We hugged and said it was great to see each other again. But, at this point, I think we both feel that our paths have diverged. I sure as hell am not the same person I was when we had dated, or tried to date, let me put it like that. Seems like forces beyond all control are putting things into chaos all of the time. I know that he is going through some things, too. But, M-town is a small place. Our paths will cross again.

Cousin Wayne. When we were kids, it was a lot different. His family is just not wired correctly. That's me saying it nicely. But, that's a family situation that you try to run away from and leave behind for good. There's always something that keeps you coming back. I try to cope with it; but as time goes on and as more of his lies surface, I have a rotten feeling inside. Like there is something deeper. Psychopathic, even. But with everything his family is involved in, I do feel cornered now that he's in the band. With that being said, I can't wait for the day when it's time to say: You're fired.

Jesus, I've said before, is the best of all of us. He's such a talented, nice dude. A great husband and father. His ex-wife, I'll rip that bitch's hair out for cheating on him and not letting him see his first daughter, and I've never met her before! But that daughter loves him to death. His new daughter loves him to death, and his wife Amy is still nuts about him. I do feel that our band is taking that family time away from him. With our goals, is it possible for him to go on the road? He swears up and down that he'll make it work. Rick likes to use the term: Yoko Ono, for girlfriends and wives getting in the band's way; but maybe, just maybe, Jesus is on to something that we just don't see. Is he breaking the deadbeat dad cycle once and for all?

I got a new place! On the south side of town. On old HWY 30. I swear, this road has got it in for me. But I had to get out of the Compound ASAP.

Annie, turns out, found some guy to shack up with in town. It wasn't like she had much to move with her. I saw her at "Wallyworld," where she works now. She partied too much at the porn shop and got canned. Her companionship for me was needed at the time. It was fun while it lasted, but mostly exhausting. She has a good heart and needs to take care of herself. She doesn't need to ruin her life with vodka.

Rick and Rosita were sitting outside the Compound when I went to get the last of my things. She came up to me all giddy and took my hand and asked me if she noticed anything different. I looked at her and she rubbed her tummy with my hand in hers.

"Dude, I'm pregnant!" she said.

I was taken aback and tried to process this gut-punch as I drifted off and thought about the future of the band. Can we have two guys in the band with kids, especially two-thirds of the core members? She was motor-mouthing at that point. I "came to," looked at her, and asked her how far along she was.

"I'm pretty sure we got pregnant the first night at the studio. You guys were asleep in the lounge area, me and Rick were in studio A and—" she kept on going. It had been a little over two months. I know they've been partying hard that whole time, and I had to fight back the vomit that I swear was coming out of my mouth.

I sighed and looked over at Rick who was sitting, facing east, in one of the filthy plastic white chairs we had out on the back porch. He had a 12-pack of PBR next to him. He had his trademark sunglasses and cowboy hat on, staring off in the distance.

"—I'm just so excited and guess what? I want to name her, if it's a girl, after YOU, Azul! Isn't that great? Since you and I are Latinas in this corn-bred state, and you've been nothing but a true sister. It would be an honor if you would be godmother!"

I heard that and licked my teeth to try to get the bad taste she had just put in my mouth. "God…" I thought. I just wanted to leave and not have to deal with this.

Then she served up another hot, steaming, shit sandwich from the What-The-Fuck Buffet…

"My daughter Rosa, back in Chicago, is gonna have a baby sister or brother! She's gonna have some kickass brothers with Rick's four sons! Isn't that amazing!?" She tufted her freshly washed brown hair, (which I've always admired and hated her for having instead of my thick black mess—)wait, what did she say?

I don't know if the surprised look gave it away, but I did not know he had kids! But, four sons!?

She giggled then said, "Oh ya know, the two he had when he was thirteen with the first baby mama. Then, the other two after that with the two others…"

I inhaled and almost blurted out, "Don't forget the stepson he has with Mandy!" But, I caught my breath, exhaled, and let out the ditziest, "Congratulations!" I could muster.

Shock-and-Awe in-motherfuckin'-deed, man! Welfare will be SO proud of you two!

He hinted at "making a mistake" a couple of times when we were drinking. Since then, I always suspected he maybe had a child back home he never talked about. But I never would've imagined FOUR! Why I was left in the dark all this time about this info speaks volumes on Rick's character. I'm surprised Jesus never told me. He has to know, right?

Maybe not telling me this fun little fact slipped your guys' minds...

...or is it, bros before hoes. Whatever, man...

* * *

My dearest little brother, Zach, his "father," was supposed to pick him up for a weekend of visitation when he was just six years old. I remember Zach being so excited to be going to his dad's place, I packed his things, and I waited with him.

He never showed up. We never saw him again. He skipped town. Another cowboy hat-wearing motherfucker. I don't know if my mom had anything to do with him not showing up. She never said. But, the fact of the matter is that piece of shit probably has like, three more kids now; and I practically had to raise Zach while our mother started drinking.

I think back to my meeting with my father. Me, my two sisters, a brother in jail. Four children also. I got another letter from him just now. He, after all of these years, finally got his NDN name. Yeah...He said his new name means: "Good Man."

* * *

So, I asked myself as I was driving away from the Compound: Is this how the thief of lives looks every time he revels in the thieves' chair? A cowboy hat on, a 12-pack by his side while staring off in the distance?

...Rick fell over in his chair after I thought this.

CHAPTER EIGHTY-SIX

Q: How long did the band last after that Slayer show?

Hmm, well after I moved out of the Compound, we continued to practice there. All the while, I was trying to raise enough money to get our CD mixed and mastered at this studio called Catamount in Cedar Falls. We did eventually make it there, but that was after eight more months of shows. We were on a roll after the Slayer thing. I mean, how many local bands can say they opened for one of the Big Four of Thrash Metal? We had some buzz and clout to go with our live reputation. We needed that elusive big CD! We opened up for so many national acts, doing the pay-to-play thing, and by our own booking.

Q: I'm sorry, explain pay-to-play...

It was what the Slayer gig was. We essentially had to sell
X-amount of tickets to earn our spot on the bill. It's an unfair
practice for bands, especially for the ones just starting out. It puts
them in a place where they're at each other's throats with other
bands trying to sell them.

Q: So what did happen to Felix, the drug dealer?

Oh, I said my piece to him after the show. To not be involved in
any more business with our band. We didn't want the police to be
raiding our practice space and put all of us in jail. One of us was in
there already. And, he stayed away. He eventually got busted. He
partied at the Marriott one too many times. Ronnie went down, too.
Spike and poor Charlie. Jail. Their Pomeranian starved to death in
their apartment at the Tallcorn.

Q: Oh my...

It's so unfortunate. Lives wasted. All of them...
I know for a fact that Rick was still dealing for a while. He laid
low after Felix and his crew got busted. He relapsed with meth a
couple of times. He was snorting it, and you could just hear and feel
the deterioration happening in his nasal cavity, vocal cords, and
lungs. After we finally did mix the CD, which was the last time the
three core members were on the same page, he was smoking pot as
well as drinking.

Q: Did you manage to stay sober after your time in the hospital?

Of course not. It's not that easy to just up and quit. I've been through the AA rodeo enough to know that it can take multiple times in, and maybe you'd get clean. Of course, the Christian eccentricities of the program didn't help me either. Imagine that. It wasn't until years later I finally did get clean. Best thing I ever did for myself. My family was there for me, and I'm lucky to still have them in my corner.

Q: I'm very glad to hear that! So, tell us a little about how the band split? Did it happen suddenly? Was there a single moment where you all decided to?

Well, we had no choice but to play without a bass player. We just couldn't find one.

We were trying out different drummers behind my cousin's back for a couple of months because the drama, lies, and creepy behavior was getting on everyone's nerves.

He even had, in a big goofy-assed font: *Wayne of M-town,* emblazoned on his bass drums. Yeah... (Laughs) Nobody liked the guy.

The tribal scandal that his family was involved in got them banned for life from the casino. It was a crazy time. Even I got interviewed about it on the AP wire! He seemed to retreat more and more into that pathological liar's world of delusion that cost him his friendships. But he brought it on himself. It wasn't the most ideal circumstance that he joined, and it was the same as when we let him go.

We fired him right after a show we did at the House of Bricks in Des Moines. It turned out to be our last.

Interesting fact about that show, Rick had this hare-brained idea where we had our whole bodies painted in black. Black clothes, black face, everywhere. We did a photoshoot before the show. Chester rejoined for that gig and brought a friend with him that we covered in black just for the photoshoot. My cousin couldn't make it to the shoot, but he came to do the show, and had to leave right after. He had no time to put on the black makeup, but we didn't care. We finally kicked him out after we played.

We have video of that show on YouTube, and it's creepy, because we're all in black except for him.

There was a definite release of tension, but we never ever found a drummer that could play our stuff. Our music was too much for most musicians in that area, but we kept looking until we just disintegrated.

Rick and Rosita's newborn kid had a lot to do with it, too. They had moved out of the Compound and went into low-rent housing in a small town in the middle of nowhere. He had stopped dealing and started bartending again. They were miserable. They had a baby boy, which they named Arnold. He told us that they were gonna move to the Chicago area that winter. We stopped practicing, and I went online to make the announcement of our demise. Wasn't too ceremonial. Shame.

Jesus had a second daughter. Beautiful child. So, that kinda sealed the deal. Those two haven't played music since.

Q: How are they doing? Have you spoke to them since?

Jesus is doing well. Real well. He made the big jump and started HRT recently. He had to move out of Iowa to get that done since intolerance got so bad in recent years.

His mom did end up beating the cancer she had and lived for a few more years and totally accepted his transition.

He's still a great family man. His two daughters are great kids.

Rick was in prison for a couple of years for getting caught with a meth lab in the trunk of a chick's car that he was bonking. I don't know what happened to Rosita and their son, or how he's getting along with his entire brood. I hope he has done some reparations since then.

Q: I see, that's unfortunate. But, you did manage to get your CD mixed and mastered later on. But it wasn't until much later that you released it online, to little fanfare, but sparked an interest to the ones that were fans of the band. How did that feel?

Ya know, I remember after that last show that I drove home exhausted. I picked up a six-pack of Heineken, got to my apartment, went to the shower to wash all of that black makeup off of my body, and just cried. You work on something for so long and you think it's gonna work out. Then when it doesn't, and you know deep down that it's over even if it's on life support, a wave of grief washes over you as you're trying to get all of the black stains off your body so you can start anew in the morning. Of course, the stains didn't come off until a couple days later, but I remember that feeling. It was something I hadn't gotten over for some time.

I fell deeper into drinking and depression. I was in my mid-twenties, and I had tried to get on the normal path of how twenty-somethings are supposed to do: Find a normal job, find someone, build a nest...

I had the master tape canister sitting with me in that apartment with the marker scribbled on the label: *The Azul Project*. When I finally released it online, after I got sober so many years later, I finally felt good about it. I feel the stains have finally washed off. So, it's how I choose to live my life now, to work from project-to-project.

Q: Life goes on indeed. I'm glad you have reached a sort of closure, and I feel that is a good segue for us to hear you perform another song for us live.

That's great. I just wanna pull out this poem that I wrote about that era real quick, since I have my trusty journal here——let me find it——here it is! I thought, since it really kinda sums up that era: What the local bands like us were doing at that time. Do ya mind?

Q: Oh no, no! We'd love to hear it!

Sorry we're too loud
We're just trying to write songs of our own
We can't stand to listen to the TV anymore
Telling us who to hate, who to root for, what to think

Sorry we're too loud
You have every right to be whoever they tell you
If you don't like what we're doing, We'll like it even more
We want to be ourselves, to plug in, to say something

Sorry we're too loud
If one kid likes one song, he finds two more like him
They'll start a band, I'll go see them play
That's the way it works, they create, we share

Not sorry that we're too loud
We're playing the songs that people want to hear
To go somewhere, feel something real, nothing fake
Ephemeral, yet everlasting

Q: That's lovely. Was that something you had written back then?

I just wrote it. Here's a song for you.

ACKNOWLEDGMENTS

At the risk of sounding arrogant, I want to thank myself for sticking to it and getting this story out to the world. Iowa isn't known as a breeding ground for writers outside of the Writer's Workshop in University of Iowa. What you have in your hand/device/listening platform is from a blue-collar worker where there are no support groups for such endeavors. In that regard I want to thank my family for being supportive throughout the process and FAS, my high school English teacher, for providing guidance in the first draft copy-editing process during the COVID lockdown. Much appreciated.

To all my band brothers and sisters who I have had the pleasure of sharing the stage with: That shit was fun! This book would not exist were it not for our good and bad times. There were too many stories left on the cutting room floor and since many would consider this a work of Autofiction because of this, I guess I would have to agree to a point. I got to say what I wanted to say in the musical tapestry of our collective adventures and it was so damn easy to write!

This book was written in the Scrivener exe. (literatureandlatte. com) Design and Layout done in Adobe Creative Cloud. Audiobook recorded and mixed with Presonus Studio One.

Now, go write your own book!

ABOUT THE AUTHOR

FORREST LONEFIGHT,

Musician, Songwriter, Artist, Union Member Blue-Collar Worker is a Native American from the Meskwaki Tribe of the Sauk & Fox of the Mississippi in Iowa and member of the Three Affiliated Tribes: Mandan, Hidatsa, Arikara. He calls his home Des Moines, Iowa. Stay tuned for new releases from his metal band Somnarsonist, as well as his solo work!
Check out the companion Original Soundtrack to LIFE BELONGS TO THE LOUD, the first novel, at:
www.forrestlonefight.com

LOW FICTION

Printed in the USA
CPSIA information can be obtained
at www.ICGtesting.com
CBHW071742020724
11025CB00006B/104